S0-ACS-682

FOR LOVE
and
COUNTRY

Center Point
Large Print

Books are
produced in the
United States
using U.S.-based
materials

Books are printed
using a revolutionary
new process called
THINKtech™ that
lowers energy usage
by 70% and increases
overall quality

Books are
durable and
flexible
because of
Smyth-sewing

Paper is
sourced using
environmentally
responsible
foresting methods
and the
paper is acid-free

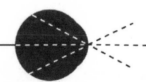

**This Large Print Book carries the
Seal of Approval of N.A.V.H.**

FOR LOVE
and
COUNTRY

A Novel

Candace Waters

Fountaindale Public Library
Bolingbrook, IL
(630) 759-2102

CENTER POINT LARGE PRINT
THORNDIKE, MAINE

This Center Point Large Print edition
is published in the year 2020 by arrangement with
Howard Books, a division of Simon & Schuster, Inc.

Copyright © 2020 by Alloy Entertainment, LLC.

All rights reserved.

This book is a work of fiction.
Any references to historical events, real people, or real
places are used fictitiously. Other names, characters, places,
and events are products of the author's imagination, and
any resemblance to actual events or places or persons,
living or dead, is entirely coincidental.

The text of this Large Print edition is unabridged.
In other aspects, this book may vary
from the original edition.
Printed in the United States of America
on permanent paper.
Set in 16-point Times New Roman type.

ISBN: 978-1-64358-667-0

The Library of Congress has cataloged this record
under Library of Congress Control Number: 2020934760

One

"Have you ever seen anything like it?" Belle Ames breathed in a tone of wonder, looking up at the giant arch of white lilies and blue hydrangeas she and Lottie were standing under.

"Mmm," Lottie Palmer said in a tone that she hoped masked her total lack of interest in both the hydrangeas and the huge party that was currently being thrown for her.

The floral arch was more than a story tall, but it still didn't come anywhere close to scraping the famous glass ceiling of the Book Cadillac Hotel's Italian garden ballroom, which hung two stories above the dance floor now crowded with Lottie's friends.

The truth was Lottie had seen something like the gargantuan flower display before. In fact, the one they were standing under wasn't even the only one in the ballroom. In a fit of enthusiasm over Lottie's upcoming wedding, Belle's mother, Annie, one of the grande dames of Detroit society, had ordered three of them. One stood at the entrance to the ballroom from the hotel. One stood at the opposite end, where another set of doors opened to the street. The one Lottie and Belle were standing under stood sentinel in the center of the room.

And Lottie wasn't impressed by any of them.

If Lottie were to be honest, which she had no intention of doing at this particular moment, the huge, grandstanding arrangements weren't all that different from the other huge, grandstanding arrangements that her father's friends had trotted out during the whirlwind of parties leading up to her wedding. It seemed like all the tycoons and would-be tycoons in Detroit were elbowing each other out of the way to host celebrations for her and Eugene. Not just her father's fellow automakers, but anyone who had anything to do with the auto industry. The men who made the tires, or the steel, or the glass. All of them wanted to throw Franklin Palmer's daughter a party. And nobody wanted to have less expensive wine, or fewer guests, or smaller flower arrangements, than the other guy.

Maybe it was because, as Belle's mother had pointed out, flowers were one thing they weren't rationing. At least not until someone in the War Department figured out a way to fight the Germans with hothouse roses and daffodils.

Rationing meant it was hard to get enough butter or sugar to serve a big party, even if you were one of the most powerful families in the city. And even if you could afford the high market prices, it was considered bad taste to flout the rationing laws that other families were obeying. So the big families of Detroit might have had to put up with serving cake sweetened with applesauce at their shindigs, but if they still felt the need to show off, they could make up for it with flowers.

Lots and lots of flowers.

Lottie wasn't even sure how many parties had been thrown that summer for her and Eugene. But she knew this was the last one. Until her rehearsal dinner, next weekend. A few weeks ago, she'd thought it would be a relief when she finally got to cross the last party off her calendar. Now, though, she just felt a growing sense of unease. When she thought about it, she couldn't tell why. So she tried not to think about it.

Belle finally glanced down from the floral phantasmagoria overhead to get a look at Lottie.

Lottie gamely tried a smile. She'd always liked Belle, even though they'd never had much in common. And she wanted to be grateful for everything Belle's mom had done to put the party together. But she wasn't sure she was going to be able to fake the kind of enthusiasm Belle so clearly expected.

So when she saw Eugene's familiar figure striding across the room, his buddy Donald in tow, she grinned with relief.

Beside her, Belle's face lit up as well, at the prospect of gushing about the flowers to someone else.

"Genie!" Belle cried as Eugene approached.

Lottie knew he hated this nickname, which Belle had dubbed him with in grammar school. With judicious threats, and a few minor fistfights, he'd actually managed to convince all the other guys in their set never to call him that.

Obviously, he hadn't been able to use either of those tactics on Belle herself, and his gentler efforts at persuasion had never succeeded in getting her to stop. But to his credit, Lottie noticed his face didn't give away even a flicker of the displeasure she knew he felt.

"Will you look at this?" Belle asked. With renewed vigor, she pointed at the flowers overhead again, her hand tracing the arc as if it were the hand on a clock.

"They're beautiful," he said. "I'm not sure I've ever seen anything like it." Somehow, Eugene always knew exactly what to say.

"That's what *I* was just telling Lottie," Belle said with a coy smile.

"And you'll be sure and tell your mother how grateful we are," Eugene said.

"Of *course,*" Belle promised.

"I told her myself just now," Eugene said. "But it's always easier to believe things when someone says them about you behind your back."

Belle's smile, which Lottie wouldn't have believed could get wider, actually did—an effect Eugene seemed to have on just about everyone.

Then he glanced at Lottie, a knowing look

peeking from behind his polite smile. "How are you doing, Lots?" he asked. "You like this sky garden they made us?"

Lottie hadn't been able to figure out a polite fib for Belle, and it was even harder with Eugene. They'd known each other since before either of them could remember, and he didn't miss much. Still, she tried her best.

"It's lovely," Lottie said.

"Of course it's lovely," Eugene said. "How could Annie Ames have thrown a party that was anything but?"

"And it's not just the flowers," his buddy Don added. "Did you see the swan chairs?"

Annie Ames's pièce de résistance for the evening was about half a dozen couches, shaped like swans, scattered around the perimeter of the dance floor. They were covered in white velvet, complete with plumes of ostrich feathers that created a delightfully scandalous effect by screening the hijinks of whoever sank into their lush cushions. She'd made it a point to say they'd come out of storage, from one of her own parties as a girl, so that nobody would think she wasn't economizing due to the war effort.

Something about the pretense and hypocrisy sat wrong with Lottie.

Eugene's lips curled and his brown eyes crinkled in a grin.

"What's this, Lots?" Eugene said. "You don't like them?"

Lottie dropped her eyes and swirled her beverage, stalling. "They're very nice," she finally managed.

"It's so hard to impress a modern girl these days!" Eugene said in a teasing voice. "Now, what would it take to upgrade those incredible confections of couches to something other than nice?"

"Live swans?" Don suggested, getting into the joke.

"No, no," Eugene said. "Far too troublesome. Have you heard the sound those things make? I'm afraid it would put the bandleader right off."

"Unless you trained them to sing along," Don said.

Lottie sighed and crossed her arms with a playfully irritated smile.

"I know!" Eugene burst out. "What this party is really missing is tigers. That would do it, wouldn't it? A tiger on every couch. Then we'd really have something going on."

"Hmm," Lottie said. "Well, at least then we'd have something to do with disrespectful young men."

"You're going to feed us to the tigers?" Eugene asked, grinning. "That's quite Roman of you. Maybe I should start calling you empress."

As he spoke, the music on the dance floor changed. The couples who had been locked together in their spins and dips broke apart and re-formed into new pairings. As they did, a young man in an olive-green army uniform came over and stood before Belle.

"May I have this dance, young lady?" he asked with a wink.

They wound through the crowd and made their way into the whirl of dancers, who were all flailing through a jitterbug.

As they disappeared into the mix, Lottie and Eugene retreated to the wall, where a group of stag men, many in various uniforms, were clustered, joking and keeping an eye on the dancers, some with idle curiosity. Others watched with a keen interest that made Lottie suspect the girl of their choice was whirling around the floor with some other young man.

Under the din of the chatter, Lottie could feel Eugene looking at her more closely.

"Come on, Lots," he said as Don scanned the dance floor, following the lithe lines of whatever girl caught his eye, until the next one did. "Can't you be happy at a party, just this once?"

"Sure," she said. With a little shrug, she tried a smile. But it twisted on her face.

She certainly didn't feel like a bride having the time of her life on the weekend before her wedding. But then again, she'd never had the time of her life at any party—and the fancier the parties got, the worse her chances were.

"Come on," he said. "What's wrong?"

Lottie took a deep breath. "It just doesn't feel right," she said, looking around.

A look of alarm flickered across Eugene's face. "The wedding?" he asked.

Quickly, Lottie shook her head. "No, of course not," she said, taking his hand.

Nothing in her life had been more obvious than that she should marry Eugene. They'd known each other all their lives, the same way she'd known all the other boys. And she knew with certainty that he was the best of them. "It's just . . ." she began, then trailed off again.

"What?" Eugene asked, a mild impatience creeping into his voice.

As Lottie's glance flitted around the dance hall, it landed on one of the swan couches, its ostrich feathers still trembling from the motion as its current resident had sunk down into its cushions.

"It just doesn't even seem real," she said, gesturing at the crowd, the band, the arches of flowers. "All this nonsense, when there's a war on."

"Well, Lottie," Don said sensibly, "this is the good stuff. It's what we're fighting for, to be able to have good times like this. And just because the Germans want to take it away from us is no reason to stop. It's a reason to keep having the best times we can, despite them." He ended his little speech with a perfunctory nod.

"I'm not even sure why we're fighting the Germans, personally," Eugene broke in. "It's not like they've invaded Michigan."

"Do you really think this is a good time?" Lottie asked Don urgently. "I just keep feeling like there must be something more than parties and music. Some kind of adventure. Something to do that *means* something. Like what the troops—"

As she said this, a soldier who had been standing within earshot turned around with a precise snap, almost as if he'd been ordered to make a quick turn in a parade line. Both Lottie and Eugene tried to offer him welcoming smiles, but his expression remained stony.

"Excuse me, ma'am. I hear you think our troops at the front are just off on some adventure," he said in a clipped voice, biting off every word. "I can assure you from my time at the front that it is not."

Lottie was so surprised by his words that it took her a minute to realize she knew him, and knew him well. It was her childhood friend Robert, whom she'd spent untold summers with shoveling sand on the beach at the yacht club. He was almost unrecognizable in his uniform and with his military haircut.

She looked closer and noticed how much older he seemed now. Fine lines had creased his forehead and the corners of his eyes. His skin was tan and leathered from many days spent in the sun. But his eyes . . . his eyes were piercing and stern. The intensity was startling.

In the same moment, a flicker that passed over Robert's face showed that he had recognized her.

"You'll excuse me," he said, and stalked away, toward the ballroom doors that led out to the street.

"Robert!" Lottie called after him, her heart sinking.

"That was Robert?" Eugene said, his voice rising in surprise. "Little Robbie Packard?"

Without answering him, Lottie dove into the crowd, following Robert's retreating form as it moved, ramrod straight, through the crush of revelers. Ahead of her, when he reached the door, it swung open, revealing a bit of the blue light of the dark street before it swung shut again.

Then Lottie pressed through the crowd and pushed the door open herself, surprised, when she found herself out on the street, by the quiet after the noise of the party.

Robert had stopped on the sidewalk, puffing on a cigarette that glowed a deep angry red.

"Robert," Lottie said. She took a half step toward him, then hesitated.

Robert took a puff and let the hand that was holding his cigarette drop to his side, where the red glow winked out.

His face was no longer stony. Now he looked

tired, and perhaps even sad. "I'm sorry, Lottie," he said. "This is your party. I shouldn't have—"

"No," Lottie said, coming up beside him to take his arm. "I'm the one who's sorry. I know what you're doing is serious. I know I don't even know how serious."

"That's why we're fighting," Robert said, his voice full of emotion. "So you won't ever have to know."

Something tightened in Lottie's throat.

Robert squeezed her hand on his arm. "It's just, at things like this, sometimes I get the feeling that nobody even cares that we're over there."

"That's not true," Lottie said. "I think about it. I think that's what I was trying to say, but it came out wrong. What you do matters so much. So much more than these—parties, and champagne. I didn't mean to make it sound like it was just some silly game. I just get so tired of all this nonsense here. I think what I meant to say was how much I want to serve, too," she said, the words coming to her just before she spoke them, so that she felt as if she were learning what she thought by listening to herself. "I want to be part of something that means as much as what you're doing. Because I can't think of anything that matters more."

As she said it, her voice broke.

"Thanks, Lottie," Robert said.

He glanced at the ballroom door as it swung

open to let a small gang of partygoers spill out onto the street, then shook his head and let his cigarette fall to the sidewalk, where he ground it out. "I think I'm going to get out of here," he said. "Give Eugene my congratulations. I can't make the wedding. They've got us shipping back out in a few days."

Lottie gave him a hug and a kiss on the cheek. "Don't do anything I wouldn't do," she said.

Robert smiled as he released her from the embrace. "Oh, Lottie," he said with a wink. "What wouldn't you do?"

Lottie winked back, giving a bright smile as Robert turned and wandered off down Washington Boulevard, toward the bright lights of downtown.

Even before he reached the corner, her smile had faded. In its place, Lottie felt sick to her stomach. It was hard to watch him walk away, knowing he was heading toward the war. And knowing that she was heading toward champagne and ballrooms.

But as she stared at his retreating form, she felt something else as well: a kind of envy at the square of his shoulders, which showed he knew that even if what he had to do was hard, it mattered.

What would that feel like? she wondered as the faint strains of the party music drifted through the glass ceiling of the Italian garden and out into the street.

For weeks now, leading up to the wedding, she'd felt like a square peg in a round hole, putting on dress after dress to go to parties full of people she'd never really felt she fit in with. But now her unease turned into a gnawing resentment. She was supposed to go back in there and pretend she cared about flowers and dresses, while Robert was going off to serve his country. But it was her country, too. And she wanted to serve it just as much as he did.

Two

Lottie took in a deep breath, leaning her head back on the driver's seat. She and Eugene spun past the water plant on the river, heading out of Detroit along the river on Jefferson Avenue. The fresh spring country air whipped around them through the lowered top of her Stutz Bearcat convertible.

It was an old car, by the standards of most of her friends. In fact, it had been most popular right after the last war. But when she'd been a girl, her father's buddy Harry Stutz had sent one of the last ones ever made up from his factory in Indiana as a gift to their family. Lottie had been years away from being old enough to drive, but she thought she'd never seen anything so pretty in her life: the rich maroon sides, the smart whitewall tires, and the creamy canvas convertible top.

Every chance she'd gotten, she'd begged for a ride in it, until her father jokingly told her that it would be hers once she was old enough to drive.

Since she wasn't even ten at the time, he likely thought she'd forget about it by the time she was sixteen—or be begging for one of the Bentleys or Cadillacs her friends were all clamoring for by that age.

But Lottie had never lost her fierce attachment to the Bearcat. Despite the teasing of her friends, it was the first car she chose to drive when she first got her driver's license. And she still drove it every chance she got—this time out to Grosse Pointe, where Eugene's parents lived, for their weekly Sunday afternoon dinner.

She'd already driven down from the Boston Edison district, full of big homes like the one where she'd grown up. And she'd stopped to pick up Eugene from the bachelor apartment he kept downtown.

But there was nothing like the feeling of leaving the last skyscrapers and homes of the city behind, especially as the Detroit River opened into Lake Saint Clair, and Jefferson wound up along it, just a hand's breadth from the riverbank.

"Ah!" Eugene said, closing his eyes against the lowering sun. "Is there anything better than this?"

Though Lottie had had the same fleeting thought a moment before, when Eugene said it aloud, something suddenly went a little awry in her chest.

Is there anything better than this? she wondered.

"I don't know," she said. "Do you really think so?"

Eugene leaned over to kiss her cheek and rub her shoulder. "No," he said. "I think marrying you will be better. And maybe a couple kids," he said with a meaningful glance at the backseat.

Lottie shifted in her own seat. Now it didn't just feel like something was wrong in her chest; it felt like something was pressing down on it. And Eugene's hand on her shoulder suddenly felt like a spider crawling over her.

"You want to have kids right away?" she asked, trying to sound casual.

"Not too fast," Eugene said, throwing his own head back to catch the scent of the river. "I mean, I'll be satisfied if we have three in the first three years."

Lottie glanced at him, and he grinned back at her, enjoying his joke.

"I mean, my family is known for production efficiency," Eugene joked. His family was one of the major manufacturers of car parts in the city. At least, they had been, until the government mandated a weapons quotient for every manufacturer. Now Eugene oversaw weapons production at his father's factory, a convenient post for the son of the proprietor, since it came with the added perk of exemption from the draft.

"Don't you think . . ." Lottie began, then hesitated, not sure exactly how to put it. "Don't you think it would be nice if we could do some other things first?"

"Like what, Lots?" Eugene asked with a lazy smile.

20

She thought for a long moment before answering.

"Like travel the world."

Eugene sighed and planted both his hands on his knees. "I've been around this world more than once," he said. "And I've never found anything I like as much as what we've got right here, in Detroit."

Lottie pursed her lips.

"Especially the girls," Eugene said. He leaned over to kiss her cheek again. "Especially one particular girl."

Lottie tried to smile. "But what about other things you've always wanted to do?"

"You know what I haven't done yet that I want to?" Eugene asked. "I want to marry the most wonderful girl in the world and raise a family with her."

"You don't want anything else?" Lottie asked.

"No," Eugene said simply. Then he turned in his seat so he could really search her face. "What have you always wanted to do?"

The question spun around Lottie's mind as the river rolled alongside them and the clouds slid by overhead.

Then the car lurched and sputtered. Lottie rolled her eyes and jammed in the clutch to try putting it back in gear again, but it was no use. The engine, which had been powering them merrily along the river road, had completely cut out.

Giving a wave over her shoulder to the traffic behind them, Lottie nosed the car off to the side of the road, braking just before she hit the fence that cordoned off a spit of private land that ran out into the river, with boats bobbing at anchor at the far end, where the river was deep enough to launch them.

"Not again," Eugene said in a tired voice.

"Your brand-new Cadillac broke down two weeks ago," Lottie snapped, feeling defensive about her beloved Bearcat.

"Yes," Eugene allowed. "But it didn't break down two weeks before that. And two weeks before that. And . . ."

Lottie pumped the gas, put the clutch in, then tried turning the ignition again. The engine coughed but then went silent.

Eugene, who was well acquainted with the moody ways of Lottie's ancient chariot, leaned back and kicked his feet up on the door.

"The good thing about all these Sunday drivers," he said, "is that someone will be along to help us anytime."

Steaming at his lack of faith, Lottie opened the driver's-side door and climbed out. "We can't be stuck here forever," she told him.

Then she walked around to the side of the car, bent over to find the release catch for the hood, and popped it open.

From beyond it, she could hear Eugene groan.

"Lottie," he called. "We can just hitch a ride to my folks' place and call a mechanic when we get there."

But Lottie was already lost in thought, poring over the engine, remembering what Gus had always told her about the first step in repairing any engine: "Take a look."

Gus was the one who had taught her everything she knew about engines, even though her father owned a factory that built hundreds of them a day. He'd been a mechanic before he became their chauffeur, which was crucial when even the best cars had a habit of breaking down at the most inopportune moments.

Lottie had numerous memories of her family all piling out of the car to find a patch of shade or flagging down other drivers who might send to the house for another vehicle to take them home while Gus worked on the problem.

Lottie, on the other hand, had always snuck around to watch Gus at work. She was fascinated by the gears and shafts, the pistons and carburetor and fuel tank, the axles and exhaust pipes. But he would never let her touch the engine herself— until she started sneaking out to find him in the garage. Even then, it took her weeks to wear him down. But eventually he put a wrench into one of her small hands and started to show her the basic elements of the engine.

By the time she had wrangled her Stutz Bearcat

from her father, at age sixteen, she wasn't just expert enough to fix it herself if it happened to break down. She could troubleshoot just about any car engine in the Detroit area. And she'd even managed to help a friend get their plane running in one of Grosse Pointe's massive yards after an afternoon party.

The pilot, a buddy of her father, had landed it there the day before, with the joke that since he knew everybody would show up to the party in the best cars in the world, he'd opted for a plane. But when he tried to take off the next day, the engine wouldn't even turn over. While all the auto execs stood around, gobbling in shock like a pack of turkeys, Lottie had been the one to quietly trace the fuel line, which led to the revelation that a local critter had gnawed a hole in it overnight.

"Take a look," Gus's first admonition, meant getting a grasp of the whole situation before you started taking things apart. The better you knew an engine, the more instinctive doing a visual check got. And Lottie didn't know any other engine better than that of her beloved Stutz, with its large, smooth engine block, silver tubes, and thick copper-colored wires.

Gus's second admonition was just as hard to forget as his first. "Look for the simple answer," he always told her. "Not the complicated one."

But she also knew after a quick glance that this wasn't going to be a simple fix. Lack of power could only come from a handful of problems. She knew it wasn't an issue with fuel, because they'd been purring along steadily before the engine choked. So it had to be something deeper in.

A minute later, over Eugene's protests, she had pulled out the small tool kit she always kept in the trunk of the car.

"Lots," Eugene pleaded with her, still with his feet propped up on the door of the car. "Darling, I beg you, wait for a proper mechanic. If only to spare that ravishing dress."

Before he mentioned it, the thought hadn't even crossed Lottie's mind. But now that he'd brought it up, she did spare a minute to look down at her outfit: a smart white spring suit with white piping and white pumps. It was the kind of getup that might make some girls hesitate to even sit on a park bench.

But Lottie just shook her head. "I can do it," she said. "Gus's uniform is always spotless."

"The first thing I'm going to do once we're married," Eugene said good-naturedly, "is fire Gus."

"Gus doesn't work for me," Lottie retorted, squatting down to get a better look at the carburetor. It was easy enough to see, a silver cylinder right on the top of the engine block. But what she was interested in was the second butterfly inside, which had a tricky habit of getting stuck. And that was going to take some time to get at. "He works for my father," she said, pulling a wrench out of her tool kit.

"That's what your father thinks," Eugene agreed. "But does Gus know that? I'm not convinced he's aware he works for *anyone.*"

"Whoever he thinks he's working for," Lottie said, "he always gets it done."

"I would just like to observe, my dear," Eugene said, "that you are one of the lucky few who does not need to work."

But I want to, Lottie suddenly thought with a fierceness that surprised her. A moment ago, she hadn't been able to think of anything in the world she'd always wanted to do. Now there wasn't anything she wanted more than to fix this crazy old car.

After a few minutes of loosening bolts, Lottie had finally opened up the belly of the carburetor. The first butterfly valve worked perfectly, as always. "Thank you," she said briskly as she continued tinkering to get at the second.

"What did you say?" Eugene called.

"I wasn't talking to you," Lottie said.

"You were talking to yourself?" Eugene asked.

When she didn't answer, he said, in a tone of mixed amusement and incredulity, "To the *engine?*"

"Shh!" Lottie said. "You'll hurt its feelings."

Just as she'd suspected, the second butterfly valve was stuck, but with a good push from her

26

screwdriver, it sprang loose. She spread an ample amount of grease over the whole thing for good measure and double-checked the action. Then she quickly screwed everything back into place and collected her tools from the grassy roadside. Feeling satisfied, she hopped back in the car and honked the horn with a grin.

Eugene sprang upright from his reclined position, dropping his feet to the floor of the car, his eyes wide in astonishment. She figured he must be thoroughly impressed at her mechanical prowess.

But as his gaze fixed not on her eyes, but on a region somewhere around her midsection, she finally glanced down at herself to see a giant smear of black grease that covered not just the jacket of her smart white suit, but the skirt itself.

Oh no.

Too bad she didn't keep a spare outfit in the trunk next to that tool kit.

"Like you said," he said wryly after a minute. "Spotless."

"That's the inside of the carburetor," Lottie said, judging from the stain. "I must have forgotten what I was doing when I pulled that section out."

"You can tell just by looking which part stained your dress?" Eugene said. "Somehow I think that puts you in a class beyond."

Lottie was about to smile at him, until he

added, "I just wish that you'd remembered who you're meeting for lunch."

At the reference to his parents, Lottie's smile died on her lips. They most certainly would not find anything amusing about her stained dress.

She turned the key in the ignition. The Stutz roared back to life and she patted the dashboard fondly. Then she turned to Eugene. "But the car works!" she crowed, pulling out into traffic. "At least we won't be late for dinner."

"That'll give my father so much more time to enjoy your dress," Eugene said.

Lottie felt a little pang as she looked down at the grease smeared all over her lap. "Maybe I can do something about it before he sees it," Lottie said.

"Like buy a new dress?" Eugene asked.

Lottie rolled her eyes.

A few minutes later, they turned onto the long lane of mansions his family house sat among and then the winding drive that led to his house, hidden among a dense growth of old trees.

Lottie parked in the circle near the front door, then steeled herself and stepped out. She scanned the yard for a garden hose or something to clean up with, but before she could, Eugene's father appeared in the front door.

The big grin that had graced his face when he first threw it open faded immediately at the sight of Lottie's dress.

"Are you all right, dear?" he asked. "What's happened to you?"

"Lottie's Bearcat failed to proceed," Eugene said, going up the walk to shake his father's hand, with Lottie trailing along beside him. "But she got it running again."

The look of concern in Mr. Grantham's eyes changed to one of consternation, then recognition. "That's grease," he said. He was one of the biggest parts manufacturers in Detroit—there was no telling him the stains were anything else, once he knew what he was looking at.

"Guilty," Lottie said with what she hoped was a charmingly self-deprecating smile. "But we got it running again."

Mr. Grantham looked from Lottie to his son in shock. "We?" he said, looking at his son. Lottie bristled at his reaction.

"I'm afraid I can't claim any credit for this one," Eugene said, raising his hands as if in surrender.

"I'm not sure this is a credit to *anyone,*" Mr. Grantham said. He scowled at her as if she were a machine that had malfunctioned and needed to be fixed—or replaced.

Lottie felt her cheeks begin to burn with frustration and shame.

"Well," Mr. Grantham said. "I think maybe you'd better go around the side and see if you can get one of the maids to help you, before you go in to Mrs. Grantham."

"Dad—" Eugene began to protest, but Lottie laid her hand on his arm.

"That's perfect," she said. "I'll see you in a minute."

Then she tramped off around the side of the house, toward the kitchen and laundry at the back.

Lottie chastised herself for letting Mr. Grantham's disapproval affect her so much. She didn't have any reason to feel a lick of shame or regret over the ruined dress. In a strange way, she was sort of proud of it.

As she traipsed through the garden to the servants' entrance, she just called up the sound of the engine in her head and felt the same satisfaction she had when it had roared to life. The sound of that gentle purr had been intoxicating. And it was worth all the grease stains in the world.

Three

"Lace from Alsace," Madame Rosetti said.

While Lottie watched in the threefold mirror in front of them, Madame draped a length of thick, delicate white frippery over Lottie's shoulder and around the curve of the neckline of her wedding dress, letting yards more of it fall back down over Lottie's shoulder, to the ground. Then Madame pinned the raveling edge of the lace firmly in place in the center of the dress and gestured impatiently at her young assistant, Vera, who scrambled to hand her another bolt of expensive trimming.

Lottie barely recognized herself: in the mirror was a perfect bride, with lace and silk cascading from her shoulders and billowing out in gigantic folds from her waist.

"English bobbin lace," Madame announced, repeating the whole operation by pinning this lace to the opposite side of Lottie's neckline, then letting the remains spill back down over Lottie's other shoulder.

When Madame was finished, she stepped away from the little round dais where Lottie was standing, which raised her a good ten inches off the floor of the room. Madame clasped her hands and closed her eyes as if she were Michelangelo regarding his statue of David. *"Brava!"* she breathed. *"Si beau!"*

Beside her, her assistant shuffled nervously, not quite sure whether she should imitate her employer's rapture or stay at attention in order to quickly meet Madame's inevitable next demand.

Lottie stifled a smile at Madame's casual switch between Italian and French. She had always wondered how someone with such a clearly Italian surname had decided to advertise herself to the world with a French honorific. But Madame's business acumen was unquestionable. Despite her French moniker, or perhaps in part because of it, she was the most in-demand bridal couturier in Detroit.

In the mirror, Lottie glanced back at her mother, who was seated on a dove-gray fainting couch behind Lottie, wearing a smart gray suit herself, her blond hair as perfectly coiffed as always.

"What do you think?" Lottie asked.

"What do *you* think, dear?" her mother replied with a gentle smile.

Lottie looked back at the mirror.

She had picked the dress out ages ago, right after Eugene proposed last Christmas. She'd watched other friends lose months of their lives to the hunt for a dress, rifling through gowns at shop after shop in Detroit and all the way out to Ann Arbor or Chicago. Before the war, she'd even known girls who took a boat or plane to the continent, so they could choose a design no one had ever seen before, from shops in Paris or London.

Lottie, on the other hand, had been both decisive and sensible. Madame's shop was known as the best, so she'd started there, looked at a dozen dresses, and chosen one: a simple design in thick white silk with princess seams, a scoop neck, and delicate cap sleeves that showed off the way tennis had toned her arms.

Initially, Madame had been effusive about the dress and appeared to be almost in awe of Lottie's levelheadedness. But over time, Madame's awe had faded into something more like suspicion. Was Lottie *sure* about the dress? she wanted to know every time Lottie came in for a fitting. Didn't Lottie have *any* opinions? Wouldn't Lottie like something to make the dress a bit more *special?*

And just as Lottie had chosen her dress with great reasonableness, she listened to all of Madame's suggestions with great reasonableness—but didn't take any of them. The truth was she *wanted* her dress to be simple. The country was at war, after all.

As a result, Madame's suggestions got more and more elaborate. Which was how Lottie had ended up there, at what was supposed to be her last fitting before the big day, with lace cascading down her back.

Madame was certain that the dress needed

a little something more, something to make it truly special, truly Lottie's. And so she'd dug up handmade lace from across the world, so Lottie could see the difference.

When Lottie looked in the mirror, she could barely see any difference between the two laces at all. One was delicate and frothy, the other handmade, faintly ivory. As far as their effect on the dress, or how either one looked on her, she was at a loss.

But it was as she looked up, from the lace to herself, that she got the real shock. For some reason, when her eyes met the eyes of the girl in the mirror, she didn't recognize herself.

She looked down at the dress, and the girl in the mirror looked down at her dress. She fumbled nervously with the skirt, and the girl in the mirror did, too. But when she looked up, back into that girl's eyes, Lottie still felt as if she'd never seen her before.

Her chest began to feel tight and her head dizzy. She took a step back, to steady herself.

"Honey?" her mother said. "Are you all right?"

"I think the Alsace," Madame said, raising one eyebrow over her practiced eye.

Lottie began to fumble with the pins that held the lace at her throat, as if removing it might make her recognize herself again.

"Oh, no, no," Madame said, rushing forward. "I will do."

But Lottie held her hands out, fending her off. "I'm sorry," she said. "I just need—"

She looked at her mother helplessly, her heart racing. She was at her wits' end with the wedding planning, especially in the face of this war, which made everything else seem so unimportant. She didn't want to ruin her mother's happiness. But she didn't know how much longer she could just stand here, acting like some kind of doll, when there were American soldiers dying abroad.

"Madame," Lottie's mother said, rising to her feet. "Could you give us a moment?"

Reluctantly, Madame backed away from the dais, somehow managing to shoo her assistant along behind her. "Of course, of course," she said with utmost politeness, which somehow still managed to register her absolute disapproval. Then she slipped out between the velvet curtains that hung over the door to the dressing room, and Lottie and her mother were alone together.

Lottie stepped down from the dais and immediately found her feet stuck in an ocean of silk and tulle.

"I can't—" she said, putting her hand over her chest, which felt so tight now she was having trouble taking even breaths.

Quickly, her mother was at her side. With deft fingers, her mother unpinned the lace from either side of Lottie's neckline, turned it quickly into neat rolls, and then unzipped Lottie's dress.

When the stays released from around her ribs, Lottie was suddenly able to breathe again. But tears sprang to her eyes. She willed herself to keep them at bay.

"Thank you," she said, hugging her mother's neck. "I don't know what happened. I just felt like . . ."

As she trailed off, her mother continued to help her out of the gigantic confection of her dress. Then she handed Lottie her blouse.

"I think you just need a little break from all of this," her mother told her. She nodded at the small service door that led from the dressing room out to the back parking lot. "Why don't you go for a little walk? I'll handle Madame."

"But the lace . . ." Lottie began.

"Did you really love either of them?"

Lottie looked from the delicate wisp of Alsace lace to the more homespun, then shook her head.

"Well, that settles it, then," her mother said, and swept them both away.

By now, Lottie had slipped into her blouse and skirt. She turned so her mother could fasten the hook and work the zipper in the back. Then she smoothed her hair down and looked in the mirror. With a sense of relief, she finally felt she recognized the girl who looked back at her, with her familiar shoulder-length russet hair and brown eyes.

Lottie's mother turned back from hanging the

dress up on a nearby rack. She threaded her arm around Lottie's waist and gave it a squeeze. Then she nodded at the delivery exit.

"Go on," she said. "Get out of here."

Lottie kissed her mother's cheek.

"Thank you, Mom," she said.

As soon as she stepped out onto the street, she felt like a new woman. The weight she had felt in the dress shop fell away from her shoulders. But in its place she didn't feel peace or calm. Instead, she felt a sense that there was something she was supposed to be doing, or someplace she was supposed to go.

But she had forgotten what it was.

She ran quickly through all the events of the coming week, between now and the wedding. There was no way she had actually forgotten anything. Her mother was running the wedding like clockwork, and Lottie wasn't in charge of any of the details.

Lottie cut through the parking lot in the back of the dress shop, then up through a narrow alley to one of Detroit's downtown streets.

In the first shop window, she saw a sign advertising war bonds, with a picture of a soldier, jaw set, looking up at the flag.

He looked so much like Robert had the other night that Lottie felt a twist of shame at her thoughtless comment. She felt worried for him all over again.

He was right, she thought. The war had been

far from her life. Her father was building trucks for the troops, and Eugene's father had converted over half his operation to supply planes to the air force. But that had actually kept the war even farther from Lottie.

It meant that nearly everyone in her life—including Eugene—was exempt from going to the front.

But now every store on the street seemed to be filled with posters urging people to join up, to find ways to work within the rations, to buy more war bonds to fund the war effort.

And with every one she saw, Lottie felt even more strongly how distant it had all been kept from her—and how much she wanted things to be different.

She suddenly saw three small faces in her mind's eye—sporting Eugene's hazel eyes and her russet hair. A feeling low in her belly told her instantly that she wasn't ready for that kind of life. Not for children. Not for any of it. Maybe she would never be ready. The thought made her shudder.

But in the back of her head, she could hear Eugene's gently mocking voice. What did she actually think she could do for the war effort? Was she actually going to go load ammunition into artillery or march through the mud at the front?

Perhaps I could plan lavish parties to lure in the Nazis? Lottie thought bitterly. It was just about all she was qualified to do.

A few blocks away from the dress shop, she came to the Downtown Theater, with its huge, bulb-studded marquee.

Without thinking twice, Lottie stepped up to the ticket booth and bought a ticket for the next show, desperate for some kind of escape.

She passed through the movie palace's gaudy entrance and sat down with relief in the darkness of the theater, just as the first of the opening newsreels began to flicker across the screen.

With a sinking heart, Lottie realized she couldn't escape the war, even in here. Black-and-white images of the war filled the whole screen.

An airplane took off from the deck of a gigantic aircraft carrier as it cut through the broad ocean that stretched away on either side. A woman saluted smartly from the deck of a battleship at anchor.

Lottie's mind ground to a halt because the image was so strange.

A woman . . . saluting?

Suddenly, Lottie found herself leaning forward in her seat as the announcer's voice came in over the patriotic background music.

He was saying something about women serving in the war.

Then the face of a handsome seaman came on the screen, with a square jaw, sandy blond hair, and blue eyes turned clear gray by the black-and-white film. "Hello, I'm Captain Luke Woodward.

Women Accepted for Volunteer Emergency Service play a vital role in the war effort," he said. "Now more than ever, we need women to help win this war."

Then a banner flashed across the screen: *Navy WAVES,* it read, followed by an image of two women in smart white uniforms walking along the shoreline of a big city. *Don't miss your great opportunity.*

Lottie's mind flashed back to the white suit she'd ruined the other day, fixing the old Bearcat. Then she imagined herself in a similar uniform, hunched over the engine of a military truck. Suddenly, the nagging sensation inside her vanished. And suddenly, she had an answer.

The newsreel ended and she sat through the rest of the movie. But when she left, she couldn't have told anyone what had happened in even one scene.

Instead, another movie had been playing in her head: all the possibilities of what it might mean for her to sign up for the Navy WAVES. The hard work, the comradery with other women, the boats and planes, the sparkling sea—and all the things she couldn't imagine, and would never know about, unless she went there to see for herself. The chance to do something that really mattered, to make a difference, not just staying in the safety of home and playing dress-up, but working to serve and help others. She saw all of it in clearer focus than she'd seen anything for ages.

When she got home, she found her mother sitting in the den that she had quietly turned into her own private library, with giant shelves of her favorite books. These books, unlike the dusty, collectible volumes stored in the cavernous formal library, were ones that someone might actually want to read.

When Lottie came in, her mother laid aside her book and held her hand out. Lottie went over and sank down beside her on the comfortable stuffed window seat where her mother loved to sit and while away the afternoon with a new story.

Lottie's mother took Lottie's hand and squeezed it. "How are you doing, honey?" she asked.

Lottie looked down at their intertwined fingers.

"Do you remember when you got married?" Lottie asked.

Her mother laughed. "How could I forget?" she said. "And I was younger than you, remember. By a few years. We thought girls of twenty-two were already old maids."

Lottie smiled. "How did you feel . . ." she asked. "Before?"

Her mother didn't answer right away. For a moment, her eyes darted out the window.

"Were you nervous?" Lottie asked.

"I think everyone's nervous before their wedding," Lottie's mother said. "How could you not be? Getting up in front of all those people."

"Were you nervous about . . . Dad?" Lottie asked.

Her mother shook her head firmly. "I knew he was a good man," she said.

Lottie felt a bit of comfort at this. She felt the same way about Eugene. And after all, her parents had been happy.

But as she thought about it, she realized that her questions weren't really about Eugene. They were about something else.

"Did you ever want to do anything . . . else?" Lottie asked.

"What do you mean?" her mother said gently.

"Anything you could have done," Lottie said. "If you hadn't gotten married."

Lottie's mother's eyes widened slightly, as if she suddenly understood something about what Lottie was asking that she hadn't before.

"I didn't mean . . ." Lottie began, then trailed off.

"I think I know what you're feeling," her mother said before Lottie could find the words. "I know you wouldn't guess it from looking at my life, but there are all kinds of things I dreamed about doing, besides what I've done. I still do, sometimes," she said with a smile. "And who knows?" she asked with another glance out the window. "I still might."

"But you don't regret this one?" Lottie said. "The life you have?"

Her mother squeezed Lottie's hand. "I don't regret marrying your father," she said firmly. "After all, if I hadn't married him, I wouldn't have you. And I can't imagine that. If I had it all to do over again, I'd do it all exactly the same, just to have you." She kissed Lottie's cheek. "But I do regret one thing," she said.

"What's that?" Lottie asked.

Her mother looked into her eyes. "When I was making the decision to get married as a young woman, I didn't think I had any other choice," she said. "Getting married felt like my only option. But it wasn't. I wish I'd known that. Because you always have a choice in life, Lottie. You always do."

"Thank you, Mom," Lottie said, giving her a hug.

The warmth and strength of her mother's embrace lingered with her long after they parted. But her mother's words stayed with her even longer.

That night, as Lottie washed her face and put her hair into rollers, she looked at herself hard in the mirror. Her mother's words echoed as if they were bouncing around the walls of a cavernous valley, first far, then so near it felt as if her mother were right there with her again.

You always have a choice in life, Lottie. You always do.

Four

"This dress is so beautiful," Mrs. Hancock said, remarking on the delicate sky-blue silk of the gown Lottie had chosen for her rehearsal dinner. "I can't imagine how you will be any more beautiful tomorrow."

Lottie bit her lip to keep from snapping back that she couldn't see what being beautiful had to do with anything. Her unease with the first parties celebrating her wedding had long ago turned to impatience, but now she was feeling an urge to dash out of the place, and it was so strong she could barely hold herself back.

Her dress was a throwback to the days before the war, with a long cascade of blue silk gores that swirled like clouds around her silver pumps. That kind of styling hadn't been seen in years, since the war had made it so much more difficult to get the yards and yards of fabric that it required.

When Lottie's mother had first picked it out, it had seemed like the perfect celebration dress to her, and a relief from the grinding monotony of the severe wartime designs, when all the relaxed frippery of the debutante's dresses had suddenly been fashioned into lines as simple as those of a man's military uniform. Her mother had planned a lavish dinner in their banquet room and on their back patio, and Lottie had imagined herself twirling the night away, under the large oak tree she'd spent so many afternoons climbing as a child, in this perfect dress.

But when she'd put it on earlier that day, she'd immediately hated it. She couldn't even walk down the steps from her room without having to gather it up so she wouldn't trip on it. It seemed like it had been designed to keep her from doing anything. Then it hit her. *That's the only reason you'd wear a dress like this.* To show that you didn't *have* to do anything.

She gave Mrs. Hancock, who was waiting for her chauffeur to bring the car around, a wan smile.

But Eugene, as he always did, knew exactly the right thing to say. "I always think she couldn't be any more beautiful than she is," he said with a quick peck on Lottie's cheek. "But every day, she somehow still manages to surprise me."

Mrs. Hancock's face lit up as if Eugene had paid the compliment to her.

"Oh, you two," she said as the lights of a car spun around the circle drive. "I can't wait for tomorrow."

"Thank you for coming," Lottie called as Mrs. Hancock hurried down the steps.

Eugene sighed as her car slipped away into the night.

Behind them, the doors to the banquet hall swung open as a waiter hurried through. The babble of the voices of all the guests who were still milling around and chatting inside leaked out into the hall.

"Do we have go to back in?" Lottie asked.

Her mother had been the one to plan this party, the final one in the endless whirl leading up to her wedding tomorrow. And because her mother had planned it, it didn't feature any of the ostentatious displays some of the others had: no giant towers of flowers; no flaming canapés; no live animals, like the peacocks that Anastasia Fremont had thought would lend a classy touch to the festivities at her riverside estate.

She'd been unaware, apparently, that the giant birds could actually fly, and instead of class, they'd lent a bit of comic relief when several of them wound up on the roof of the Fremonts' carriage house. They'd then begun to dive-bomb guests, making their eerie calls, until one of them knocked off Mrs. Anderson's wig, and Anastasia Fremont called the peacock handlers to come collect them.

But despite the simple, elegant gathering in Lottie's own home, featuring her favorite lemon ice cream and some of their closest friends, Lottie felt a sense of dread at returning to the house.

"Come on," she said, pulling at Eugene's hand. They were standing beside the door to the kitchen, which a servant had just passed through and where most of the family servants, as well as a few dozen who had been hired just for that night, were busily entering and exiting, clearing the hall of the night's plates and silver. Inside was a little vestibule, designed to give servants a place to wait for guests to arrive at the front door and then quickly disappear again while members of the family greeted the newcomers.

It had always been a favorite haunt of Lottie's, and when they were kids, she had introduced it to Eugene as their special secret: a place to disappear for an instant when the big gatherings her family was always throwing got too boring, or noisy, or overwhelming.

Eugene hesitated. "People are waiting for us," he said. But he gave in as Lottie pulled him into their hiding place.

Inside, she gave him a kiss on the cheek, then sank down on the little wooden bench built into the wall just inside the door.

He sat down beside her.

"So?" he said, an edge of impatience in his voice.

Lottie took a deep breath.

"Eugene," she said in a rush. "I saw an ad for the Navy WAVES when I went to the movies. Earlier this week."

"What's that?" he asked. His tone was polite as ever, but she could tell he thought she was just making small talk—and barely paying attention himself.

"It's women," Lottie said. "Women in the Navy."

"Women in the Navy," Eugene mused, his tone shifting to disapproval. "It's about time this war got over."

"I think I could do it," Lottie said.

"Well, of course you could, Lots," Eugene said, chucking her under the chin. "You could do just about anything you put your mind to."

Lottie hesitated. She'd braced herself for an objection, but his easy agreement stymied her for an instant.

But suddenly the words rose up, not out of her thoughts, but out of her heart. "I want to," she told him. "I got an application at a recruitment office, and I already sent it in. I want to join the Navy WAVES."

"Join the Navy?" Eugene said, sitting up so that he could look her in the eye. His own eyes sparkled slightly, as if he were already amused by whatever joke she was trying to play now.

Lottie nodded, her jaw set.

As Eugene recognized the seriousness in her eyes, his own smile faded. "Lots," he said, taking her hand in his. "We're getting married tomorrow."

"But what if we didn't?" Lottie said.

At the surprise in his expression, she gave his

hand a quick squeeze. "I mean, what if we didn't right now?" she said.

Now Eugene took a deep breath, shaking his head. "Lottie—" he began.

"No, listen," she interrupted. "Our whole country is at war. The whole world is. Robbie's going off to fight it. But I never do anything."

"What about me?" Eugene asked, his tone turning sharp. "Do you think I don't do anything?"

Lottie stopped, confused. "No," she said. "You work for the war every day, at work."

As she said it, she felt her certainty about that slipping away. Lottie had always thought of Eugene's position as a clever way to *keep* him from the war. Mr. Grantham certainly agreed. He had absolutely forbidden Eugene to have anything to do with active duty, even though he was unquestionably of age and so many of their friends were serving now, themselves.

But this wasn't about Eugene. She was trying to tell him how she felt, about her own life. "I have skills," she said. "They need people. I could help. I might not be able to do much, but I could do something."

"Skills?" Eugene repeated, raising his eyebrows.

"I can repair engines," Lottie said. "They might need mechanics."

Eugene played with her fingers on his knee.

49

"Lots," he said, "I'm not sure how many Stutz Bearcats the Navy's employing these days . . ."

"You know I can repair other engines!" Lottie said indignantly. "You've seen me."

Eugene held his hands up in self-defense. "I know, I know," he said. "You got Bob Spratt's Cadillac up and running again when it broke down after that picnic on the Rouge River."

"And Emmeline Fairchild's convertible," Lottie reminded him. "When it broke down last year. And I repaired Jim Trinkle's plane engine, remember that?"

"I remember you found the hole a groundhog chewed in his fuel line," Eugene said.

Lottie nodded with satisfaction that he seemed to be taking her point.

"But I remember other things, too," Eugene added gently.

"Like what?" Lottie asked.

"Remember what you wanted to be when you were ten?" he asked.

"A cowgirl," Lottie answered promptly.

"That's right," Eugene said. "And so your dad got you Star, and then you begged him for Bullet."

"Star was too short to do a real jump," Lottie said.

"And you got good at jumping," Eugene said.

"I won a Michigan Equestrian cup that year," Lottie said proudly.

"I know," Eugene said. "I was there, remember?"

Lottie smiled. He'd shown up with a bag of apples for Bullet, and it had been a trick to get the grateful horse away from him, over to the competition. "I do," she said.

Eugene nodded. "And remember what you wanted to be when you were thirteen?" he asked.

"A nurse," Lottie said. But this time she felt a little uneasy.

"And if I wanted to see you," Eugene said, "I had to go over to the Grosse Point Hospital, where you were volunteering, and roll bandages with you."

"I loved volunteering," Lottie said. When she'd participated in the program, which brought young students into the hospitals as volunteers, it had been the first time in her life that she'd really felt anything she did might really be making a real difference.

"You were wonderful at it," Eugene said. "I remember every time you went into a room, they always said, 'Thank God you're back!' If it'd been up to the patients, they would have hired you full-time."

Lottie smiled. Eugene was making a better case for her than she even could for herself. She'd always wanted to be part of something that mattered. And he had known that, she realized, even before she did herself.

"And remember what you wanted to be when you were sixteen?" Eugene asked.

"An Egyptologist," Lottie said.

"Hieroglyphics," Eugene said. "And pickaxes. Everywhere."

Lottie laughed. "And you said you'd buy me a ticket to Cairo, even if my dad forbade it."

"But I didn't have to," Eugene said. "Because by the end of that summer you were going to become a master jeweler."

At this, Lottie's heart dropped in her chest. She could see where he was going, and she didn't like it.

"And the next year you were going to be a reporter," Eugene said. "So you spent a summer writing society notes at the *Free Press*, until you got to college and took your first class on astronomy . . ."

"This isn't like that!" Lottie said angrily, pulling her hand away from his.

Patiently, Eugene reached for her hand again.

This time, she let him keep it.

"Isn't it?" he asked. "Are you sure about that?"

Lottie took both his hands in hers, kissed them, and looked pleadingly in his eyes. "What if we just waited a year?" she said. "Just a year. The war has to be over in a year. I can join the WAVES, and once it's over, I'll come back, and we can pick up right where we were."

Eugene didn't object, so she rushed on. "It's

not that I don't want to marry you," she said. "It's just that I feel like I need to do something, to be part of something that matters. That's all I want. Like you. You've already gotten to do so much."

Eugene stared back into her eyes. "So have you, Lottie," he finally said, quietly. "So have you."

Lottie sighed. "If we could just . . ." she began again.

But Eugene shook his head, this time with a firmness that let her know she needed to listen.

"Lottie," he said. "I don't care what you want to do. When you wrote me letters in hieroglyphics, I got a book to decode them, hoping you might be too shy to tell me you were in love with me in regular old English." Eugene smiled. "I drove you to every party in Detroit when you were working the society beat for the paper." He looked down at his lapel, where a pin she'd made him from a flawed emerald glimmered. "I've worn this pin of yours for years," he said.

"If I'd known you'd really wear it I would have used a better stone," said Lottie.

"I don't need a better stone," Eugene said impatiently. "I only want you. And I don't care what you're up to next year, or the next, or fifty years from now. I just want to be part of it."

"Well, then we just—" Lottie began.

Eugene raised his hand. "But this isn't just another of your whims," he said.

"No," Lottie said, hurrying to agree.

"It's a war," said Eugene. "It's something some men won't come back from. It's serious. And it's dangerous."

"I know," Lottie insisted.

"I'm not sure you do," Eugene said. "I'm not sure anyone does, until they're part of it. Which I pray you never are." He took a deep breath. "And this wedding isn't just another whim," he said. "At least, not for me. I'm serious about you, Lottie. I always have been. Our wedding's tomorrow. Of course you're going to feel some nerves. Everyone has them. That's only natural. But it's time for us to get married."

Lottie felt tears spring to her eyes. A flood of emotions washed through her. Her feelings for Eugene but also a growing sense of frustration at his words.

"I'm sorry," she said.

Eugene wrapped her in his strong embrace. "You don't have anything to be sorry for, Lots," he whispered in her ear.

When she pulled away, he smiled. "You'll see," he told her. "All those things you want to do, you still can. We'll just do them together."

But not the WAVES, Lottie thought. You had to be a single woman to join them.

Eugene took a deep breath, stood, and held out his hand. "Come on," he said. "We're being rude to our guests."

Tears sprang to Lottie's eyes. It had seemed like Eugene was really listening to her. But now she felt like he hadn't heard a thing. "You go back to the party," she said. "I'm going upstairs."

"Lottie," Eugene called, but she just pushed through the door and raced up the stairs, then down the long hall that traversed the mansion's second floor, to her room.

When she got there, she sank down on her bed, lay there for a minute, then rolled over and turned on her bedside light.

With a gasp, she realized that one of the maids must have brought her freshly pressed wedding dress to the room while she was gone. It was hanging on the door of her closet, the hem floating several feet off the ground, so big that it felt like a stranger had stepped into her room with her.

She looked away. Outside her window, on the otherwise dark front lawn, was the American flag her father flew there proudly, illuminated brightly by lights shining up from the ground.

She didn't have any idea how long she sat there, staring at the fluttering bands of red, white, and blue, while memories of Eugene and thoughts of the war spun through her head, while her heart tugged, restless, in her chest, almost as if it were being blown about by the same wind that caught the folds of the flag beyond her window.

Five

It was still dark when Lottie woke up. She lay there for a long moment, waiting for her eyes to adjust to the dawn light, which she thought must have awoken her, but it was still pitch-black outside. As she stared through her bedroom window, into the night, her eyes eventually began to pick out the stars in the sky beyond the dark branches of the trees nearest the house. But there was no hint of daylight yet.

Lottie sat up.

Despite the darkness, and despite a fatigue in her bones that let her know she had barely slept, she was wide awake. And she knew what she had to do. It wasn't even so much that she had thought her way to a decision. It was simply that the path before her was suddenly clear.

And it didn't lead down the aisle to Eugene.

She wasn't sure where it led. She just knew she had to follow it—this voice in herself that had started as a whisper but was now impossible to ignore, telling her that she was built for something more than anyone in her life believed—including her.

She stared out into the night.

Then she reached over and turned on the small light on her bedside table. She pushed away the covers, got out of bed, and stood face-to-face with her wedding dress in the dim light.

After a long moment, she reached up and unhooked it from her closet door, and threw the gown and its piles of tulle underskirts on her unmade bed.

She opened her closet, pulled out a simple blue shift, and got dressed. She knelt beside her bed and pushed the skirts of her wedding dress aside to root around under the bed.

The first piece of luggage she pulled out was rich red cordovan, decorated with shining brass. With a little shake of her head, she pushed it back and reached deeper under the bed. This time, she pulled out a somewhat battered blue canvas satchel, one of her father's that she had rescued from the trash heap when he decided it had gotten too worn for him to travel with it.

She'd never actually traveled with it herself before, other than to parade around the house or the yard with it when she was small. But now she set it on the foot of her bed, flicked the latches, and flipped it open to reveal the faded gray satin lining within.

Quietly but quickly, she began to fill it. She piled in some underthings, a pair of cotton pajamas, and a handful of socks. She stacked a few blouses on top of a pair of shorts and a pair of slacks. She pushed aside the rows of silk and velvet and chiffon party dresses in her closet and pulled out another simple shift, this time olive green. Then she slipped a pair of Mary Janes onto her feet.

As she did, she noticed her jewelry box, which she'd left open the night before, on the vanity at the foot of her bed. It was large, about the size of a bread box, and lined with dozens of velvet cubbies big enough to fit one necklace, or brooch, or pair of earrings. In the faint light that reached all the way from her bedside lamp to the cubbies, her gems gave off a faint glow: glimmers of sapphire, ruby, turquoise, and diamond after diamond, her father's favorite gift to her on almost every birthday since she had been a little girl.

Without taking anything out, she closed the box.

She twisted the engagement ring on her finger once, twice—and dropped it on top.

Then she went over to the little writing desk beside her bed.

The other furniture in the room was all the best available, from Hudson's, a department store downtown. The wood shone, the detail was exquisite, and the upholstery was lush.

But her desk was from another time and place. It had been built by her mother's father, for her mother's mother, when they were first married. Unlike the luxurious pieces the family could afford now, the joinings weren't cleverly hidden. The varnish wasn't perfect. And the signs of all the years that her grandmother had used it were clear: dings and scrapes on the legs, ink spots soaked into the wood. But it had always been Lottie's favorite piece of furniture in the whole room.

She sat down in the little chair her grandfather had also made. It looked so rickety that it might barely hold the weight of a child, but Lottie knew it was as sturdy as anything else in the room.

She pulled out the single rough drawer in the center of the desk, removed a few sheets of her monogrammed stationery, and picked up the pen she had left lying there.

For a moment, she bowed her head, covering her eyes with her hand. Then she lifted her chin and began to write.

Dear Eugene,

Tears sprang into her eyes as she looked down at the blank page. She shook her head and her glance landed on her wedding dress, with the little bag she'd packed just beyond it. Pen still in hand, she wiped the tears away from her eyes.

Then the thoughts that had filled her mind all night, and were still there roiling when she woke again before dawn, began to fill the page.

I wish that I could be in two places at once today. But there's only one of me, and there's something I feel I have to do. I've

never felt so strongly that I need to be part
of something bigger than myself. I want to
try to be of some help in this world.
   I want you to know that you'll always
be in my heart. I hope one day you can
forgive me.
   Your Lottie

She laid the pen down, folded the page over without reading it again, and slipped it quickly into an envelope. Then she wrote Eugene's name on it, sealed it, laid it on her desk, and stood up.

She went over to the bed and picked up the small valise she had just packed.

As she crossed to the door, she looked back at Eugene's name on the letter. Her mind flashed forward to what it would feel like for him to hold it in his hand, to open and read it. She could see the way his face would fall and how he would quickly try to cover his sadness, so as not to distress anyone else who was there with him.

The guilt nearly stopped her in her tracks. But something else tugged at her even more strongly, pulling her urgently toward the door, and she followed it out, into the hall.

She paused after she pulled the door to her room shut behind her, listening to the sounds of the rest of the house. A bit of very early light was starting to dawn now, pouring faintly into the hall from the large windows at either end. But nobody else seemed to have awoken yet. No boards creaked, no electric lights hummed.

Quickly, she slipped through the hall to the stairs and down to the main entryway. It was also deserted, with the early sun just beginning to pick the buffets and chairs out of the darkness.

She ducked into the vestibule where she and Eugene had sat the night before, then passed through it quickly to the kitchen, heading for the garages that opened off them, so that deliverymen could easily stock the big larder and refrigerators.

But just a few steps before she reached the delivery entrance on the opposite side of the kitchen, a shadow separated itself from the counter with a happy cry, and the overhead fixtures flicked on.

Squinting in the sudden light, Lottie turned around, already forming the excuse she'd give to whatever cook or kitchen maid she'd surprised with her early morning foray. After all, brides were liable to do all kinds of eccentric things on their wedding day. An early morning drive was hardly the strangest thing a bride had ever done.

But when Lottie turned and saw her mother's face, she was speechless.

Her mother smiled as she swept over to embrace Lottie in a long, warm hug. "Oh, sweetheart," she said, smoothing Lottie's hair before she released her. "You're up so early. Did you get any sleep at all?"

Lottie stood frozen. Her mind was racing. She had never lied to her mother. But if she told her the truth, what would her mother do?

Lottie had barely had the strength to write the message to Eugene, even when she wasn't there to see his face. If her mother tried to stop her, she didn't know what she would do.

Maybe, she told herself as her mother gave her another squeeze and stepped back, she wouldn't notice that something was wrong.

But as soon as her mother gave Lottie a quick once-over, Lottie knew that was a foolish hope.

At the sight of Lottie's simple dress, and the valise in her hand, her mother's smile vanished.

"Lottie," she said. "Where are you going?"

All kinds of half-truths spun through Lottie's mind: that she was going out for a drive, that she just needed a moment to clear her head, that she had to go out to get something she had forgotten.

But when Lottie was confronted with her mother's clear, questioning gaze, the truth began to tumble out.

"I'm joining up. The Navy is taking women now," Lottie said. It sounded so foolish as she said it, even to herself, that her heart fell. And everything else that she wanted to add—that she'd finally found a purpose, that she needed to do good in the world—sounded so flat in her own mind that she couldn't even bring herself to say them.

Her mother's expression made Lottie's heart twist in her chest. When Lottie had first come down the stairs, her mother's face had been compassionate and open. Now it took Lottie a moment to recognize the look in her mother's eyes, because she had never seen it before. It was fear.

"You don't have to marry Eugene," her mother said softly.

"I know," Lottie said, tears springing into her eyes.

"And you don't have to join the war, either," her mother said. "When I said you always had a choice . . ."

She trailed off, but Lottie didn't need her to finish the sentence to understand what she meant. When her mother had told her she always had a choice in life, she hadn't ever expected it to be this one.

"I know," Lottie said, squaring her shoulders with a slight lift of her chin. "I want to."

Her mother bit her lip, blinking back tears. But then she nodded and took Lottie's hand.

"Does Eugene know?" she asked.

"I tried to tell him," Lottie said. "He didn't understand."

Her mother took a deep breath. "Well, maybe one day he will," she said.

"I have to go," Lottie said, her voice breaking.

To her surprise, her mother's face broke into

a small smile. It was laced with traces of other things: worry, sorrow. But it was still a smile.

"Well," she said. "I see you've made your choice."

She turned away for a moment, rummaged around in a drawer, and then tucked something in the pocket of Lottie's shift. When Lottie put her own hand in to investigate, she discovered it was a small wad of bills.

"Just in case," her mother told her. Then she gave her another hug, this one even longer than the last. She pulled back and put her hand tenderly on Lottie's cheek.

"Be careful," her mother said, her eyes brimming with tears. "I'm letting you go, but I expect you to come back."

Lottie looked at her mother long and hard. Her heart swelled with gratitude for the woman staring back at her.

Then her mother cleared her throat and shook her head, the spell of the moment broken.

"Love you," Lottie said.

She expected to hear the same familiar "I love you" her mother had always answered her with, but when her mother opened her mouth, nothing came out. Her mother pressed her lips together, as if she was struggling to hold something back.

"Mom?" Lottie asked.

Her mother shook her head, and when Lottie

reached for her again, she stepped back, out of Lottie's grasp.

The gesture wrung Lottie's heart, even though she knew it was her mother's way of letting her go.

It took everything Lottie had to pick up her valise again and go out the door.

The top of her Bearcat was already down. She tossed her valise in the back, then made her way over to the door behind it by the early light now spilling through the big square panes of glass. It only took her a moment to undo the latch and let it swing wide enough to ease the car out safely.

The keys were in the ignition, where she'd left them. This time, the engine caught as soon as she put the clutch in and turned the key.

Suddenly, the weight in her chest that had grown more and more crushing with every day that led up to the wedding vanished. In its absence, she felt content. A smile spread across her face, and she felt hope for the first time she could remember. It was such an unfamiliar feeling that it took her a moment to recognize it: the swelling in her chest, the dizzy feel of freedom, and the sense that suddenly all doors were open and everything was possible.

A moment later, she was winding down the long drive from her home and turning onto the main road. She was headed due east, into the sunrise.

Six

Lottie stepped into the small room off the narrow dormitory hallway, dropped her little blue valise on the bare mattress of the nearest bed, and sighed.

It was hard to believe the whirlwind she'd been through since she first carried that bag out of her bedroom at home. The tough test they'd given her to check her math and writing skills once she arrived in New York, where the WAVES housed their training base, at Hunter College in the Bronx. The interview they'd given her, once she passed the test. And then the waiting to hear whether she'd been accepted—weeks of it.

She would have liked to do it all on her own, but the fact of the matter was that she had never held a job before and didn't know how long she could promise to stay at one. So one of her first calls home, a few days after the canceled wedding, was to her mother. Her mother's voice had been strained, but she'd tried to stay cheerful—like the mothers of so many who were already off at war. And when Lottie told her she'd spent the night in a single room down the hall from a shared bath, her mother had insisted that she check into a private club in the city where her father was a member.

Lottie knew she'd created so many worries for her parents that she couldn't bear to create another one now, so she'd complied. But as soon as she got there, she regretted it, feeling more and more friction between the lavish lifestyle of the people who frequented the club and the war she knew was raging abroad. She read the papers every morning, from front to back, but she was still restless.

So she'd started going to the recruiting office every day to see if there was any word about her case. And eventually, they'd gotten so tired of her questions that they put her to work, signing up other volunteers who came in—a handful of women who had heard about the WAVES program, but mostly young men.

Every day, she'd checked the mail at the front desk at the club—sometimes twice a day—waiting for word from the Navy. For weeks, all that had come was mail from her mother, little notes on her familiar stationery. They arrived every few days with cheerful updates, letting her know that the maples on the golf course had all turned red with an overnight cold snap, or that the Beauforts' new puppy had chewed up the leg of their Louis XIV couch.

But her mother's letters gave Lottie an uneasy feeling. That was partly because they deliberately made no mention of the war, as if Lottie were just out for a long visit to the city. And partly because an update about Eugene or the aftermath of the canceled wedding was noticeably absent.

Despite her mother's attempt at cheery small talk, Lottie could feel the strain in her tone, just like she had over the phone. She couldn't let her mind dwell on what it must have been like for her mother to let her go, even for a moment. If she did, it would be crippling. It was easier to simply throw herself into her work and try to forget everything—and everyone—she'd left behind. So she wrote back, not as frequently as her mother did, with her own newsy letters, full of any jokes or silly moments she could scrounge up from the pattern of her days.

Then, finally, the official letter had come, ordering her to report to the training program at Hunter College and giving her the address of one of the apartments near the campus that the Navy had also taken over as housing for recruits.

She'd always dreamed of having a little apartment in New York. But as she unfastened the latches of the valise, Lottie realized she'd never thought it would be one like this: so far away from the heart of things, back in Manhattan.

The room was dingy, nothing more than two twin beds, one dresser, and one desk. A small window looked out at an alleyway and a small mirror hung above the desk on the pale yellow wall. It was clearly a dorm room—furnished, but not with any thought or love. Even the personal marks that might have made it feel homey had vanished along with the previous inhabitants.

Despite this, or perhaps because of it, Lottie realized she'd never been so pleased to step into any room before in her life.

Lottie plopped onto the mattress, the springs squeaking cheerfully. It felt like she had just reached the end of a long race. And although this seemed like some kind of a finish line, she knew the real race was still to come. Basic training hadn't even started.

She figured she'd better unpack and make her bed. She'd just begun by unfolding one of the sheets that were neatly piled at the foot of it when she heard footsteps in the hall.

She turned to see a young woman in a red midi dress, with frizzy red hair and a broad face full of freckles.

"Hello," Lottie said, turning on her warmest smile. "I'm Lottie. Lottie Palmer."

"Yeah, I got that," the woman said in an unmistakable Southern drawl. She tapped on the wall in the hallway, then stalked into the room. "Says it by the door."

"It does?" Lottie said. Somehow, she'd managed to completely miss it.

Her smile faded as she darted back into the hall, where she discovered the newcomer was correct. Two names were hand-lettered on a placard outside: C. Palmer, for her full name, Charlotte. And M. Duckworthy.

"So you're . . . Duckworthy?" Lottie tried.

Somehow, her new roommate had already managed to snap the sheet onto her bed and was tucking the perfect hospital corners under the mattress. She gave a crisp nod.

"What does the M stand for?" Lottie asked.

"Maggie," the woman said, then dropped her own bag on the bed.

Lottie couldn't help but notice that it was even smaller than her own, and even more worn. Its rickety sides seemed to be made out of actual cardboard, and it was held together not by its latches, but by a piece of thick string.

And further conversation seemed to be the last thing Maggie was interested in.

Lottie stepped back through the doorway into the room and finished making her own bed, then opened her valise on the thin blanket. She couldn't help feeling a little grateful that she had thought to choose a bag that wouldn't give away her family's wealth. It felt good to earn her place in this room, and she wanted to earn everything else the same way.

She'd pulled her small collection of simple clothes out of the bag and started to hang them in the small shared closet when she heard a snort behind her.

"Rich girl, eh?" Maggie said.

Lottie stared into the closet, which contained nothing more than her Navy-issue suits and shirts, her Navy topcoat and rain cover, and the gloves, stockings, and shoes that the Navy had assigned her. Just the standard issue and a few simple dresses of her own. She felt heat rising in her cheeks, surprise and shame chased by indignation.

How did Maggie know?

She glanced back at her. She'd never heard that word—*rich*—sound so ugly before. Maggie's wardrobe was already closed, with her empty bag settled neatly beside it, wilting a little bit without any contents to give the tired sides structure.

Maggie nodded at the open door. "You'll get along real well with Miss Prissy across the hall, then," she said. "You should see all the stuff she brought for the war. You'd think she got an invitation to a garden party."

Lottie glanced through the door, across the hall. A tall, willowy blonde was struggling to lift a large Louis Vuitton bag off her bed. And Lottie immediately recognized her dress from the window of Barneys.

She looked at the woman's luxurious accouterments and thought of her own simple collection of belongings, wondering what similarity Maggie could even see in them. They seemed so different to her that part of her wanted to start an argument about it. The only thing that stopped her was that, despite it all, Maggie was still right: she and the woman across the way were both undoubtedly wealthy.

Lottie spent so much time puzzling over this that the woman across the hall must have felt her gaze somehow. She turned around and waved. "Hi!" she said. "I'm Pearl Florence."

"Lottie Palmer," Lottie said, and crossed the hall to shake Pearl's hand.

"Where are you from?" she asked. "I thought I was from New York City, until I got up here to the Bronx. Now I'm realizing I'm not sure I even know what that means."

Lottie couldn't tell if the girl meant to be a snob or if she really was just marveling at how much she didn't know about the world. Maybe it was some of both. Maybe Pearl didn't really know herself.

"Detroit," Lottie said.

Pearl smiled amiably, but then her eyes widened. "Did you say Lottie *Palmer?*" she asked. "Of the Detroit Palmers?"

Lottie had only met Maggie a minute ago, but somehow she could still see the wicked grin spreading across her new roommate's face, behind her back. Lottie tried to smile in a way that acknowledged Pearl was right but got her to stop talking as soon as humanly possible.

"You're from Manhattan?" Lottie asked quickly, hoping that would get Pearl off the topic of Lottie's own background.

Pearl nodded. "Which makes it even more tempting to think about how close my own warm bed is right now," she said, looking down on the flimsy mattress that had been issued to her. "I knew I wanted to get away when I joined the Navy, but they didn't send me very far."

She looked up at Lottie ruefully, and Lottie felt a little tug in her heart. She didn't like the way it sounded when Pearl said she'd joined the Navy to get away—like a poor little rich girl on yet another exotic adventure. But was she in a position to judge? Lottie asked herself. Was she anything different herself? Lottie wanted to believe that there was more to herself than met the eye. So it was only fair that she give Pearl the same benefit of the doubt.

"I'm just trying to figure out where to put everything," Pearl went on, looking around at her stacks of boxes.

"The only thing you need," Maggie pointed out from behind them, "is your uniform." As if to illustrate her point, she'd already changed into hers.

"Oh my goodness," Pearl said. "Don't you look smart. But is it really time to . . . ?"

Maggie looked down at her watch with what could only be described as military precision. "Depends on how long it takes you to get to lunch," she said. "It's twelve ten. First mess is at twelve thirty. In uniform."

Then she stalked off, down the hall, as Pearl and Lottie scrambled to their closets.

In the crush of figuring out where the mess hall was, and figuring out how to find anything in it, Lottie was relieved she didn't see Maggie at lunch. And she didn't see her in any of the orientation classes she'd been assigned to that afternoon, learning basic facts about the Navy and the subjects they'd be focusing on as possible areas for study: secretarial, accounting, coding, and transmission.

Lottie knew that she was one of two thousand women who had shown up for the first time on the Hunter College campus that day. And two thousand new women showed up every two weeks, for the six-week training program, which meant there was a total of six thousand women on campus at any given time. So she started to hope that maybe she wouldn't ever have to see her unpleasant roommate during daylight hours.

But then, in the late afternoon, it came time to line up in formation for drills.

The officers rounded them up by dorm. And then they split them up by floor and room, which meant that Pearl and Lottie were both reunited with Maggie in the ranks of the drill exercises, Pearl and Lottie side by side, with Maggie walking right behind.

In the heat of the late afternoon, when Lottie was feeling about as hungry as she ever had, she tripped in the course of one of the exercises. She heard Maggie snort behind her. "You usually pay someone to walk for you, too?"

The comment stung so much that when Lottie got back to her room after dinner that night, she changed out of her uniform and climbed into bed without giving Maggie much more than a polite nod. For her part, Maggie ignored the fact that Lottie might want to simply go to sleep and kept the light overhead blazing so that she could read a book.

"Could you turn that out, please?" Lottie asked after what seemed like hours of tossing and turning under the bright light.

"Did you bring a servant with you?" Maggie cracked in return. "That's funny, I don't see one here."

Lottie rolled over, giving up. It wasn't like she could have slept, even if the light had been out.

Her mind kept looping back, like a broken record, to the question of how in the world Maggie had known she was from a wealthy family. She didn't have expensive luggage. She hadn't brought a ton of unnecessary clothes, like Pearl had. Was it that obvious, just by looking at her? Was it something about her face or just the way she was? And if Maggie could see it at a glance—could everybody else?

Finally, Maggie turned out the light and put her book down beside her bed.

Before Maggie had a chance to fall asleep, and before Lottie could lose her nerve, she turned over, propping her head up on her arm.

"Maggie," she said.

"Mm," Maggie said in a noncommittal way that acknowledged that was, in fact, her name.

"How did you know?" Lottie asked.

"Know what?" Maggie asked, irritation in her tone.

Now that she had to say it out loud, Lottie wasn't exactly sure how to put it. "That my family has money."

For some reason, Maggie found this amusing enough to warrant what sounded like a full-fledged belly laugh. "Oh, honey," she said. "It's as clear as day. You didn't starch that uniform yourself. Only a service could get corners that crisp. I'm the only person in the world who's ever done my ironing for me. And I did all the ironing for all my eight brothers, because I'm the only girl. Not that there's much call for wearing anything that requires ironing out on a dirt road in Georgia."

While Lottie's mind worked, taking this in, Maggie went on. "And your shiny shoes. Of course you probably could have done those yourself. But you didn't, did you?"

Lottie thought back to the woman who had arrived at her hotel room to take the uniform and shoes away for pressing and shining, and the man she had tipped when he returned them, the uniform wrapped in thin crinkling paper printed with the hotel's emblem.

"No," she said quietly.

"I didn't think so," Maggie said with satisfaction. "Sweet dreams, Your Highness."

Suddenly, in the darkness, Lottie felt a deep longing for Eugene. No matter the differences between them, he'd always been absolutely on her side, even when they were kids, before anything between them had turned romantic. She felt so friendless and alone right now. She wanted to turn to the shelter she had known with him. But the thought of him caused an even deeper ache in her heart.

He was probably hurting, too, she realized. He'd never asked for any of this. All he'd tried to do was give her a good life—and his heart. He didn't deserve to be stood up on the eve of his wedding. At the thought of it, tears sprang to her eyes. She blinked them back quickly, worried that Maggie would somehow realize she was crying.

A moment later though, she realized Maggie had already dropped into sleep, given away by the slightest of snores.

But Lottie stayed wide awake, trying to figure out how in the world she was going to survive the next six weeks. It wasn't the training that worried her anymore.

It was her roommate.

Seven

Lottie took a step inside the new classroom and looked around, trying to get a sense of who was there, and what was going on, before she sat down.

Her left arm, which cradled her notebook and pen, still throbbed from the typhoid shot they'd given her that morning. And it was just the first of a whole slate of inoculations they'd handed her, all marked out on a single sheet: different shots every day. As far as she could tell, basic training might just have been one big excuse to make sure all of the women were up-to-date on their vaccines, before shipping them out.

The classroom was small, and looked like it was used for science classes under normal circumstances. A plastic model of a human body, with the belly cut away so the plastic organs were exposed, stood in the front of the room, turned so that it seemed to be looking out the window, down into the leafy collegiate courtyard below. A large chart of various phyla and kingdoms hung in the back of the room, illustrated with beautiful colored drawings of leaves, snails, insects, and birds. In the glass cases that lined the side walls were smaller glass cases, each filled with specimens: feathers, branches, tiny creatures floating in formaldehyde.

It was a small classroom, not a lecture hall, and most of the thirty or so seats were already filled, but Lottie didn't see an instructor yet in the front of the room. She also, to her relief, didn't see Maggie.

After their conversation the night before, Lottie hadn't even dared to ask Maggie about her class schedule. Instead, the two of them had gotten ready in stony silence. There was no reason to believe that Maggie would be in her class, with two thousand women all starting new schedules. Still, Lottie was glad to see that she'd be free of Maggie's disapproving presence, at least for this hour of the day.

The room appeared to be filling up from the back, with the empty seats mostly in the front. Lottie normally would have chosen a spot in the middle of the class, but she gamely walked up and took one of the spots just behind the front row.

As she did, she heard the click of heels behind her. The head of every girl in the room swiveled as one, to see a tall woman, probably ten or fifteen years older than most of them, striding up to the front of the room. Her dark hair was tucked neatly under her cap, and her uniform was spotless and completely devoid of wrinkles.

But that wasn't what captured Lottie's attention the most. It was something about the way the woman carried herself. Lottie knew all kinds of powerful women. The ones in her mother's circle could make or break a man's career, just with the right invitation or the wrong comment behind closed doors.

Lottie couldn't tell at first what was different about this woman. She just knew she'd never seen anything like it.

But as the officer dropped a stack of books on the desk at the front of the room and looked up to scan the class, something snapped into place in Lottie's mind: It wasn't that she was particularly this way or that. It was that this woman seemed to be completely herself, not putting on any kind of show for anyone else.

"Good morning, ladies," the officer said. "I'm Lieutenant Brown."

As the class murmured a greeting in return, the door at the back of the room creaked again. This time, the whole class and Lieutenant Brown turned to get a look at the unlucky student.

And with an unpleasant charge of recognition, Lottie saw her roommate standing in the doorway.

Lottie hadn't seen this expression on Maggie's face before. All her confidence was gone. It was replaced by embarrassment as she stood in the doorway, as if held there by the gazes of all the other women.

She didn't stay there long. After a moment, she steeled herself. Her expression became smooth and impassive, and she hurried up to the front of the class, where she slipped into the seat beside Lottie.

Lottie glanced at her, ready to offer a smile of welcome, but Maggie was so busy staring straight ahead that she didn't even recognize her.

"Glad to see you could make it," Lieutenant Brown said with clear sarcasm.

Maggie just flipped open her notebook on the desk and took out her pen.

Lottie had to admire her coolness. "Hey," she whispered in a sympathetic tone. "You have trouble finding the room?"

But when Maggie finally glanced over and realized whom she'd sat down beside, the disdainful curl of her lip drove away any sympathetic feelings Lottie might have felt toward her.

"I guess I had trouble finding a good seat," she said with a snarl.

By now, Lieutenant Brown had come around from behind the desk and leaned back on it, getting closer so that she could address them more directly.

"Name," she said, looking at Lottie.

At first Lottie looked up at her blankly.

"You have a name, don't you?" Lieutenant Brown demanded.

"Charlotte," Lottie stammered. "Charlotte Palmer."

Lieutenant Brown looked at Maggie, who said, "Maggie Duckworthy," with a smirk.

Then Lieutenant Brown continued around the room, taking in the names of all the other girls.

"Don't expect me to remember all this," Lieutenant Brown said. "If you want me to know your names, I expect you to make your name worth remembering."

She looked around the room, pausing to search the face of each woman.

"I'm going to be initiating you into the finer points of military discipline and etiquette," Lieutenant Brown said. "Which I suspect wasn't a big topic of interest at whatever nurseries or finishing schools you came from."

The way Lieutenant Brown said *finishing schools* made Lottie's pulse lurch. Had she been talking about her? In any case, Maggie clearly gave Lottie a sidelong glance in response.

Lottie's blood started to boil. She didn't judge Maggie for where she came from. So why did Maggie feel she had the right to judge her? A person can't help where they're born. But Maggie's attitude made her even more bound and determined to prove she'd earned a spot in the WAVES, fair and square.

"But before we get into the details of military discipline," Lieutenant Brown said, "I want to talk with you about war. Because this isn't just another topic for you to bone up on, like history or geology, where it doesn't matter much if you get a question wrong. War is life and death. That's the whole point of it. You may not be in the line of fire yourself—we hope," she added in a way that sent a shiver down Lottie's spine. "But the things you do, and how well you do them, can be a matter of life and death for someone else."

She'd joined the WAVES because she wanted to do something that mattered. And getting all the way to New York already felt like it had split her life apart. But she couldn't even imagine what it would be like to be part of the noise and confusion and danger she saw on the newsreels about the war. And suddenly she realized how naive she'd been to think that she could really be sure that same violence would never touch her. War was unpredictable. That was what made it so terrible.

"For the men in the field, in our planes and on our ships: every message you send, every figure you calculate, everything you do, it has to be right. And it has to be done without dramatics. If you've got nerves, or worries, or tears, this isn't the place for them. It's time to give all that up and leave all that behind."

Lieutenant Brown glanced around the room. "You girls have what it takes?" she said.

Lottie, thinking back on everything she had given up to be here, gave a vigorous nod.

To her surprise, Lieutenant Brown's steely gaze

fastened on her with a curl of the lip that looked all too much like Maggie's.

"You understand all that?" Lieutenant Brown said. "Leaving it all behind?"

Lottie looked up at her hesitantly, waiting for Lieutenant Brown to say something else or ask another question.

But Lieutenant Brown just stared at her. The blood began to pound in Lottie's ears, and in the silence of the classroom she could hear the other girls begin to shift in their seats.

"I do," Lottie said quietly. "I gave up my wedding to come here."

The smile that spread over Lieutenant Brown's face surprised Lottie. It was so twisted it looked more like a grimace. "Oh, princess," Lieutenant Brown said with evident sarcasm. "That's a lot to give up."

Lottie felt a pang at the mockery. For a second, she longed fiercely to be back with Eugene, where everything was familiar and safe, and nothing she did was ever wrong. And in the next second, she hoped passionately that nobody else in the class had noticed what the instructor had called her, that nobody would remember it, and that she'd never have to hear it said again.

Now Lieutenant Brown looked out over the class, glancing over the faces of the other girls. Lottie didn't dare look back at them over her shoulder to see their expressions. She didn't even want to try to imagine what they might be thinking.

"Did anyone else in this class give up anything to be here?" Lieutenant Brown said.

By now, the other girls had wised up. None of them were going to be foolish enough to fall into Lieutenant Brown's trap.

So Lieutenant Brown began to point. "You," she said, jabbing her finger over Lottie's head, toward one of the women seated behind her. "What did you give up to be here?"

"I just got into law school," the woman said. "But I wanted to help fight this war. I don't know if they'll let me in again when I get back," she added more quietly.

Lieutenant Brown pointed to someone else. This time the voice had a Southern accent, like Maggie's. "My mom's real sick," she said. "I don't know if she'll still be there when I get home."

Lieutenant Brown pointed to someone in the back. "You," she ordered.

"My brother's at the front," Lottie heard the woman say over her shoulder. "So I'm Daddy's only help on the farm. But if we don't win this war, it won't matter whether we can keep the farm or not."

Something strange was happening to Lieutenant Brown as each woman spoke. Lottie had expected her to get steelier. But instead, her eyes were softening. With each new story, Lottie felt like a new layer was peeled back, revealing the woman behind the reserve that Lieutenant Brown maintained in order to teach the women what they needed to do to survive in the military.

Finally, Lieutenant Brown looked down at Maggie, still seated in one of the front seats. By now, her expression was almost tender.

"You," she said. "What did you give up?"

Maggie looked up at Lieutenant Brown with none of the challenge that Lottie was used to seeing in Maggie's eyes.

"I didn't have anything to give up," Maggie said simply.

Eight

"Right!" the drill sergeant called through the bullhorn. "Left! Right, left, right!"

On the large Hunter College ball field that served as the parade grounds for the WAVES, Lottie stepped and turned with the hundreds of other women who had made it through the last six weeks of training and were hoping to pass their final unit test today.

As they listened intently for the commands, ready to turn at a moment's notice, Lottie's lips curled in amusement as she thought back to the most memorable drill of their training.

She and a few hundred other women had been mustering in the Hunter gymnasium, because a heavy New York rain was falling outside. But their instructor had gotten distracted in the middle of the drill and failed to tell them to turn.

But that didn't stop the WAVES. They just kept marching, straight toward the wall, with the first few of them even climbing jokingly up some of the sporting equipment piled at that end of the gym when they got there, to indicate that they were unstoppable. When their drill leader looked up and finally realized what was going on, the whole drill had dissolved into laughter.

On the field today, the sunshine was bright—

an unseasonably warm late-spring day. Although it was only early afternoon, Lottie was already hot in her dress-blue uniform. And she wasn't the only one. All around her, she could see the other women shifting and perspiring as they tried to keep their movements crisp and their eyes straight ahead.

Then the instructor called a halt, and the true test really began. One hour at attention, in the afternoon sun, for their final formal inspection.

In the weeks before, they'd done practice drills, but never anything this long. And even in the practice drills, women had been forced to drop out. For some of them, it was just too much to stand that long. And some of them actually passed out while trying.

"If you see someone fall," the drill sergeants had instructed the women, "catch her. Then lay her down on the ground and stand back at attention. And don't lock your knees."

As Lottie snapped to attention and took her first deep breaths, trying to stay calm and cool, she felt a knot of nervousness in her stomach. After all they'd been through in the past six weeks—the classes, the drills, the vaccines, the instructors who encouraged and hassled and shouted at them to learn more, stand up straighter, get it right this time, it could all come down to the next few hours.

Lottie had been determined to get through the training itself, and she had. All along the way, other women had dropped out, unable to do the work, or stand the homesickness, or master the fear of what would come next if they actually were sent into active duty.

But she was still here.

She knew that some of the women who had washed out already had been just as determined as her. She'd seen other women stand at attention, their eyes as steady and their jaws just as set as hers—right until the moment when they crumpled to the ground and washed out of the program, despite all the dreaming and planning and hard work they'd done to get there.

The first few minutes weren't so bad. They'd all stood at attention for long periods before, and Lottie had developed a strategy for it: she just picked one thing and concentrated, very hard, on it.

But she'd found that she had to be careful what she picked to concentrate on. One day it had been a cloud, which moved imperceptibly across the sky while she watched, and drew her gaze imperceptibly with it, until the bark of a drill leader had snapped her back to looking straight ahead.

But as the hour wore on, she didn't have to choose what to concentrate on, because so many things began to hurt at once. Her eyes stung from the sun, which managed to slip in under the brim of her cap. Her hamstrings felt tight and her back had a dull ache, while her fingers and toes itched for any kind of action. And she was exhausted, wishing again and again that she could relax, even just for a moment.

But it was as the sun began to slide down the sky toward evening that the real fight began. Most of her various aches and pains had faded and transformed into a strange sense of numbness.

But the real battle wasn't physical. It was in her mind. Without any new information at all, stuck in one place for so long, her mind had gotten tired of casting around for memories or hopes and was now demanding something, anything, to amuse itself.

And when Lottie continued to stand at attention, her mind began to come up with all kinds of unhelpful thoughts. She began to worry over how strained her parents' voices had sounded the last time she talked to them on the phone. Was something wrong back home? Something they were keeping from her? Or did all that pain come from the choice she'd made? Then her mind turned to the fact that she hadn't talked to Eugene at all. He hadn't been angry, her mother had said: "He was just—quiet."

But Lottie knew what that meant. The more Eugene was feeling, the quieter he got. She just wished she knew if he'd forgiven her. The thought that he might hate her made her tremble—although, she deserved it if he did. She'd never wanted to leave him. It was just that she couldn't go where she felt she had to without leaving him behind. And now that she was out in the big world, she couldn't believe how often her mind returned to him, wondering what he would think about the things that were going on around her.

Part of what kept her in line, at sharp attention, was the fact that Maggie was still standing directly behind her. Their relationship hadn't warmed any in the last six weeks. They were polite enough to each other in the room, but even after all this time, they still treated each other like strangers, as if they'd just met that day.

And that was on the good days. On the bad ones, Maggie had made it clear that it would give her great pleasure to see Lottie wash out—or Pearl, who stood just to Lottie's left on the parade field.

It was a surprise to Lottie that Pearl had made it this far. All along the way, Pearl had struggled with the basic secretarial tasks and almost always seemed to come in last or close to last in the athletic events, struggling to complete the ordered number of calisthenics or laps around the track. And she seemed to struggle with things the other girls didn't even give a second thought.

Most of them dove right in when they were assigned kitchen duty or had to clean the halls or bathrooms. But Pearl had clearly never done a lick of that kind of work in her life. And not only did she not know how, she didn't like it. But to her credit, she didn't give up.

Now, though, Lottie saw Pearl begin to move out of the corner of her eye. It seemed a reasonably safe time to do it, if you had to let off some steam, because the nearest drill sergeant had just stalked around their quadrant of the field with a clipboard and was now heading away, back up toward the front of the formation.

But Lottie had also seen Pearl faint before in formation, when they didn't have to stand for nearly as long as they did today. And this was how it started. The tiniest tremor, then some shifting, and suddenly, she would be toppling over. Other times, the other women had caught her, to the point where it had become something of a joke. But now they'd have to step out of formation to do it and risk their own status in the final exercise—which was no joke at all.

But Lottie could also see another one coming, marching toward them from the back of the column. "Pearl," she hissed. "Snap to."

"I can't do it," Pearl said, her voice high with stress.

"Shh!" Lottie said, her eye on the drill sergeant striding down their line.

Then, to her surprise, she heard a familiar voice behind her. "Yes, you can," Maggie shot back at Pearl. Her voice was forceful, but it had none of its usual sneer. She was dead serious. And she was risking her own parade standing, Lottie realized, to bark at Pearl not to lose hers.

"How much longer?" Pearl asked.

"Doesn't matter," Maggie snapped. "Don't you dare move."

"Ladies," a voice boomed. "Would you care to let us in on your conversation?"

Somehow, Pearl suddenly found it in herself to snap back to perfect attention.

Beside her, Lottie did the same, hoping that maybe the approaching sergeant, a heavyset woman with red hair and an even redder face, hadn't really seen exactly who was talking.

But her heart sank when the woman came to a stop right in front of her. "Do we have conversations while we stand at attention?" the woman asked, her face inches away from Lottie's own.

"No, ma'am," Lottie said, staring straight ahead.

"But you were talking," the sergeant said.

Lottie hesitated for a moment, then decided the only thing she could do was fess up. "Yes, ma'am."

"You understand what that means?" the sergeant asked.

The tight knot that had been sitting in her stomach since the opening of the exercise felt as if it had just doubled in weight in that single moment. Was this it? After all she'd done to get here, was she about to wash out because of a stupid whispered comment?

But before Lottie could answer, the sergeant answered her own question. "It means your exercise is going to last longer than all the rest," she said. "After we're dismissed, I want to see you stand here at attention until final bell.

"You and your friend here," the sergeant said,

slapping Pearl on the shoulder so hard that Pearl lost her footing and had to come back to attention again.

Then the sergeant sauntered off, back up the line.

Lottie would never have believed that her heart could leap for joy at the prospect of standing at attention for another three hours. But it did.

Pure relief carried her through to the end of the exercise, when all the girls marched off the field and began to disperse back to the dining hall, where a special celebratory dinner was being served.

And it even carried her as the sun slipped behind the buildings and night fell.

But by the time the other WAVES trailed past to their dormitories, full of celebratory good cheer, Lottie felt dizzy and nauseous.

The sergeant returned, her face impassive. After a few more minutes, or perhaps several, the bell finally rang.

"I'm so sorry," Pearl told her as they shuffled toward the dormitory. "You would have had a perfect final inspection if it weren't for me."

That was true, but Lottie didn't care. Though it would have been nice to have the perfect marks Maggie no doubt had gotten.

Lottie's stomach let out a rumble.

"I made you miss dinner," Pearl groaned. "On top of everything else."

Lottie's stomach grumbled in agreement, but she shook her head. "Don't worry about it," she said. "We both made it through. That's all that matters."

Pearl glanced away from her, her expression guilty.

"Hey," Lottie said, giving her a quick hug. "Please. Don't worry."

"I didn't deserve it," Pearl said quietly.

"You just get out there," Lottie said, "and do everything you can to help our boys win."

Pearl nodded, still looking down as she reached for the door to her room and slipped in.

Lottie opened the door to her own room. Maggie didn't even look up from the book she had her nose buried in when Lottie entered, and Lottie didn't dare to interrupt her with a greeting.

But when Lottie looked at her own bed, there was a small plate sitting on it, holding a drumstick and a small pile of green beans. And beside that, slightly smashed on a paper napkin, was a hefty slice of chocolate cake with thick chocolate frosting.

"What's this?" she asked, her voice loud with surprise.

"Chicken," Maggie said as if she were talking to a very small and very slow child. "Green beans. Cake."

"But why?" Lottie said, turning around.

Maggie still didn't look up from her book,

but she raised her eyebrows in annoyance. "Did they feed you dinner out there on the track?" she asked.

"N-no," Lottie stammered.

"Well," Maggie said. "There's your dinner."

Suddenly, Lottie felt an unexpected rush of warm feeling for her roommate. Maggie had saved all this . . . for her?

She sat down on the bed and dug into the meal. It was lukewarm but more delicious than any meal she could remember having, no doubt thanks to all the stress of the afternoon.

After a few bites, something began to tug at her. "Did they have a lot left over?" she asked. Maybe someone had insisted she take it with her.

But Maggie just gave her head a little shake. "I had to sneak it out under my jacket," she said.

For the first time, she looked up from the book and met Lottie's eyes. "I saw what you did out there," Lottie said. "Trying to help Pearl."

Maggie snorted. "I just didn't want to see her waste all of Uncle Sam's money," she said. "Like you rich girls waste your own."

Somehow, because Lottie had thought Maggie might actually be trying to do something nice for her, the sting of this sharp comment was worse.

Quietly, she got up and dropped the remains of her dinner in the little trash can under their shared desk.

"Princess," Maggie added.

Nine

"California," Lieutenant Brown said.

Lottie was so surprised that she wasn't sure for a moment whether Lieutenant Brown had actually said anything at all, or whether Lottie had just been so nervous that she'd imagined the craziest thing possible while she was waiting for Lieutenant Brown to tell her what her actual assignment was going to be.

The two of them were sitting in a small office that, by the looks of it, had belonged to a classics professor before the WAVES took over this quadrant of the campus. The shelves were stuffed with leather-bound books with Greek lettering in black or gold on their spines, and black-and-white postcards of Roman ruins were scattered haphazardly around the shelves.

Lieutenant Brown herself was seated behind a small desk, piled high with more leather-bound books and papers, where she'd managed to carve out a small space of her own, probably by piling the books that had been there even higher on either side.

On the desk beside her was a small replica of what appeared to be the explosion of the volcano at Pompeii, complete with brightly painted red and yellow plaster spurting from the mouth of the volcano, in place of the ancient lava.

Lieutenant Brown raised her eyebrows. "I thought you'd have *something* to say about that, Palmer," she said.

So she really *had* said California. Visions of palm trees and wide beaches and unfathomably blue skies began to unfold in her mind, but she still didn't manage to come up with anything to say.

Lieutenant Brown looked down at her papers. "You'll be in the airplane mechanical division," she said.

For the second time in as many minutes, Lottie was sure she was hearing things. She knew how to fix a Bearcat engine, and she was pretty sure she could figure out a jeep. But Eugene had been right that she hadn't really touched an airplane engine, just managed to find the broken fuel line on her family friend's plane.

Besides that, she hadn't known being an airplane mechanic was even a possibility. All the classes and aptitude tests they'd taken had been about shorthand, and typing, and accounting, with a bit of coding thrown in for good measure.

Happiness and confusion struggled on Lottie's face. "But," she said carefully, "I didn't know they tested us for mechanics."

Lieutenant Brown cracked a brief smile. "We test for everything," she said, glancing down at

Lottie's papers. "And you scored quite high on mechanical aptitude."

As Lottie sat there in wonder, Lieutenant Brown's expression turned more severe. "You think you can do the job, Palmer?"

"Yes, ma'am!" Lottie said immediately. Her confidence came from her heart, but after a moment, Lieutenant Brown's very first words in their first class came back to her: this was a war, and a matter of life and death. Lottie was confident she could do whatever was asked of her. But she didn't want her overconfidence to lead to disaster for some American pilot.

"But I've never really worked on a plane engine before," she confessed quietly.

Lieutenant Brown let out a bark of laughter. "I've never met a debutante who has," she said. Then her expression softened by a fraction. "Don't worry, Palmer," she said. "They'll teach you everything you need to know. Whether you like it or not."

Lottie wouldn't have believed that Lieutenant Brown's face could get more serious, but when her brief smile vanished, her features turned even more severe than they had been. "This is a specialized post," she said. "So you'll have quite a bit more contact with the men than the other WAVES. I guess I don't have to tell you what that means."

Lottie nodded, her mind racing to catch up,

although she had no idea what Lieutenant Brown thought that might mean.

"More opportunities to fraternize," Lieutenant Brown said. "Which I'm sure you understand is grounds for discharge."

"Yes, ma'am," Lottie answered promptly.

Lieutenant Brown pulled a page from Lottie's file and held it out.

"It's quite an assignment, Palmer," she added. "You should be proud."

Then she flipped Lottie's file folder shut and jutted her chin toward the door. "Dismissed," she said.

Lottie stood, took the paper, and walked out the door. Even in the hallway, reading the letters on the page in all caps for herself, she still couldn't quite believe it: *NORTH ISLAND*. The naval air station in San Diego.

Her first thought was how surprised Eugene would be. For a full second or two, she wondered about where she could find the nearest phone, to call him and share the news. Then she came to her senses.

She hadn't spoken a word to him since she'd walked out on their wedding. But the grooves their long relationship had worn in her heart were still deep. Until now, she'd managed to block out her memories of him almost completely. And something about the victory of actually finishing training must have set them free.

So she pushed the thoughts of Eugene aside and called up images of California—the beaches, the sunshine, and the boats on the endless sea.

By the time she reached her room, the shock had started to wear off, replaced by a growing sense of excitement and a good dose of pride.

All her life, Lottie had been drawn to machines, especially engines. It was in her blood—after all, that was how her father and his father before him had made their fortunes.

But all her life, people had been looking askance at her for her interest in mechanics—sometimes even when it was *their* car she was in the midst of fixing. She was so tired of the world constantly underestimating her.

But now the US Navy would certify her as a bona fide mechanic. Or at least someone who had enough aptitude to be a mechanic. It was a totally different feeling than any she'd ever had before—a deep shift in the way she saw herself.

For all her confidence, which was famous back in Detroit, and her opinions, which were infamous, there had always been some part of her that wasn't absolutely sure what she was worth. All her life, she'd been treated as if she were special, simply because of who she was.

Some of the people she'd grown up with seemed to think they mattered more than other people because they had the right clothes, the right address—or the right car. But Lottie felt none of that even mattered at all.

She knew how to do so many things. But how was she supposed to use her talents? What was it all for?

She might not have even been able to put any of this into words—until Lieutenant Brown put her orders in her hand. But as soon as Lieutenant Brown did, Lottie suddenly knew what she had been missing: purpose. A sense of what it was she was put here to do. A sense of how that might actually, ever, help anyone else.

The feeling of knowing her part in things, of having her own special assignment, was so unfamiliar, and so powerful, that it filled her with warmth that radiated toward everything, and everyone, she saw as she headed back to her dormitory.

The peeling paint on the walls looked no longer dingy but homey, and the press of women milling about, crowing about their own orders, or dragging their suitcases and uniforms out of their rooms, seemed like not a crowd but a community.

When Lottie caught sight of Pearl struggling through the door of her room with three pieces of her Louis Vuitton luggage dangling from her arms, she brightly waved and headed toward her.

"Pearl!" Lottie said, running up to give her a hug.

Pearl looked down, but Lottie just grinned.

She could barely remember the day before, when they'd spent the extra hour together at the track. How could that matter, now that both of them were off to their new assignments?

"Did you already get your assignment?" Lottie asked. "What did they give you?"

"Virginia," Pearl said. "Storekeeping."

From their training, Lottie knew this meant accounting or bookkeeping, to keep track of supplies that were supporting their men at the front.

"That's wonderful," Lottie said. "You can do that in a heartbeat. You were always one of the first ones finished with those math tests, and I bet once—"

Pearl looked up and met Lottie's eyes, and something about the look in them stopped Lottie midsentence.

"Lottie," she said. "I'm not going."

"Not going?" Lottie repeated. Her mind ground to a screeching halt, then started to cast around in shock. All that work, all those weeks, all those other women who had washed out—the risk Lottie had taken with her *own* hopes and dreams, trying to help Pearl reach hers. "Why not?"

Pearl looked down at the scuffed wood of the dormitory hall, shaking her head. "I'm not sure I can do it," she said.

"Well, the Navy thinks you can," Lottie insisted. "And they weren't doing anyone any favors along the way. There were other women who never made it this far."

"I know," Pearl said quietly. "But I almost didn't. I'm not sure I should have."

"Of course you should," Lottie said impatiently.

"But what if . . ." Pearl said, then trailed off.

"What if *what?*" Lottie said.

"What if I can't do what I need to do?" Pearl said. "When it really matters? When someone's life is on the line?"

It was a good question, even though Pearl would be stationed far from any battle. Any mistake any of them made along the way, now that they were really part of the war effort, could be a matter of life and death. But still, it seemed to Lottie like Pearl had chosen the wrong way to think about it.

"Think about all the things you know you can do," Lottie said. "You know we need someone who can do them. What if we need you, but you don't come? What happens then?"

Pearl couldn't bring herself to look back up at Lottie.

"I can't," she mumbled. "I don't think I can."

For an instant, Lottie could feel the pull that Pearl was giving in to. It would be so easy just to go back to the life she'd known before, a life free of drill sergeants, and mockery, and angry roommates—and danger. A life with her parents, and Eugene. At the thought of him, her heart tugged, as it always did, both drawn back and pushed away by the pain she knew she must have caused him.

But even deeper was a feeling that had gotten her where she was right now: the sense that she had something to give, something to do. She grasped onto it now and pushed away her doubts. And she knew that if she could do that, Pearl could, too.

"Pearl," Lottie pleaded.

"I'm sorry," Pearl said, and started off down the hall.

As Lottie watched her go, frustration mounting, she caught sight of Maggie, watching her from their room across the hall.

It was hard not to feel any sense of companionship with someone who had been through everything they'd been through in the past weeks together. And she was still grateful for the kindness Maggie had shown her the night before—even if it had been followed by a nasty swipe.

But when Maggie opened her mouth, she managed to blast away all goodwill with a single comment.

"Princess Pearl tell you she was jumping ship?"

Hot words in Pearl's defense rose to Lottie's lips.

But when she looked at Maggie's face, she couldn't bring herself to say any of them. Maggie was right. That was exactly what Pearl was doing.

Feeling defeated, Lottie stepped into their room.

"Whatcha got there?" Maggie asked, nodding at the paper with Lottie's orders on it, which was still in her hand.

Lottie sat down on her bed.

"They find some palace good enough to send you to?" Maggie asked.

But even Maggie's teasing couldn't spoil the satisfaction Lottie felt in the place she'd earned for herself. "I'm going to be an airplane mechanic," she said.

"Mechanic?" Maggie repeated, incredulous. "I never saw you pick up a wrench."

"They never gave any of us a wrench in basic training," Lottie pointed out.

Maggie raised her eyebrows, acknowledging the point.

"But I've got my own toolbox at home. I can fix just about anything that's wrong with a car, if I've got enough time."

"Car and plane engines, they a lot alike?" Maggie asked.

It could have been another one of her sarcastic comments, but this time the question seemed sincere. "I guess I'll just have to get there to find out," Lottie said.

Lottie took Maggie's silence as a good sign.

Maybe she'd finally earned some respect from Maggie. Or maybe it was just easier for both of them to get along, knowing that they'd never see each other again after the next few hours, since their orders would no doubt send them to opposite sides of the continent.

"What station did you get?" Lottie ventured. She was curious. And after she'd told Maggie all about her own orders, it seemed impolite not to ask.

"Yeoman," Maggie said. Lottie nodded. That meant Maggie would be doing the administrative and communications work that kept the whole system running, making sure all the i's were dotted and t's were crossed, that everyone knew everything they should and nothing they shouldn't, and that everything got where it was going.

"They assign you to a base?" Lottie asked. Not all of the women she'd talked to had been. One of them had even been assigned to support a university program in Boston that was doing work the Navy thought might help in the war effort.

But Maggie nodded. "San Diego," she said.

"San Diego?" Lottie repeated. "In California?"

Maggie raised her eyebrows. "Is there more than one of them?" she asked sarcastically. "I hadn't heard that."

"I can't believe it," Lottie said, shaking her head.

"What?" Maggie asked, a challenge in her tone. "You don't think I can handle it?"

Lottie lifted up the orders she had just been given, pointing at the block letters at the top: *SAN DIEGO*.

The two of them stared at each other.

Ten

As she stepped out into the dazzling California morning, Lottie drew in a long breath of the sea air, scented with salt. All around her, other women streamed out of the barracks, laughing and talking as they headed to their posts in the big military office buildings.

For a few steps, Lottie walked along with them.

But then, at the rough path that led to the airfield and hangars, she turned from the main walkway and headed off by herself.

She was the only woman on the base who had shown enough mechanical know-how to qualify for classes as an aircraft mechanic.

That had been a source of a lot of teasing, because most of the women on base were in classes with other women, not with the enlisted men. "Leave one or two for us, will you?" they asked when they found out Lottie had been posted to the mechanic's hangar.

But until this morning, her first day of classes, it hadn't actually occurred to her what it would be like to walk into the training bay alone, as the only woman.

Lottie did some quick reconnaissance. The hangar itself was a giant cavern of a building, its gigantic bay door at least two stories high and already wide open to the breeze that swept in off the sea.

A few aircraft sat inside the bay, in shadows. Others had been parked nearby, in the sunshine. A few men were still walking in after her, but a good number were already at work. That came as a relief. She hadn't wanted to arrive too early and stick out like a sore thumb. But she never wanted to be late, especially on the first day.

She seemed to have timed it just right. The little knot that had formed in her stomach when she'd first walked onto the airfield started to ease.

"Morning," she said, nodding at the guard on duty as she passed through the airfield gate, then headed toward the repair hangar.

He nodded back without a flicker of friendliness on his face.

Lottie lifted her chin and tried to tell herself not to take it personally.

Not all men had been thrilled to see women join the Navy. Maybe this guy was one of the ones who wasn't thrilled to see "a girl" on the job.

But she'd always gotten along well with men, Lottie reminded herself. At parties, when she wasn't out on the dance floor, she was often in a corner with a bunch of stags, sipping whiskey and puffing cigars with the best of them.

It might take a little time, she told herself. But she was sure that—

"Missy!" someone shouted nearby, breaking into her thoughts. "Hey, missy!"

For an instant, every man in the vicinity of the hangar seemed to look up from his work, hoping for a glimpse of a pretty girl.

When they saw it was only Lottie, in her workman's overalls, they turned back to their tinkering with a collective mutter of disappointment.

As they did, a short, skinny guy came striding up to Lottie, squinting at her from under a mop of greasy black hair.

"You got a message to deliver or something, missy?" he asked with an expression halfway between a leer and a sneer.

"I'm reporting for duty," Lottie said, reading the name sewn on his overalls: Pickman. "I'm assigned to this team."

Pickman raised his eyebrows. "A pretty girl like you?" he said. "Working in this dirty old repair bay?"

He let out a long, wondering whistle.

As he did, someone began to clap and shout over in the corner.

Lottie turned quickly, bracing herself to fend off the next insult or catcall. But instead, she saw a young man with a confident air waving his hands for attention, just outside the hangar. And all the dozens of other men were clustering around him.

"Who's that?" she asked Pickman.

Pickman himself had straightened up and was headed over in that direction. "That's Captain Woodward," he said. "Our commander."

Lottie trailed after him, taking up what she hoped was an inconspicuous spot near the back of the gathered crowd.

"Gentlemen," Captain Woodward was shouting.

Around her, a couple of the men glanced at Lottie and snickered. Lottie felt a pinprick of irritation, both at them and at Captain Woodward, for ignoring the fact that she was there. Although a small part of her suspected her reaction would've been the same if Captain Woodward had singled her out.

As the men finally piped down, Lottie realized that there was something familiar about Captain Woodward. She felt like she'd met him before, but she wasn't sure where. Had they crossed paths at some party in Detroit? Or somewhere else in her travels: New York? One of her European trips?

"Welcome back, Captain!" one of the men shouted.

Where had Captain Woodward been? His face was so tan, he looked like he had spent pretty much every day of the past year here in California. And the tan made his strong jawline even clearer and his blue eyes seem even more blue.

Captain Woodward didn't answer. He just held his hands up, waiting for complete silence.

When he finally got it, he dropped them.

"I see some new faces here," he said, looking around the hangar. "And some of you who probably already forgot everything I ever said, even if you heard it a hundred times."

Laughter rippled through the crowd.

From the looks on the men's faces, Lottie could see that Captain Woodward was well liked. And he'd clearly been here for some time. So she probably hadn't crossed paths with him in New York, at least not while she was at training.

"We're going to get to work here in a minute," Captain Woodward said. "But since it's been a while, and since some of us don't know each other yet," he added, "I want to stress a point I don't think we can ever stress too much."

He looked around the gathering, and Lottie was both relieved and a little put out that his gaze didn't even seem to flicker as it passed right over her.

"This shop is a good mechanic's shop," Captain Woodward said, to the rumble of cheers and approval from the crowd. But his own face stayed stony. "But that's not enough," he said. "We have to be the best in the world. We're not just mechanics. We're mechanics at war. So everything we do is a matter of life and death. We can't be lazy, or careless, or just plain wrong. Because people are counting on us for their lives. Not just the men in the sky. The people they're fighting for, all over the world."

He glanced to the side, giving a clear view of his distinguished profile, and suddenly Lottie realized where she knew him from: the Navy WAVES newsreel. The one that she'd seen all those months ago, in the theater near the dress shop her mother had helped her escape from.

The recognition gave her a sense of vertigo, but it didn't seem to affect anyone else in the hangar.

"You got that?" Captain Woodward said, scanning the crowd again.

Lottie glanced to her side. All the men were staring back at him, their faces just as determined as his.

Captain Woodward clapped his hands. "All right, then," he said, finally breaking into a grin. "I know you've missed me."

As the crowd laughed, Lottie asked the man next to her, "Where has he been?"

The man did a double take when he realized she was a woman. Then he laughed as if she'd just told him a joke. "I would have thought you knew, lady," he said. "He's been away getting some R & R. Helping set up the mechanic tests for the WAVES."

"So," Captain Woodward was saying from up front, "I've got a new challenge for you." He pulled the corner of a large piece of tarp away from a mass of metal that Lottie quickly recognized as some kind of engine on a test stand.

It glinted in the sun.

"Who wants to take the first crack at this beauty?"

A murmur spread through the crowd.

The guy next to Lottie shook his head.

Lottie felt the same curiosity and determination she always did when presented with a broken engine. It felt like a thrilling puzzle. But the lines of this one were totally unfamiliar to her. And she wasn't about to raise her hand in front of all those men during her first day on the job. She was going to take her time and prove her worth, not go down in flames on a problem the rest of them were clearly too scared to solve on their own.

She could tell this because not one of the men in the group had raised his hand, either.

"Really," Captain Woodward said, a smile playing around his lips. "Not one of you boys thinks you're up to the task?"

The men in the audience shuffled their feet, looking from side to side.

That meant that Pickman, who was standing beside Lottie, got a look at her while he was trying to avoid the captain's gaze. And that, apparently, gave Pickman an idea.

"Hey, why don't you try it, missy?" he asked, giving her a shove forward that almost sent her toppling into the guy in front of her.

As Lottie got her footing indignantly, Pickman

had what he thought was an even better idea. "Ladies first!" he shouted, pointing at Lottie.

Lottie froze in place while the guys around her looked back, realized she was there, and began to chant. "Ladies first, ladies first!"

Lottie tried to keep her features steady, not to give away her anger at being singled out—or her fear.

She looked up at Captain Woodward. For the first time, their eyes met. But she didn't see any of the mockery or suspicion in them that she saw in the eyes of the other men. Instead, she thought she saw concern, and calculation, as he quickly ran through his options.

Before he could decide, she began to push her way through the crowd. "All right," she said as the men parted around her on either side. "Let me through. I'll do it."

By the time she reached the front of the group and was face-to-face with the engine, Captain Woodward's expression had turned impassive. "Name?" he asked.

"Palmer," Lottie said.

Captain Woodward nodded at the engine. "You'll find tools in that box," he said, pointing to a nearby kit. "Go ahead. Get started."

Lottie took a step toward the box, trying not to show how self-conscious she felt in front of all those men. But before she took another one, Captain Woodward clapped his hands again.

"All right," he said. "Get to work."

A chorus of complaints and boos bubbled up as the men began to disperse to their various posts. "You didn't think we were all going to stand around and watch one person work all day, did you?" he called after them.

Lottie knelt down, opened the tool kit, and pulled out a wrench so she would look like she was working, even though she had no idea yet if she was going to need a wrench or not.

When she stood back up, Captain Woodward was standing next to her.

"It's a Merlin engine," he said to her. "You think you can handle that?"

With gratitude, Lottie realized he'd just given her a huge clue. Before this, she'd had no idea what she was looking at. But from his expression, she couldn't tell if he'd meant it as a favor or a challenge.

"A Merlin's nothing more than a big old Packard block," Lottie said over her shoulder as she turned back to the engine. "And I learned how to fix one of those when I was seven years old."

This wasn't quite true. The Packard auto company had started manufacturing the Merlin engines after the Brits invented them. And she knew Packards because her father's buddy, who owned the company, had given one to her family as a gift. The thing broke down all the time, which was how she had learned the basics of the engine, looking over Gus's shoulder as he tinkered to get it running again. Her father had never been upset when the Packard broke down, though. Every time the car his friend manufactured failed, he just took it as a victory, with competitive glee.

No aircraft engine, Lottie knew, was remotely as simple as an automobile's. And she knew enough about Navy engines already to know that a Merlin wasn't standard in the Navy. It was water-cooled, unlike the air-cooled engines she'd been trained on, so one of the first things she'd need to do would be rig up a makeshift cooling system, to even test it. But she wasn't about to let him see her sweat.

Captain Woodward just raised his eyebrows. Then he turned around and walked off, without another word or a backward glance, leaving her alone to begin to test the shafts and pistons.

As she jerry-rigged a cooling system and caught on to the ins and outs of the engine, she began to seethe.

This was a job for an experienced mechanic. No one should have been asked to do it alone. Let alone someone who was brand new to the class. She knew unfairness when she saw it. It always made her blood boil. And this was no exception.

She pulled the whole thing apart, trying every trick she knew. But an hour later, all she could do was get it to cough.

That was enough to get Captain Woodward's

attention. "What have you got here?" he asked as a group of other men drifted over to see what kind of progress she'd made.

"Same thing I had an hour ago," Lottie said. "Busted engine."

The nearby men laughed, but she wasn't sure if they were laughing with her or at her.

"All right," Woodward said. "Nice work. Come on and join one of these other teams. You might learn something."

"I can get it," Lottie protested, looking around at the smug faces of the surrounding men. None of them had even been willing to take the chance. But now they were all looking at her as if they would have known how to do it better than she did. "Just give me another few minutes."

"No," Captain Woodward said firmly. "Head over there. Rick's showing some guys how to repair a broken propeller."

"But—" Lottie tried again.

"Palmer," Captain Woodward interrupted. "Didn't they teach you how to follow orders in basic training?"

"Aye aye, sir," she said.

Exasperated, Lottie dropped the greasy wrench she had been holding back into the toolbox and stalked off in the direction in which he had pointed.

For the rest of the day, she did her best to put a good face on it. She even managed to learn a thing or two about the differences between a car engine and a plane engine: the way they were configured differently to fit in the different spaces; the fact that plane engines typically ran at a lower rpm than car engines, even though planes traveled so much faster than cars did.

But all the while, she was struggling to fend off feelings of humiliation. She felt like every time anyone looked at her, they just saw the girl who had made a big fuss about how she was going to solve the tough challenge—and then failed, in front of everyone.

It didn't help that it seemed like every time she turned around, someone was staring at her— or refusing to look at her, as if she weren't even there at all.

Or that Captain Woodward didn't give any other sign that he knew she even existed, for the entire rest of the day.

She kept a brave face on when she walked out of the hangar and all the way back to the women's barracks. But when she got to her bunk, she couldn't keep it up any longer. She threw herself down on her bed and burst into tears.

She'd never cried like this before. The deep, wracking sobs shook her to the core of her being. She longed for her mother's embrace. And with a deep ache, she missed Eugene. What if she just went back? she wondered. Would there still be any room for her there? Not just in her home, but in his heart?

She didn't know how long she'd been there crying when she heard footsteps coming down the row.

Quickly, she wiped her eyes and sat up.

The person she locked eyes with was the last one she'd expected to see: Maggie.

Lottie hadn't crossed paths with her once since they'd arrived in San Diego. And yet here Maggie was, at the moment Lottie least wanted to see her.

Predictably, Maggie didn't even ask her what was wrong. Instead, she just said gruffly, "Stop that, princess."

Then she looked down the aisle, toward the door that led out to the base. "You didn't let those men see you cry, did you?" she asked.

Wiping her tears away, Lottie shook her head.

"Good," Maggie said. "Don't you let them. They'll think you're weak."

What if I am? Lottie thought. But as she listened to herself, she realized how much that sounded like Pearl. She shook her head, to shake that thought out of it, and lifted her chin.

"That's right," Maggie said, and started off down the aisle again.

But after a few steps, she looked back. "You know," she said, "some princesses grow up to rule."

Eleven

It was still dark when Lottie opened her eyes the next morning: true dark, without a hint of dawn.

But she didn't close her eyes again. Instead, she groped blindly for her work uniform, put it on, tied her hair back under a bandana, and slipped out of her room while all the other women in the barracks still breathed deeply, in the grasp of sleep.

Outside, there was the dim light from the fading stars but no electric path lights to guide the way. The base was on a perpetual blackout by night, so as not to attract enemy attention.

It was unlikely the enemy would ever get close enough to stage an attack on California like the one that had devastated Pearl Harbor. But the United States Navy didn't plan to be surprised again, by anything.

And neither did Lottie.

The guard at the gate to the repair hangars wasn't quite asleep at his station, but he wasn't exactly on full alert. When Lottie walked through the gate, he scrambled upright on the chair he'd been slumped on, then did a double take when he realized she was a woman.

From the expression on his face, Lottie could see that he was wondering whether she was just another part of some dream. She also wondered with amusement, as she walked by, whether he thought it was a good one or a bad one.

She just pointed at the name sewn onto her work uniform and kept walking. In the darkness, the repair and storage hangars rose around her. It was strange, Lottie thought, how much a place could change from day to night. In daylight, she barely noticed the size of the hangars. She was too busy trying to figure out her place among the men and the machines that the hangars sheltered. The hangars hung overhead, easy to forget, just like the sky. But by night, with no one else around, the shapes of the buildings were so big they almost seemed like they were made by God himself—as if they must have been part of the land somehow, like small mountains.

When she got to her assigned hangar, she felt a burst of nerves when she laid her hand on the lever of the entry door. The giant hangar doors were safely closed against the night winds off the bay, and even if they weren't locked up, she wasn't sure she knew how to open them herself.

But mercifully, the lever turned easily under her hand. She opened the door and stepped into the shadows of the hangar.

Enough moonlight poured through the hangar's big windows for her to make her way over to the engine that had defeated her the day before. When she got there, she didn't hesitate. She simply found a nearby lantern, flicked it on, and found a tool kit in the harsh light from the naked bulb.

Then she went to work. By the time sun was streaming brightly through the windows of the hangar, it looked like she had dismantled about half the engine block, part by part. She had thoroughly checked both rotors, worked her way through every connection in the fuel system, and was in the process of trying to look deeper into the recesses of the engine when she heard a footstep behind her.

She glanced up at the clock on the wall beside her makeshift workstation. It was still over an hour before any of the other men were expected to report for duty. She laid down her wrench and turned around.

As she did, Captain Woodward, who had just walked in the nearby door, leapt back, startled. He stood frozen in the square of light from the door for a moment, then recognized her.

"Palmer," he said. "What are you doing here?"

Lottie started to give him a friendly smile by way of greeting, but as he stalked over, scowling at her, she scrambled to her feet, wondering if she should come to attention or not. She wound up doing some approximation of it, while trying not to trip over the engine parts she still had scattered all over the floor.

"Just working on this engine, sir," she said. "I

didn't get it finished yesterday, so I thought I'd come in this morning."

"Did I order you to keep working on this engine?" Captain Woodward asked, still stone-faced.

"You ordered me to fix it yesterday," Lottie said. "And I haven't fixed it yet."

She braced herself for some kind of blast from Captain Woodward, but to her surprise, it didn't come.

Instead, he just looked down at the parts, now with some curiosity.

"What are you doing here?" he asked, surprise in his voice.

"I already tested both rotors," Lottie said. "They're moving freely. All the connections in the fuel lines that I can see are tight. Everything I can get at right now performs as expected. So I'm trying to get a look at what I can't see from here. The problem has to be deeper in the engine."

Captain Woodward raised his eyebrows.

"I'm a good teacher," he said. "But even I know I didn't teach you all that yesterday. You've had some training."

He stated this flatly, as a fact. But in his eyes she also saw the question carried with it: *Where did a little lady like you learn your way around an engine like that?*

Lottie's mind flashed back to all the afternoons she'd whiled away with Gus in the family garage, or crouching on the roadside with her head in an engine. "I've had some training," she agreed. "Back in Detroit."

Captain Woodward nodded appreciatively, gazing down at the pieces she'd removed from the engine, apparently calculating what she must have been working on and giving a slight nod as he took each piece in.

But then his expression changed. His eyes went wide. Wide enough that his stony expression betrayed a hint of vulnerability.

"Detroit . . ." he said. "The Detroit Palmers?"

People had been asking Lottie this all her life, and she had a whole series of deft or coy ways to answer, depending on how she was feeling. Sometimes she said, "Not many people have heard of us," as a joke, because it was so obvious that almost everyone had heard of the Detroit Palmers. Sometimes she simply said yes and hurried the conversation past the moment as quickly as possible. Sometimes she shook her head no, just to see what they did then.

But this time, she felt a sinking feeling. She didn't want to be a Detroit Palmer to Captain Woodward. This time, for a change, she wanted to stand on her own two feet. And she still couldn't seem to escape the extremely long shadow cast by her family name.

Then her debutante training kicked in. If you didn't like where a conversation was going, her mother had always told her, just change the subject. "Where did you get your mechanical training?" she asked.

Surprised, Captain Woodward met her eyes. Even in the early light, they were just as blue as the sky that was starting to peek through the high windows of the hangar.

"To tell you the truth," he said, "I was too young to remember most of it. Out on my dad's farm in Nebraska, we had to know how to do everything, because everything else was miles away. One of my first memories is climbing around in the engine of my dad's tractor. I think they might have handed me a wrench when I was born."

"Nebraska?" Lottie said with a wry smile. "Hmm."

Suddenly, for the first time she'd ever seen, Captain Woodward cracked a smile. She was surprised by how handsome he suddenly seemed. And how her heart flipped in response.

"Now, don't you go getting any ideas," he said.

What did he mean by that? Lottie wondered, panicked that she had somehow given her sudden attraction to him away.

But as he went on, she realized he had no idea. "You might be from the jet set in Detroit," Captain Woodward said, "but we farm boys are a lot more sophisticated than you might think. You know the difference between a Guernsey and a Hereford cow?"

127

Amused, Lottie shook her head.

"I didn't think so," Captain Woodward said.

Then he knelt beside the half-dismantled engine. "And more to the point, I can pull a Merlin like this apart and put it back together in just under an hour," he said.

Lottie lifted her chin. "I might not be able to do that yet," she said. "But I'm going to learn. The Navy won't be sorry they took me."

Something flickered in Captain Woodward's eyes at this. He glanced away from her.

"You think they will?" Lottie said, then bit back her next words. She was already out of line, she knew, talking to an officer in that kind of tone.

But Captain Woodward seemed to have forgotten the fact that he was an officer, at least for the moment. His eyes had gone distant, and almost sad.

He shook his head. "They won't be sorry they took you," he said. "But you might."

Lottie's brows drew together. "I'm not giving up, if that's what you think," she said. "No matter how hard it gets."

"There's a kind of hardness in war," Captain Woodward said, still not meeting her eyes, "that no one can know until they see it."

Suddenly, Lottie realized that they weren't talking about her and her capabilities, but about something much more.

"It might be hard," she said. "But it's an honor

to be part of it. And we can't give up. We have to fight."

Captain Woodward gave his head a quick shake. She had the sense that he wasn't even responding to her, but to something in his own mind.

Then, finally, he met her eyes. "I appreciate the spirit, Palmer," he said. "But I wasn't looking for you to get this old thing up and running. I saw the work you did. Your instincts are good, and your troubleshooting was smart. That's what I was looking for: the courage to try and not give up. And you already passed that test."

This was the first praise Lottie had heard from anyone since she joined up. But something about it rankled her. She knew she'd passed the test already. She wasn't trying to impress him. She was working something out on her own. And she knew she could do it. She didn't need him to tell her that. And something about the way his handsome features had thrown her off balance a moment before made her even more irritated.

"Well," she said, an edge of sarcasm in her voice. "I'm glad to hear I passed the test."

Instantly, all the friendliness vanished from Captain Woodward's face. He took a smart step back, and for an instant, Lottie was afraid that he was going to snap to attention himself, or even worse, bark an order to her.

"That was yesterday," he said. "This is today."

He looked down at the parts spread over the ground again.

"You've made a real mess here," he said. "I want it all cleaned up before any of the other men get here."

Lottie bristled a bit at the phrase "other men." Did he mean other men besides him? Or besides her? And if he was thinking of her as one of the men, should she take it as an insult—or a compliment?

When she didn't start moving instantly, Captain Woodward barked, "Now!"

Lottie actually jumped. Then she crouched over the thick chunks of metal and tiny screws that she'd scattered over the floor. She picked one up blindly and began to fiddle with it, her face so hot with irritation she knew it must have turned a deep shade of crimson.

As she did, she could hear Captain Woodward's boots slap the concrete as he stalked away.

When he was finally gone, safely doing something else at the opposite side of the hangar, Lottie finally figured out what was in her hand: a valve for reducing fuel pressure that she'd removed in hopes of getting a better look at the engine workings.

As quickly as she could, she began to fasten it in place, trying to beat back her frustration, which mingled with her determination to do even better today than she had the day before. She would prove that she deserved her place here. She would do it whether he wanted her to or not.

So he might try to make her life miserable from now on, she realized with a sinking feeling. He clearly thought she was an incapable girl. He might have liked to pretend to be the fair one in front of the other men. But when it came right down to it, it was clear he had the same opinions about women as the rest of them—and he wasn't thrilled to have her in his shop.

But no matter what happened, she told herself, her training here in California couldn't last forever. When it was done, she'd never have to see Captain Woodward, or remember this day, ever again.

And that couldn't come soon enough for her.

Twelve

When Lottie walked into the women's barracks, she thought at first that she'd accidentally stumbled into one of the large, lavish dressing rooms outside the ladies' restroom of a tony hotel or private club.

The beds were normally neatly made, in reverent fear of the patrolling officers, who were always on the lookout for a messy blanket, a disreputable-looking kit, or a wayward towel. But now they were piled high with stockings, brushes, lipstick, and even high heels.

And the women themselves, usually neatly arrayed in the sober blue or white of their dress blues, had suddenly blossomed into all kinds of glorious colors: a red pencil skirt, a green silk blouse, a boatneck dress in a beautiful deep shade of turquoise.

As she slipped through the chattering, laughing crowd, heading for her own bunk, Lottie realized she was one of the only women still in uniform. The women on the base who were working desk jobs, which was almost all of them, had been let off at a normal hour. But Captain Woodward had kept his class late that day, insisting that nobody could go home until they'd finished work on an old bomber that nobody in the class had successfully managed to get running. By the time they finally did, the California night had already set in around them.

Apparently, that was why all the women were dressing up. Not only was it night. It was Friday night.

When Lottie finally made it to her bunk, Frances, a friendly brunette who bunked nearby, grinned at her while unpinning her own locks to reveal freshly minted pin curls.

"Where's your uniform, recruit?" she asked.

"I didn't realize we had to muster this evening," Lottie shot back.

"Muster," Frances said with a laugh. "I guess that's one word for it."

"What's going on?"

"Evening pass!" Frances said. "We're all going out to some clubs on the bay. You better get changed if you don't want to miss it!"

Lottie looked around at the whirlwind of activity. "They should hire us on as smugglers," she said. "I can't believe what these girls have been hiding in their kits."

A woman with short blond curls walked by, with a huge rhinestone clip in the shape of a swallow holding back one wing of her hair.

"Is that military issue?" Lottie asked Frances jokingly.

"If it is, we need to join that branch," Frances said with a wink. She pulled the last plain bobby pin out of her own hair, gave it a shake, and then patted it into place. "You better hurry up!" she said, taking a bright red alligator clutch from her bunk. "If you don't want to miss all the fun."

Lottie stepped back as Frances brushed past, not wanting to spoil Frances's pretty gold blouse with the grease on her hands and overalls.

Frances wasn't the only one on her way out the door. All over the barracks, women were putting the final touches on their evening's attire and streaming out the doors into the night.

Quickly, Lottie grabbed her towel and soap, heading for the showers.

By the time she returned, pulling her hair down from the scarf she'd tied it up in to keep it dry, the place was almost deserted. A few stragglers were laughing as they headed out the door together.

Other than that, it looked like she had the place to herself, the whole giant barracks as her own very large but very unglamorous dressing room.

With a sigh, she dropped her overalls onto her bunk and knelt to pull out her kit. But as she was foraging through her clean clothes, looking for one of the few dresses she had brought with her to training, she saw something out of the corner of her eye.

A figure was coming out of the women's bathroom, which was odd, because Lottie hadn't noticed anyone in there when she left herself.

Even odder, the woman hadn't been there to

check her hair or outfit one more time, or put on a last smear of lipstick. Instead, she seemed to be the only woman in the place still in uniform.

As Lottie looked at her, puzzled, she realized with a shock that, even at a distance, she recognized the woman's red hair and freckled face.

It was Maggie.

"Hey!" Lottie said, waving, as Maggie came down the wide aisle between the stands of beds on either side. She pulled an evergreen dress with short sleeves and pretty magenta piping on the collar and cuffs on over her head.

When her head popped out again from the fabric and she settled the knit fabric over her hips and let it drop to her knees, Maggie had frozen where she was standing, several rows away.

"I never thought I'd be ahead of you at *anything*," Lottie called, full of excitement at the chance to go out and just a little pleased to be in a position to tease Maggie about something for a change. Part of her, though, felt uneasy as soon as she said it. Maybe it would have been better to just let Maggie walk on by. They'd both made it clear enough that they weren't thrilled to be stuck in the same place together again.

Maggie just looked at her, stone-faced. Then she went over to her bunk and lay down on it, and tilted the brim of her uniform cap over her eyes for good measure.

Surprised, Lottie slipped on the one pair of brown Mary Jane heels she'd allowed herself when she left home. Some part of her was tugged toward the door and the adventure beyond, telling her to let sleeping dogs lie.

But something else drew her, step by step, over to Maggie's bunk. Maggie had never been easy to get along with, but by herself in the barracks, surrounded by the empty bunks, she suddenly looked smaller than Lottie had remembered. And Lottie couldn't think of any reason that any of the women would miss the fun tonight, unless something was really wrong.

"Are you feeling okay?" Lottie said, sinking down onto the mattress across from Maggie's. "Do you want me to go fetch a medic?"

"No," Maggie said in a voice that made it very clear she still had all the vigor Lottie remembered.

Irritated, Lottie thought about grabbing Maggie's hat away from her face and demanding she sit up. But Lottie wasn't sure she wanted to find out what Maggie's reaction might be to that.

Stymied and mystified, Lottie just sat there, wondering what she should do.

A minute later, Maggie removed the hat from her face with a sigh and looked over. "You're still here," she said, deadpan.

"Yep," Lottie said. Then, mildly encouraged by the fact that Maggie wasn't outright ignoring her, she tried to give her what she hoped was a playful chuck on the shoulder. "Come on," she said. "Get changed. I'll wait for you."

But when she said "get changed," she noticed something flicker in Maggie's face. Maggie rolled over. "I'm too tired to go out," she said.

Suddenly, Lottie thought back to the day they'd both unpacked at basic training. She remembered Maggie's pair of neat uniforms—and the fact that the rack where they had hung had been empty of anything else.

Lottie suddenly realized she might be treading into very dangerous territory, but she couldn't leave Maggie there alone without giving it a try. "Listen," Lottie said. If all else failed and Maggie got furious at her, she thought ruefully, they weren't exactly friends to begin with, so no harm done. "I've got a dress I always thought would look nice on you. It's just simple, but it's a beautiful royal blue. Would you try it on for me tonight?"

Maggie turned and met Lottie's eyes. Lottie saw the unmistakable brimming that came with the start of tears. Not wanting to embarrass Maggie, Lottie glanced away.

"Maybe it's a silly idea," Lottie said. "But I'd love to see it with your hair."

To her surprise, when she looked back, Maggie was sitting up.

"I know what you're doing," she said.

Lottie thought about feigning ignorance, but the words died on her lips. Instead, she simply offered a small smile. "Well?"

"I'll look at it," she said finally.

"You will?" Lottie said. Then, before Maggie could change her mind, Lottie was on her feet, hurrying over to her own kit. In a flash, she had the blue dress in hand and was shaking out the wrinkles.

When she turned back, there was Maggie.

"If I'd known I was going to loan it out, I'd have tried to steam it just a little bit," Lottie said.

"No need to apologize, princess," Maggie said. But this time, the nickname didn't have the edge Lottie was used to hearing when Maggie said it.

Without another word, Maggie accepted the dress from Lottie and returned to her bunk to change. When she stepped out into the aisle again, she looked like a new woman.

Lottie had just been making an excuse to get Maggie to try on the dress, but she was more right than she had known that the royal blue would look fantastic with Maggie's red locks. And although Lottie hadn't thought to worry about a pair of shoes for Maggie, the navy-blue pumps that the Navy had issued for their dress blues had just enough of a heel to create a nice effect with the royal-blue dress.

"Wow!" Lottie said as Maggie came down the row. "That looks great."

Maggie gave her a smile, but when she got to Lottie's bunk, she didn't even stop, heading for the door.

"Come on, princess," she said. "What are you waiting for?"

When they finally got to the civilian club where the other women had headed, with some help from a few of the officers from base, who were also headed that way, the club was already packed.

Under normal circumstances, Maggie might have made a beeline as soon as they got there for whatever part of the club was farthest away from Lottie. But there were so many people there that it was impossible.

They managed to get through the door together, and Maggie muscled their way up to the bar, where eventually they wound up with drinks in hand, courtesy of some seamen who waved to them from farther down the bar but couldn't come over, because it was just too hard to move around.

So the two of them wound up talking all night to whoever happened to be around, which was mostly other WAVES. In their immediate vicinity were women from Boston, Albuquerque, North Dakota, and Louisiana—all with their own stories of how they'd gotten there.

When someone asked where Lottie was from, Lottie hesitated for a minute before she said

Detroit, hoping that maybe the other women would have forgotten her name by now or wouldn't connect it with the city she was from.

But sure enough, someone in the crowd yelped, "Detroit? The Detroit Palmers?"

Lottie smiled, hoping she could just keep it pasted on her face long enough for the conversation to move on to something else without having to answer any more questions about where she'd come from.

But the woman who'd made the connection, a blonde with a narrow face and a bottomless well of curiosity, just kept asking questions.

No, Lottie said, she didn't get to design the company cars. No, her father didn't either. Yes, it was fun to go to all those big parties, sometimes.

No, her father hadn't made a phone call to get her the best assignment. With every question, her smile faded just a little more.

And apparently, Maggie noticed. Because just as the blonde opened her mouth to ask another one of her interminable questions, Maggie jumped in.

"None of this has anything to do with whether Palmer here can do her job or not," she said. "And let me tell you, she can. I never saw anyone so determined to make it through at that whole basic training camp."

Lottie shook her head. "That's only because you couldn't see yourself," she said. "I was the one who had to stand behind you the whole time."

The blonde looked from one of them to the other, obviously calculating that Maggie didn't seem to be an obvious choice of companion for someone of Lottie's pedigree. "Oh?" she said. "And how long have you two been friends?"

Maggie looked at Lottie, her eyebrows raised in surprise and amusement. And when Lottie's eyes met hers, the two of them started to laugh and laugh.

Thirteen

For one moment, as Lottie gazed out of the huge door of the hangar at the flashes of blue bay and the few fronds of palms that waved between the grim gray buildings of the aviation repair complex, she wished passionately to be down on the beach, any beach, relaxing in the beautiful, brand-new red swimsuit she had left behind, along with so many other things, in Detroit.

What she wouldn't have given for even ten uninterrupted minutes of sun. Not to mention a glass of something cool, served by a handsome and attentive stranger.

Then, with a sigh of determination, she looked back at the half-built engine in front of her. This was the part she liked the least. Tearing an engine open to figure out what had gone wrong with it was like a treasure hunt. Even the tiniest action, like unscrewing a bolt, setting a part aside, was charged with excitement, because it could be the piece that revealed the mystery or solved it all.

And taking steps to fix the problem once she'd solved it had a kind of drama of its own. Had she made the right diagnosis? Had she chosen the right patch? Had she executed the fix correctly? All that was more than enough to keep her mind engaged and alert.

But sometimes the problem was buried in the engine, under piston after piston or the entire carburetor. In which case she didn't just have to go in and make a fix. She had to put the whole thing back together again.

Quite often, she couldn't really know for sure whether she'd fixed the thing or not until she got it put back together. Which meant that she could be doing all the boring scut work only to discover it all had to be taken apart all over again.

And Lottie wasn't the only one who hated this part of the process. The master mechanics who were moving through the trainees, pointing out their errors, helping them when they were stuck, and giving them tips along the way, would often tear an engine apart, get to the heart of a problem, and then call over one of the mechanics in training to reassemble it for them.

But Lottie wasn't a master mechanic yet.

So it came as a relief when a shadow fell over the engine as she was bolting in a fuel-filler gasket, because it meant that someone was there to help.

Until she looked up and saw whose shadow it was.

Captain Woodward was looking down at her. Or at least looking down at the engine she was working on. He hadn't actually met her eyes since the day she'd come in early to get a jump on the old Merlin block. But that didn't mean he'd forgotten she existed.

In fact, to her, it sure seemed like he always had time to go out of his way to find something wrong with whatever she was doing, whatever it happened to be.

He'd picked on her for heading straight to a plane's engine block when the propeller wasn't working, instead of first doing a manual check of the propeller itself. He'd called her on the carpet for not trying to fire an engine up before she started to troubleshoot, even though the guy who'd assigned her to the case had told her it was completely dead—and when she checked it, it was. He'd hassled her about fuel intakes and cylinder cases, valves and pistons and gaskets, rpm, horsepower, and miles per hour.

So it was no surprise that he found something to frown about when he looked at the engine she had just torn apart now.

Lottie just stared up at him, waiting for his verdict.

As usual, he looked at everything but her.

For a minute, when he couldn't seem to come up with anything she'd done wrong, Lottie thought maybe she'd finally stumped him. She felt a tiny kernel of pride in her chest.

But then Captain Woodward crossed his arms. "You call that a clean engine, Palmer?" he asked.

Lottie looked back at the engine, surprised. This engine wasn't particularly clean, but it wasn't particularly dirty, either. She'd seen engines that looked a lot worse. And she'd seen Captain Woodward give praise or blame for them, without ever mentioning the cleanliness of the engine, or lack of it.

"Sir?" she said.

"I don't just want to see this engine working," Captain Woodward said. "I want it showroom clean."

Lottie looked back at the engine, which was covered with grease.

Gamely, she picked up the next piece that needed to be fit in and wiped it down with a rag.

"No," Captain Woodward barked. "The whole thing."

"You want me to take it apart again?" Lottie said, trying to control the irritation in her voice. "Just to get it clean?"

Was he doing this because she was a woman? she wondered. Was this some backward way of letting her know he thought she was only good for cleaning?

"That's right," Captain Woodward said, and stalked away.

As he did, she heard a giggle behind her.

She didn't have to turn around to recognize it. She'd heard it too many times before in the last few weeks. It was Pickman, who also seemed to have made it his personal mission to make her life in the repair bay miserable.

But at least when Captain Woodward picked on her, she usually learned something.

Pickman, on the other hand, just got in the way of whatever it was she was doing.

"You better do it, too," Pickman said. "He made me do that last week. And he spent ten minutes taking it apart himself to make sure I actually cleaned under the carburetor."

That actually came as a comfort to Lottie. At least it meant the assignment wasn't a personal slight to her.

"Yeah," Pickman went on. "I had trouble getting some of that burnt grease off so I just used my face cream. You know. That real nice stuff, from Paris. Works like magic on an engine."

"How do you know where the best face cream comes from, Pickman?" Lottie asked.

This strangled Pickman's laughter at his own joke, midgiggle.

To her satisfaction, as she continued steadily working on the engine, dismantling the pieces she had just reinstalled, part by part, he eventually ambled away.

But before Pickman got very far, she heard his footsteps stop. And then she heard a general murmur spread throughout the crowd of mechanics in the hangar.

When she turned around to see what the fuss was about, a black shadow filled the door of the hangar bay. A twin-engine bomber plane sat just outside.

"That's a PBJ Mitchell," Lottie heard one guy tell another.

Captain Woodward began to clap his hands for attention.

"All right, all right!" he said. "Gather 'round."

As the trainees crowded near, Captain Woodward turned back to give the Mitchell an admiring glance.

"What we have here," he said, "is a PBJ Mitchell bomber. One of the great standbys of this war. And our very own Navy plane."

He walked around the front of the plane and gave one of the propellers a swat that seemed almost affectionate.

"This one," he said, "is distinguished by the fact that neither of the engines work. Our pilot brought it in with only one in service. By the time we tried to fire it up in the repair bay, the other one had gone out, too. You boys like a good race, don't you?"

A series of whoops and cheers went up from the crowd.

"All right," Captain Woodward said with a grin.

Lottie had seen a smile on his face so rarely that she hardly recognized him. But suddenly her memory was thrown back to the dark movie theater where she had seen him for the first time. What had happened to that charismatic man who had so much to say about the importance of women in the war effort?

"So I need two volunteers," Captain Woodward said.

All around Lottie, hands went up.

Lottie's memory of the last time she'd volunteered was still strong in her mind. And it didn't give her a lot of incentive to try again. But at the same time, she didn't want to back down from anything all the other men were gunning for. And so many hands were raised, she reasoned, there was no way Captain Woodward was going to pick her again.

"Palmer," Captain Woodward barked the instant her hand rose above her head.

A grumble rippled through the crowd as Captain Woodward scanned the other faces for his next victim.

But when Captain Woodward said, "Pickman," cheers broke out again. There were lots of other men in the bay who had given Lottie the cold shoulder or made comments that made it clear she wasn't exactly welcome there. But nobody in the hangar could have missed the fact that Pickman was her chief antagonist. He was the loudest voice cutting her down, and he did it multiple times a day.

Carrying her tools, Lottie made her way to the plane in a daze, not sure if the cheers were because the men thought Pickman could take her down or they thought this was her chance to give Pickman his comeuppance.

Probably, she thought as she came to a stop in front of the Mitchell, *a bit of both.*

But right now, she didn't have time to think about who was on whose side.

She looked over at Pickman, who was standing under the other wing of the plane, beside the opposite engine.

He gave her a wink with a threatening grin.

"Ready?" Captain Woodward was saying. "Set . . . go!"

Pickman was already twisting screws off the nacelle that surrounded the Mitchell's engine before Lottie even had her screwdriver out.

When Lottie broke into the engine itself, she found a Double Wasp, known for its reliability. So she wasn't dealing with a famously temperamental engine, she reasoned. And the solution, whatever it was, should be a simple one. That had always been Gus's advice when he was teaching her about engines. She smiled as she thought of him.

All around her, she could feel the eyes of the gathered crowd.

"You want us back to stations, Captain?" someone called.

Captain Woodward shook his head. "What fun is a race if no one's watching?" he asked.

So everyone stood there watching as she checked her fuel lines and seals—all good. She double-checked the valves and the gasket between the engine head and the engine case.

From Pickman's side of the plane, she could hear him swear as something dropped to the ground: a tool or a part. She didn't have time to bother looking.

She started to check the spark plugs. And there, she found it: an unseated plug, just waiting to be knocked back into place.

Her heart beating hard, she yanked the plug and cleaned it with hands that tremored with excitement, until it looked, as Captain Woodward had said so recently, factory clean. Then she pushed it snugly back into place.

For a moment, she hesitated, the sound of her own blood echoing in her ears. How sure was she that this was the fix? Did she want to take the risk of claiming her victory in front of everyone, when she wasn't absolutely sure the engine would work if she fired it up?

It only took a moment for her fear of losing the race to win out over her fear of getting it wrong.

She threw her hand up in the air. "Captain Woodward, sir!" she called. "Permission to try the ignition, sir?"

Captain Woodward looked at something over her shoulder, his face stone. "If you think you're ready, Palmer," he said.

"There's no way," Pickman sneered.

Lottie took a deep breath. Then she climbed up over the wing, stuck her head in the cockpit, and fired the inertia starter. When she saw the mixture advance, she waited for the ignition to spark.

For a sickening instant, she didn't hear anything. Then there was a slight hum that turned from a purr into a growl.

When she pulled her head back out of the cockpit, the propeller on her side of the plane was spinning merrily.

The one beside Pickman stood stock still.

"It wasn't fair," Pickman complained. "Hers is probably the side that only broke after landing. It probably didn't even need fixing."

Captain Woodward walked over as a smattering of applause broke out among the gathered men, tepid at first, but then growing. "Actually," Captain Woodward said, "that was your side, Pickman."

Then he looked up at Lottie, meeting her eyes for the first time in weeks.

With a little shrug, Lottie turned her back on him and stuck her head into the cockpit to shut the engine down.

When she turned back, he offered her his hand, to help her down.

"I don't need a hand, Captain," she said. "I can do it by myself."

Then she jumped down without his help and started putting the engine back together again, part by part.

Fourteen

The mess hall was never a quiet affair. The seamen who had ruled the San Diego base before the WAVES got there to train were a rowdy, rough-and-ready bunch to begin with, and when the women of the WAVES had arrived, they'd brought their own feisty spirit right through the door with them.

But Lottie had never seen the women as keyed up as they were this morning. And she knew why. Today was the last day of training for the women who had arrived with her on the base. Their permanent assignments had been dropped off sometime during the dead of night in the mail room. So everyone had stopped there to pick theirs up on the way to breakfast. And everybody was asking and telling everyone where they had been stationed, all at once.

In Lottie's pocket was the letter she had just picked up from the mail room, with her permanent assignment in it.

Machinist's mate.

That was Navy-speak for airplane mechanic, and it didn't come as a surprise.

But the location of her station did: Pearl Harbor. Hawaii.

A few years ago, that would have conjured up

nothing more than images of travel agent window posters of smoky volcanoes over sparkling blue water and pristine beaches.

And Pearl Harbor should have conjured the prettiest images of all—a beach strewn with pearls, or a harbor filled with oysters full of pearly treasure. But now nobody in the country—or probably the world—could hear the name without thinking of the Japanese surprise attack on the base that had killed thousands of American naval officers.

Her mother had been hoping that Lottie would be assigned to one of the stations on the East Coast, about as far from the front as you could get anywhere in the world. And that was a very sensible hope. Most of the girls whose assignments Lottie had overheard had wound up at stateside bases, where they'd be doing secretarial or accounting work, to free up men for active duty.

But Hawaii was the only part of the United States that had actually seen open conflict in this war. It was the most dangerous place in the whole country. It wouldn't settle her mother's fears.

It would make them worse.

And her father—Lottie could hardly think about how worried he'd be. He'd be tempted, she knew, to try to buy the whole base up and shut it down, just to keep her out of harm's way.

But this wasn't a competitor that he could drive

out of business. This was the war: something far bigger than Lottie or her father. And the fate of the whole world depended on the choices that all these individual people, even ones as small and insignificant as Lottie, were making, at any given moment.

Lottie hated the thought of worrying her parents. But at the same time, it felt right. So many other parents were worried. So many parents had lost so much to the war already. Wasn't it right that their family should give something that really mattered, that really cost them something, despite all their wealth, as well?

What still didn't feel right to her was the break with Eugene. Just like when she'd gotten the assignment to San Diego, some deep part of her now wanted to share her new assignment with him. For so long, he'd been the first one she'd told about almost everything. It almost felt as though if Eugene didn't know about something in her life, it might not be real. But at the same time, the life she was living felt more real than anything she'd ever experienced before in her days as a socialite, which now seemed more and more like a dream. And even though she missed Eugene, she didn't have any desire to return to that life—or to live as his wife.

The only good thing about Pearl Harbor was that she'd be away from Captain Woodward, his constant hassling and disdain. It was a wonder that she'd been able to learn anything in his shop, when he so clearly wanted to see her fail. And she couldn't wait for a fresh start, to prove herself in a new shop.

As she sat down at a nearby table, the other girls were eagerly swapping their assignments.

"Parachute rigger!" one of the women said, laughing. "I mean, my brother always said I was the best in the family at folding the laundry. But I thought that was because he didn't want to do it himself."

"Both of those things can be true," the woman next to her observed.

Lottie's table was crammed with yeomen, who would be serving as secretaries, doing administrative work; women in storekeeping, who would be keeping the books with careful accounting; a few coders; one woman assigned to radio transmission.

Maggie walked up, carrying her tray full of what the Navy insisted, against all evidence to the contrary, was breakfast.

"You get your assignment?" Lottie asked Maggie as Maggie tucked into a pile of rubbery yellow flakes that the Navy liked to describe as scrambled eggs.

"Yeoman," Maggie said ruefully. "Apparently I didn't manage to convince them I was qualified as a mechanic with my excellent skills putting papers in files."

"You do a lot more than that," Lottie said.

Maggie shrugged. "Oh sure," she said, brushing Lottie's compliment off, as she always did. Lottie wasn't sure if Maggie would have called them friends or not, exactly. But since that night at the club, there had been a noticeable thaw. They'd at least gotten to know each other, to the point where Lottie could recognize certain of Maggie's habits.

Maggie brightened at another thought. "But at least my station is a little exotic."

"Oh?" Lottie said.

Maggie nodded. "Pearl Harbor," she said.

Lottie's eyes widened. "You're kidding," she said.

Maggie's brow furrowed. "What?" she said. "You think I can't take the Japs?"

"No," Lottie said. "It's just . . ."

But by then, Maggie's quick mind had put two and two together.

"No," she said. "You aren't—"

Lottie nodded, and the two of them burst out laughing.

"What's so funny?" the woman next to Lottie demanded.

Lottie shook her head, fighting back her laughter to answer. "We're both stationed at Pearl Harbor," she said.

"Pearl Harbor's no laughing matter," the woman said, and looked away in a disapproving manner.

When Lottie looked back at Maggie, she was mildly gratified to see Maggie's evil eye turned on someone besides her, at least for the moment.

"You know," Maggie said, "there was a time when I thought I couldn't wait until I never had to see you again."

"You weren't the only one," Lottie quipped, and waited for a second, bracing for a blast of Maggie's temper.

But Maggie's grin just got wider. "Ha!" she said. "You've always got more spirit than I thought. And you know what? Maybe it's not so bad, having to see you again."

"Maybe not," Lottie allowed with her own grin.

"But first we have to get through our last day of training," Maggie said. "We're taking an exam on a list of Navy rules and regulations the size of the encyclopedia. What's your final test?"

"I don't know," Lottie said. She hadn't even thought about what Captain Woodward could be cooking up for them.

She walked into the hangar at high alert that morning, eyes peeled for any clue about whatever devilish puzzle Captain Woodward might throw at them this time, as a farewell present.

But when she got there, it looked just like business as usual.

Did everyone know something she didn't?

In the few months she'd been there, she hadn't made friends with any of the men in particular.

She didn't want her questions to be misconstrued as "fraternizing." And she didn't want people thinking she didn't know her stuff just because she was asking questions.

That actually made it harder to learn. All around her, she could hear the men educating each other, all the time. It was like they didn't know how to talk to each other unless they were explaining how something worked.

But she was good at eavesdropping. And it wasn't worth it to get into any sort of misunderstanding with any of the men.

Today, though, on the last day, she decided she could risk at least one question.

"Is there some kind of test today?" she asked one of the men when she came in. "Some kind of exam?"

This didn't seem to have occurred to him, but once the thought struck him, he wasn't a fan of it.

"Hey, Larry," he asked the guy next to him. "You heard anything about this test today?"

"Test?" Larry yelped. "There's a test?"

Within a matter of moments, the chatter about a phantom final test had traveled all the way around the hangar, to Captain Woodward, who shook his head in amusement and climbed up on the wing of the bomber he happened to be standing by to get a bit of elevation over the gathering.

"All right, all right," he said. "Settle down. What's this about a test? Who's giving it?"

"Is there a test today?" someone shouted.

"A final exam?" someone else added.

Captain Woodward gave his head a definitive shake.

"This whole training has been a test," he said. "Every day you've been here. Today's no different. Whatever you've been working on, I want you to finish it. Top quality. Like your life depends on it. Or even better, like someone else's does. Because other peoples' lives do depend on our work, every day. That's your test."

Then he swung down from the wing and turned his back to the crowd, who began to disperse to their own stations with a mutter of relief.

So Lottie went back to the project she had been working on the day before: getting the fuel gauge on a little SOC Seagull amphibian working again—or actually, rebuilding the plane's dashboard, which she'd had to dismantle in order to get at the wiring that had gone faulty in the intrepid little plane.

That took her until about ten a.m.

But when she hopped down and looked around at the other groups to find another one to join, which was the common practice in the apprentice-style shop Captain Woodward was running, her eyes fell on something else: the old chunk of Merlin engine from her first day on the job, still standing on its test stand, still silent.

It had seemed impossible to fix. But he'd also

told them, over and over again, that there was nothing that was impossible to fix.

A stubborn knot of determination began to form in her chest.

She'd been given the assignment to fix it, she told herself, the very first day she walked in the hangar. Nobody could deny that it wasn't fixed yet. And Captain Woodward had just told everyone to finish up anything they'd started while working in the shop.

So it just stood to reason that taking another crack at that Merlin was her next assignment.

At least, that's what she told herself as she made her way across the shop, trying not to make eye contact with anyone else who might call her over into some other job.

When she got to the Merlin, the sun had already moved across the morning sky to create a wedge of shadow that the Merlin was half lost in.

It was not the ideal light for working. But on the other hand, it was ideal light for her to slip into unnoticed.

Within a few minutes, she was dismantling the engine. But she knew from her training that it could take days to really test every element—especially if there was some secret flaw, as Captain Woodward seemed to suggest.

So she began to flip through the various systems in her mind, trying to think which ones would cause a total failure of power, and how easy they were to get to, as she dismantled the engine piece by piece, looking into the heart of the machine.

Then suddenly something snapped into focus.

The piston.

On the Double Wasp in the Mitchell. Which had also totally "failed to proceed," as Rolls-Royce and her own father liked to put it. "A car made with Palmer parts doesn't *break down,*" he used to say with a shudder.

There were no guarantees, but the pistons on the Merlin were reasonably close to the surface on the B-side of the engine, and therefore pretty easy to examine. And when she dismantled the engine far enough to get a look at the pistons, she knew immediately why the engine had seemed impossible to fix.

Each piston was attached to a connecting rod by a floating pin, and machined with three compression pins on one end and a scraper ring on the other. All the pistons moved freely, which she had tested before. But when she checked the connections on each piston, she discovered that one of the three pistons was missing a compression ring. No matter what else she did to the engine, without that ring, it wouldn't work properly.

But that didn't mean it was impossible to fix. That just meant it was impossible to fix without the right ring.

Nearby was an area the men called "the Junk Box"—a large, only marginally organized workbench full of cubbies large and small that were themselves in turn filled with spare parts in varying degrees of disrepair.

It only took a few moments of sifting through a box of compression rings to find one that matched the one Lottie had unscrewed from the Merlin engine for comparison.

And it only took her a minute longer to put them both back in place when she got back to her workstation.

Rebuilding the rest of the engine took her longer—over an hour. The thrill of the victory of discovery had long vanished, replaced by the deadening work of strategizing which pieces went where, in what order.

So before she flicked the makeshift ignition that the hangar mechanics had rigged up to test engines that had been removed from their planes, she felt a wash of familiar self-doubt.

Lottie had a nagging fear that she'd just gone on a fool's errand. Was some other, much worse flaw still hidden deep inside the machine?

As she wheeled the engine out of the hangar into the open air to test it, she was grateful for the fact that, for once at least, she wasn't working in front of a crowd.

She sent up a prayer and tried the engine.

When Lottie heard the sweet, familiar hum of

the machine coming to life, she couldn't resist letting out a little yelp of celebration.

And that started to draw a crowd after all.

"Hey," one of the guys working nearby called to her. "Palmer! Ain't that the Merlin? You fix that old Merlin after all?"

Suddenly, all the determination that had brought Lottie to this point melted away. Now she was just uncomfortable. And she was suddenly worried about what Captain Woodward would say. She had the sinking suspicion that this would be seen as some kind of insubordination. Had she just risked everything she'd earned at the last minute, just like Pearl?

"Hey," the guy who had noticed the engine start up called to the guys he'd been working with. "Look at this. The little girl fixed that old bastard of an engine."

Lottie thought ruefully about what Eugene had always said, based on his experience of the all-men's clubs the power brokers of the city frequented: men were even worse gossips than women. And judging by the way the word spread like wildfire around the hangar, it was true.

But before she could think anything else, Captain Woodward was standing in front of her.

She lifted her chin, ready to take whatever he had to throw at her: anger, mockery, or anything else. And she felt indignation rise in her own chest in response to what she knew was coming. What kind of a teacher gave students a deliberately impossible task? What kind of a man set people up to fail on purpose? What could a student ever hope to learn from that?

But Captain Woodward just stared, bug-eyed, at the machine. And then at her. And then back at the Merlin.

"How did you do that?" he demanded. "It's missing an O-ring. I took it out myself, to keep the cocky ones humble."

Lottie had a crazy, panicky thought that she was about to be accused of witchcraft. But luckily, she had a perfectly reasonable explanation to offer. "I saw that," she said. "So I replaced it."

Lottie shifted uncomfortably and looked at the men around her. Some of the faces were astonished. Some seemed resentful. Captain Woodward's eyes filled with an admiration that she might have found gratifying earlier in her training but now found irritating.

She was done proving herself to men who didn't think women were as good as them. It was a lesson that didn't need proving. Now she just thought of how glad she was never to have to see him again, since training was finally done.

"Good work, Palmer," he said.

"I know," she said, and walked away.

Fifteen

Lottie stood on the beach, feeling the sand between her toes, trying to understand how Hawaii could feel so different from California.

Both of them had beaches and palms, and balmy breezes. Both of them had stunning sunsets, like the one that was starting to paint the sky she was looking at now, across the seemingly endless stretch of silver and blue water, with fabulous splashes of pink and gold and lavender.

Both of them, at least in her experience, were crowded with Navy military personnel.

But somehow, Hawaii felt different. Maybe it was the crenellated, deeply forested mountains of the island of Oahu, where Pearl Harbor nestled in a natural arch in the shoreline. Maybe it was the lushness of the vegetation and the steam that rose from the forests in the early mornings, in contrast to California, which always seemed a little parched. Maybe it was that so much of the natural beauty of Oahu was still preserved, while San Diego, at least from the base where she'd trained, was wharves and city as far as the eye could see.

Maybe it was the simple fact that, just about anywhere you stood on Oahu, once you got out of the shelter of the harbor, you could tell you were on an island. Before she got here, Lottie had always taken it for granted that the land she stood on stretched as far as she could see, even when she was standing on a beach at the edge of the continent. But here, no matter where she looked, the land was always giving way to the ocean, which curved in around the island on every side. It was a kind of thrill, to be so perfectly cut off from the rest of the world. She'd wanted to leave everything behind and start a new life, and this was even farther than she'd ever expected to get in her wildest dreams. But all that water, and the sense that she was only standing on a tiny scrap of land, gave her a strange feeling.

After living a life where she was almost always at the center of everything, it was strange to discover herself out on the edge of the world. For once, she felt so small.

It felt freeing, not to have all eyes on her, not to have everyone think they knew everything about her, or her family, before she even opened her mouth. It left her with a lightness, as if she wasn't quite sure what she was made of or who she was. But also hope, that now she might have a real chance to find out.

"Palmer!" Maggie's familiar voice called from behind her. "You planning to swim back to the mainland? At least have a hot dog first."

With a grin, Lottie turned around.

In the few minutes it had taken Lottie to walk

down to the water and dig her toes into the sand, the other WAVES she'd come with had transformed the beach they'd all just arrived at, after commandeering a small fleet of jeeps. The base itself was nothing but piers and concrete— not the kind of place you'd want to relax in a bathing suit.

But it had only taken a drive to reach a pristine beach, where other WAVES had decided to throw a barbecue, for a suite of reasons that included welcoming the new women who had just arrived on the base the day before and the fact that it was Friday.

As Lottie had been staring at the water, the other women had already filled their quadrant of the beach with Navy blankets and tarps, and gotten several respectable fires going in small metal barbecues.

"I'm waiting till you have a beer," Lottie shot back. "And then I'm going to convince you to swim home, and hitch a ride."

Maggie raised her eyebrows in respect for this rejoinder, and Lottie sank down beside her and another young woman, whose smooth black hair was tied back in a blue bandana that made a patriotic contrast to her bright red bathing suit.

"I'm Carmen," she said, sticking out her hand.

Lottie reached over Maggie to shake it.

"Nice to meet you."

"She's a yeoman," Maggie explained. "Like me."

Carmen smiled. "What's your assignment?" she asked Lottie.

"I'm a machinist's mate," Lottie said.

Carmen grinned. "She's a pharmacist's mate," she said, pointing to a woman in a smart black bathing suit who was using a pair of bellows to warm up the coals in her barbecue, to great effect. Then Carmen dropped her voice. "But I think I'd rather mate a machinist, myself," she joked.

Lottie shook her head. The girls who worked in bookkeeping and administration had trained in big groups, with dozens of them together at the same time. And when they got to base, they were still with other women.

They seemed to think that the girls marooned out in other jobs, where it was just them and a bunch of men, were living in some kind of romantic film. But the reality of Lottie's life couldn't have been farther from that. The last thing any of those men in the mechanics department had wanted, she thought, was to marry her. Most of them had wanted her to disappear.

Her first day in aircraft repair here in Pearl Harbor wouldn't be until Monday. But she doubted it would be any different here.

"Oh, oh!" one of the girls shouted before Lottie had to come up with something to say in reply. "Incoming!"

For a second, Lottie looked to the sky, feeling a

sickening sense of dread. But when she heard the other girls laughing and shouting, she looked to where they were pointing, down the beach, and saw a group of young men, dressed for working out, but in telltale navy blue, jogging down the shoreline.

"Just ignore 'em," Carmen muttered. "Maybe they'll go away."

"I don't find that tends to make them go away," Maggie said.

By this time, the men had caught sight of the WAVES. In their pedal pushers and bathing suits, the women weren't wearing nearly as much telltale blue as the men. But perhaps they were given away by the Navy blankets spread all over the sand. Or perhaps it was enough that they were a big gaggle of young and attractive women.

In any case, without anyone seeming to give any kind of direct order, all the men in the group, about fifteen of them, seemed to break out into catcalls at the same time, a combination of whistles, whoops, and specific observations about the merits of the women's figures, faces, and bathing suits.

Some of the women smiled. Some of them frowned. Some of them looked away.

But Lottie stared straight back at them. And when she did, she recognized one of them: Pickman. Her heart sank. She had hoped to leave him behind, just like she'd left Captain

Woodward and the rest of them. It wasn't the best news she'd gotten that day, but she held out hope that he'd be assigned to a different shop.

But at the same time, the stubborn determination that had spurred her on to beat him in the shop challenge began to form in her heart now.

"Ah, honey!" he called with a long wolf whistle. "I like that red suit! Whoo-ee!"

Maybe he thought it was a compliment, but beside Lottie, Carmen curled up like something had stung her.

Lottie's blood began to boil.

"Hey, Pickman!" she yelled back. "Is that how your mama taught you to talk to a woman?"

Pickman was so startled to hear his name that he stumbled in his jog, craning his neck to see which of the women knew his name. By this time, the pack of guys had pretty much drawn up to where the women had spread their little picnic and were about to run past them, on down the beach.

But when Pickman caught sight of Lottie, he didn't just stumble. He stopped dead. The guy behind him almost crashed into him, lurched around him, then came to a stop himself and turned back to see what in the world was going on.

Lottie took in Pickman's running garb with a quick glance: a pair of ragged gray shorts and an ill-fitting navy tank top.

"Wow, Pickman," she said, raising her voice and doing her best to imitate the tone the men had been using with the women. More of Pickman's band of runners began to double back down the beach, to see why their buddies had stopped. "Nice shorts. I really like the way you fill them out."

Pickman must have made it through basic training at some point, but he hardly had the build of a working seaman. All the hours he'd spent crawling around under airplanes hadn't done anything to improve his tan—or his physique.

He looked down at his pale, skinny legs.

To Lottie's satisfaction, he looked like he'd have done just about anything to curl up on himself and disappear. It was exactly the same kind of expression that had appeared on Carmen's face after he'd catcalled her. And thanks to her, both the women *and* the men were now staring at him.

When she saw that, Lottie couldn't help feeling just a little sorry for him.

And apparently she wasn't the only one. Because as she and Pickman stood there, facing off, Lottie's hands on her hips and Pickman trying to sink into the sand, some woman Lottie didn't know called, "You boys hungry?"

Suddenly, the awkward standoff was broken. The guys whooped and began to trickle over toward the girls, the catcalling forgotten, now introducing themselves politely and thanking the girls who scooted over on the blankets or handed them cold bottles of beer.

As the sun set and the stars came out, brighter than Lottie had ever seen anywhere on the mainland, because there was no light at all coming off the vast ocean to compete with them, the little picnic turned into a real party. A couple of the guys made a foray back to the base and returned with another big case of meat and potato salad, along with a couple of volleyballs that they kicked around, swatted at each other, and sometimes overshot into the ocean, where someone would have to swim out into the dark water to retrieve it before the tide carried it out forever.

And as the evening went on, as the new women met the ones who had been stationed there for months and strangers became friends, it was actually Pickman who came over to talk to Lottie, carrying a bottle with him.

"Cold beer?" he asked.

Lottie smiled and shook her head. "Not while I'm working," she said.

"Oh, you're working now?" Pickman said with a grin. "I guess that's how you got so good."

Lottie looked at him in surprise. "I never would have thought I'd hear you admit that," she said.

Pickman shrugged, looking out at the ocean. "I'm not as stupid as I look," he said. "I just want to see us send our boys up in the best planes we got. No matter who does it."

"Hm," Lottie said, watching him out of the corner of her eye. Pickman had hassled her so much, for so long, that she was waiting for the other shoe to drop—some big twist of the knife. She'd have been a fool to think about letting down her guard.

When Pickman looked over at her, she was sure that was what was coming.

"Besides," he said. "You'd have to be pretty damn good to ever beat a mechanic as good as me."

It took Lottie a minute to realize what he was saying.

"Be careful, Pickman," she said. "Someone'll think you're paying me a compliment."

"Naw," Pickman said, waving her suggestion away. "Everyone knows I'd never do that."

She smiled at him, for perhaps the first time, and looked out onto the blackness of the ocean.

Then he glanced at her again. "So what do you think the shop'll be like here?" he asked. "I've been trying to think how it'll be different."

Before Lottie could answer, a terrible shriek filled the night. It had the strange rise and fall of an ambulance or a police car racing down some street in the distance, except that it was about a hundred times as loud, so much sound that it felt like no matter how far Lottie ran, she would never be able to get away from it.

All around her, women and men clapped their hands to their ears. The new ones, like Lottie and Pickman, looked at each other, dumbfounded.

But others began to scramble to collect anything in reach: blankets, bottles, baskets. A few of them started to dump the barbecues out and bury the cinders in the sand.

In the melee, Lottie could see Maggie pull away from the fray to come find her. Then the two of them raced, along with everyone else, back to the cars.

When they were safely sheltered within the metal and glass of the jeep that had brought them there, the siren was still deafening but muffled enough for them to communicate.

"It's an air-raid warning?" Lottie guessed.

The woman at the wheel, Anne, nodded grimly. Then she began to back the car out of the parking spot, into the dark lot.

"The lights!" Maggie said, warning her that she'd started moving without turning them on.

But all around the lot, Lottie realized, all the other cars had started to move without turning their lights on as well, even though all the headlights had already been painted over, except for a tiny slit.

"No lights," Anne said over her shoulder in a clipped tone. "We don't want to give them a target they can see from the air. But we're not going to sit on the shore and wait for them to come."

As she slipped into the darkened line of traffic, Lottie looked back over her shoulder at the dark water, which had seemed like the perfect playground just a few minutes before.

Were there really enemy planes coming for them out of that darkness now?

This wasn't a game.

It wasn't even training.

This was war.

Sixteen

The first thing Lottie saw when she walked into the repair bay was a snarl of twisted, blackened metal.

It took her a minute to realize that that snarl of blasted steel had once, in fact, been a plane wing.

Like the repair hangar in San Diego, this one, at Kaneohe, just a short distance from Pearl Harbor, had a giant door that opened to the world outside, filling the entire place with the tang of the sea air, the sun-warmed breezes, and the faintest trace of the pink plumeria that grew in patches around the base. But unlike the one in San Diego, it opened almost directly onto the harbor and the ocean beyond, with no major structures to block the view of the sparkling blue water from the workshop.

But that wasn't the biggest difference from the shop she'd grown used to in San Diego. The biggest difference was that, on every plane she could see from where she was now standing, she saw actual signs of battle: not just the twisted steel of the plane wing that was closest to her, but tail ends ventilated by bullet holes, cracked windshields, sprays of shot all along the belly of one bomber.

The problems she'd grown expert in fixing in

San Diego were all mechanical—the work that was necessary to keep a fleet in shape far from the heat of battle.

But she'd never seen planes with damage like this before.

"How did it even stay in flight?" she murmured, mostly to herself, as she looked back at the twisted wing that was closest to her. She wasn't an expert in aerodynamics, but she couldn't imagine a plane doing anything but falling out of the sky when it was compromised like that.

"What, missy?" someone said from behind her. "Don't you know how a plane works?"

When Lottie turned to see who'd said it, she caught sight of a skinny guy with a narrow face and greasy blond hair. He gave her a nasty view of his teeth, with something between a leer and a grin, as he scampered by, heading toward the knot of men inside the hangar at the beginning of the day.

Color rushed to Lottie's cheeks, and hot words rose to her lips. She'd known that she wouldn't be welcome in this shop, either. But she hadn't thought the trouble would start so early in the day.

But before she could say anything, she heard another voice behind her. This one had a Midwesterner's faint twang. "The pilot," the voice said. "He could have bailed out, but he didn't want to lose the plane. So he risked his life, bringing her down safe."

When Lottie turned to look, she was surprised to see a man about her own father's age, with a lined face and salt-and-pepper hair. It came as a pleasant surprise after all the guys she'd been spending so much time among, who were usually not much more than boys themselves.

But she couldn't tell from his expression whether he was pleased or not to be dealing with a woman in the shop. So she looked at him warily, trying to read his face for any signs of where she might stand. The name tag on his overalls read *Cunningham*.

"Now it's our job to fix her up," Cunningham said.

Lottie relaxed a little bit at this. Cunningham seemed to be eager to get to work. And work was something she could do. There wasn't a hint in his expression that when he said "our job," he meant only men.

But before she could reply, he turned away and let out a piercing whistle that instantly silenced all the morning chatter in the shop.

As faces throughout the hangar turned to look at him, Lottie did her best to fade into the crowd, so that all the eyes in the place wouldn't be on her, too. But even though she managed to find a place behind the wing of a nearby plane, she could still see some of the glances flickering over her, which looked a whole lot less than friendly, even as Cunningham began to address them.

"All right," he said, clapping his hands, then rubbing them together. "We've got an aircraft carrier shipping out this week. And you know what needs to be on it?"

He scanned the crowd, but nobody was brave enough to raise a hand or shout out.

Cunningham's face twisted into a wry grin. "It wasn't a trick question, sailors," he said. "An aircraft carrier needs aircraft. Not much point in using up all that wartime fuel to pilot a boat over the Pacific with no birds on it.

"And at this late date in the war," he went on, "there's no such thing as a plane that doesn't need repair, unless it just came off the factory line at Willow Run."

Lottie felt the hair on the back of her arms stand up. Willow Run had been a big Ford factory before the war. But once fighting broke out, the powerful industrial technology had all been refitted, not to build cars, but to build planes for the war effort. She'd toured the factory herself not long ago and was stunned that the planners had been able to convert the giant campus to wartime use so quickly, and by the dedication and nimbleness of the factory workers. They had learned virtually a whole new trade in order to make planes instead of cars. And not only that, but they were all working incredibly long hours, to get as many planes as they could to the front as quickly as possible.

But with the charge of hometown pride, she felt the weight of responsibility herself. Those workers back in Michigan could build the planes. But once they got to the front, keeping the aircraft in the air was another full-time job. And Lottie itched to get started.

"Until the carrier goes out next week," Cunningham continued, "we'll be working double time."

As a murmur rippled through the crowd, Cunningham raised his hand. "That doesn't just mean you'll be here as long as I say every day. It means you'll be working twice as fast while you're here. Got it?"

Around the crowd, the men nodded in assent, their faces determined.

"All right," Cunningham said with another clap of his hands. "Get to work. Except you new recruits," he added as an afterthought. "To me."

As most of the men strode away, heading toward the various planes scattered around the hangar, a handful of men, including Pickman, straggled up toward Cunningham, who was now consulting a clipboard he'd picked up from a workbench nearby. Lottie took her place among them.

"Hanson," Cunningham said. "Looks like you've got years of experience with bodywork."

A freckle-faced kid with a spike of straw-colored hair that looked like it might as well have been picked from whatever hayfield he came from nodded eagerly.

Cunningham looked at the plane with the damaged wing that had confronted Lottie when she first came in.

"See if you can't help get that Helldiver back in action," he said.

"Aye aye, sir!" the blond kid yelped, and jogged over to the plane.

Working down the list, Cunningham assigned each new recruit to a project that had at least something to do with their proven skills. After he'd sent half a dozen guys off to various planes, he said, "Palmer."

"Yes, sir," Lottie said.

The man next to her shuffled in surprise. Behind her, she thought she heard a muffled snicker. Was that Pickman, about to start up again? she wondered wearily. Well, if he wanted any more punishment, she already knew how to deal with him.

"Looks like you know your way around an engine," Cunningham said. When he looked up, his eyebrows were raised in question, but Lottie thought she saw a hint of respect in his eyes, too.

Polite protests rose to Lottie's lips. If this were a dinner party, she'd have been expected to put on a show of modesty and pretend that she didn't have any skills at all. But something told her this wasn't the time to pretend she didn't have skills.

She did, and she was ready to put them to good use.

"Yes, sir," she said, raising her voice so there could be no chance he wouldn't hear her.

"All right," he said. "I've got a knotty problem on that Wildcat in the corner."

Lottie smiled. The Wildcat was built by General Motors—another Detroit contribution to the war effort.

"All right," Cunningham said, nodding at her. "Get to it."

But as Lottie turned to go, she heard a voice behind her. "You only gonna make another problem," someone said. "Putting a girl on that job."

Lottie spun around, eyes blazing, and found herself looking directly into Pickman's eyes.

But then she realized Pickman wasn't talking.

And the voice still was.

"My wife tried to add oil to our car once," whoever it was said. "Time she got done, I almost had to buy another one."

Lottie scanned the small knot of new recruits and figured out who was speaking just as the voice dissolved into an ugly snicker. It was a pasty-faced guy with dirt-colored hair who had somehow managed to get through basic training with much of his figure still just as doughy as his face. The name on his overalls was *Simons*.

Sometimes, Lottie had had to bite back the

words that came to her lips. But now her whole mind just went blank. She felt a sting inside her chest and heat rise in her cheeks.

Everyone, she realized, could see the flush spreading across her face. She felt the threat of tears in the back of her throat and prayed she wouldn't give them the satisfaction of seeing her cry. Especially not now, on the first day.

She'd gotten through so much before, without ever letting them see her crack. Why was she having so much trouble now? Maybe it was because, after everything she'd already been through and fought for, here she was again, feeling like she was right back where she had been when she first started. None of the respect she'd managed to wrest from the men back in California mattered here.

She was going to have to start over, from scratch, and earn it from all of these new men.

She took a deep breath and took another step, but as she did, she heard Pickman's voice.

This time, fury flooded her heart. Pickman should have known better. After all the times she'd bested him back in the other shop, after their conversation on the beach once they'd arrived here together, he was really going to keep bullying her now?

The anger gave her the strength to narrow her eyes and raise her chin, ready to stride away.

But then she heard what he was actually saying.

"I don't know you," Pickman said. "But I know Palmer. And if you want to get this job done, you want her on it."

Simons treated Pickman to the same sneer he'd been reserving for Lottie. "How you know Palmer?" he asked with an ugly suggestion in his tone. "Sounds like she's got you whipped, for sure."

Lottie winced internally at Simons's insinuation that Pickman must be involved with her. But she managed to keep her features placid.

Pickman looked at Lottie. There wasn't exactly sympathy in his glance, but something else: the kind of look men give to one another when they know they're on the same team, and something important depends on it.

"Maybe," Pickman said. "But you better watch yourself, or you will be, too."

"Whooo-eee!" Simons said, leaning back in what was clearly a warm-up for another barrage of mockery and abuse.

At this point, old Cunningham broke in.

"Palmer," he said. "Didn't I just tell you to get at that Wildcat?"

"Yes, sir," Lottie said promptly.

"Why are you still here, then?" Cunningham asked.

"Sorry, sir," Lottie said.

She glanced at Pickman. She didn't have time to thank him. And maybe he didn't deserve a thank-you, yet. Maybe this was just what she had earned from him, after all the mockery he'd subjected her to back in California. But in any case, she'd have to talk with him later.

For now, her job was just to walk away, head held high.

But before she got more than a few steps, she heard another voice that stopped her in her tracks.

This time, she was sure she must be hallucinating.

"Palmer," the familiar voice called. "Where do you think you're going?"

Lottie shook her head, in hopes of knocking this hallucination clean out of it, and kept walking.

But then Cunningham started in. "Palmer," he barked. "Captain Woodward asked you a question."

By now, Lottie was a good fifteen feet from Cunningham and the other unassigned men.

She hoped blindly that at that distance, she'd misheard him, and that he'd said anything, anything else at all, other than "Captain Woodward."

But when she turned back, there was Captain Woodward, grinning at her.

With irritation, she pushed down the part of her that could never help being surprised by how blue his eyes were.

"I'm assigned to that Wildcat over there," Lottie said, gesturing behind her.

But it was clear by now that Captain Woodward's question had never been anything more than rhetorical.

Cunningham was busy giving Captain Woodward a hearty handshake. "Welcome back to paradise," Cunningham said. "I think I managed to keep the place running while you were on R & R."

R & R? Lottie wondered. Was that what they thought of the demanding training Captain Woodward had just put her whole team through?

Captain Woodward was looking around the shop with an appreciative air. "I bet it's running better than it ever did when I was in charge," he said.

In charge? Lottie thought with a sinking feeling. Was there any place in the US Navy where she *wouldn't* be forced to work with Captain Woodward?

But old Cunningham already looked antsy to get back to work.

"We got a big carrier going out," he said. "Gonna be working double time till it ships."

Captain Woodward grinned. "In other words," he said, "no more R & R?"

Cunningham's lined face cracked a smile.

"I wouldn't expect anything less," Captain Woodward said.

"Pick your team," Cunningham said. "Get to it."

"Aye aye, sir," Captain Woodward joked, then looked at Lottie. "Palmer," he said.

"Sir?" she said.

Captain Woodward gestured for her to join him. "Let that Wildcat be," he said. "You're on my team."

"Your team?" Lottie repeated, still certain that she'd misunderstood something.

"Why do you think I had you stationed here in Pearl Harbor?" Captain Woodward said. "I wasn't going to let them send my best mechanic off to some other shop."

Lottie's head began to spin, and the ground felt like it was shifting underneath her. Captain Woodward had been making her life miserable pretty much from the day they'd met. He'd made it perfectly clear that he didn't want a woman in his shop, and she was no exception.

So what was he doing picking her for his team? And picking her first? And what had he just said about asking for her to be assigned to his shop? *He* was the reason she'd been stationed at Pearl Harbor?

As Lottie stood there in shock, Captain Woodward pointed at Pickman, then at three of the other new recruits who hadn't been part of the shop in California. "Pickman," he said. "You, you, and you."

Beside him, Cunningham offered him the clipboard full of background facts on the new mechanics. "You wanna see their skills?" he asked.

"Naw," Captain Woodward said. "If they're any trouble, Palmer will whip them into shape."

Lottie's mouth fell open. With a gulp, she closed it.

"You got a plane for us?" Captain Woodward asked Cunningham.

"I got a Grumman Avenger no man in this place can get running," Cunningham said, and pointed to the large shape of a torpedo bomber shrouded in tarps at the back of the shop.

"Maybe you need a woman," Captain Woodward said. "Get over there," he said to the men he'd just chosen, who scuttled off in the Avenger's direction, then started to stride after them himself.

But when Lottie didn't immediately follow, he stopped and looked back over his shoulder.

"Come on, Palmer," he said.

Startled, Lottie jerked into action, hurrying to catch up with him and the other men.

At the wide-eyed expression on her face, Captain Woodward laughed.

"What's the matter, Palmer?" he asked. "You already forget everything I taught you?"

A strange cocktail of determination and rage bubbled up inside of her. If Captain Woodward thought this was some kind of joke, then she was going to make darn sure that the joke was on him.

Seventeen

Lottie stared out at the dark water. Her bare feet were planted on the last little scrap of asphalt before the macadam gave out to the beach and ran down to the incredible sweep of the Pacific.

It felt good to be alone.

She could see glimmers of moonlight reflected again and again on the midnight-blue waves, but the horizon itself was lost in the darkness. On either side of her, the lights of the island curved away down the coast, then stopped abruptly when the dancing moonlight began at the shore.

Even in darkness, the wind still whipped the waves, and they still crashed on the beach in a constant roar. As she stared into the darkness, she knew that, miles and miles beyond, the war still raged, on land and on the sea.

Sound always carried over water in the spookiest of ways. When she'd been a girl, she'd learned that the hard way, when she'd confessed to her friend that she was sweet on Greg Roth while they were rowing out on a lake. When they'd gotten back to shore, everyone already seemed to know it.

She knew it was impossible that any sound should carry over the water from the war to her across so much distance. But she couldn't help thinking of it. And in the darkness, her mind played tricks on her and made her wonder if the roar of the water on the sand was actually the roar of far-distant engines and explosions. Sounds that hadn't been distant at all not long ago, on this very land.

She took a deep breath, then stepped barefoot onto the sand. She always felt a feeling of freedom at the touch of sand on her bare feet. And that was true, she discovered now, even in the darkness, when the sand was cooler than she ever remembered it feeling, even during the last days of summer in Michigan, up on Mackinac Island. It wasn't the way the girls' athletics coach, Miss Spriggins, had trained her to run—Spriggins was always breathing threats about the dangers of girls training barefoot.

But Lottie wasn't training now. This was the real test. She just wanted to get away from everything: the base, the guys at the shop, the women in the dorms, Cunningham, the whole war itself, even if just for an hour.

And Captain Woodward. Captain Woodward, most of all.

For the rest of the day, he'd been unusually complimentary of her. At first, she'd thought it was a joke, another way he could privately mock her. But he was so insistent, so specific, that Lottie began to suspect that it was sincere. Ever since, she'd felt uncomfortable, vulnerable even.

And all the feelings of hatred that she'd been harboring toward him had been replaced with another feeling. The kind of feeling that seemed forbidden. That made it hard to do her work. That made her head spin with questions that she didn't have answers to.

So she'd slipped away during the women's few free hours that night and taken a jeep down to the nearest beach.

It hadn't taken her long to jog across the virtually empty lot and kick off her shoes.

And now, once she had the feel of the sand on her feet, she ran: First down to the shore itself, so that she was only a few steps from the surf that hissed and fizzed as it sank into the sand with each wave. Then along the line of the coast, with the lights of the island flickering to her left, and the giant naval base up ahead, and the slivers of moonlight dancing in endless patterns on the water.

As she pounded down the beach, feeling the sand slip and grate under her, her mind became a merciful blank, filled only with her own breathing and heartbeat. The sights and sounds around her were different with every step, but also comfortingly steady—the waves new, but the sounds the same. As she ran, she could feel the stress slide from her shoulders, as if an actual weight had been lifted. She drank in the night air, and the cool darkness, as if they were a kind of medicine for her spirit.

The curve of the swimming area began to run out, and big outcroppings of black rock rose up from the sand, crowding the beach. But there was still a strip of navigable sand, even though some of it was so close to the shoreline that it was still clumped and damp.

So Lottie simply darted around the big formations, splashing through the surf until the rock receded again, revealing a little cove, sheltered on both sides by big chunks of stone. Beyond that, Lottie could see that the rocks got even larger, and the sound of the waves against them was far louder than the dull roar the water made on the sand.

If she went any farther, she might wind up dashed on those rocks herself.

So she came to a stop, squinting into the darkness, then turning her back to the ocean to get a better look at the cove.

And as she did, one of the rocks on the sand, sheltered by the curve of the larger stones, seemed to stir.

Startled, Lottie let out a shriek and stumbled backward, not stopping until the chill of the dark water closed around her ankles and drew her up short.

By this time, the rock was talking as well. In fact, it seemed to have gained the power to move and took a few steps toward her, almost as if it were a man.

"Palmer?"

There was only one person it could be.

"Captain Woodward?" she yelped into the darkness just as the captain stepped out of the shadows of the rocks into a patch of moonlight that illuminated his face enough for her to realize it really was him.

"Palmer?" he asked. "Are you all right?"

"What are you doing here?" Lottie demanded, indignation rushing in as the fear began to seep away.

Captain Woodward laughed. "I guess I could ask you the same thing," he said.

"I'm going for a run!" Lottie said, the irritation in her voice still clear.

"In the middle of the night?" Captain Woodward asked. "How do you see where you're going?"

"Probably the same way you do," Lottie snapped back. "I know the boys in the shop love to point out all the differences between men and women, but even I haven't heard anyone say that a woman can't see just as well as a man."

As soon as the words flew out of her mouth, she regretted them. If she'd said it in the shop, it would have been rank insubordination. She wasn't sure what military etiquette required when you ran into your commanding officer in the dark on a beach, but she suspected that insolence was never looked on kindly at any time. And she hated the idea that he might think she was complaining about her treatment by the men in the shop. Because she could stand up for herself. And she had every intention of proving that here at Pearl Harbor, just like she had in California.

"Captain Woodward," she began, "I—"

"Please," Captain Woodward said. "It's Luke."

Lottie stopped, openmouthed.

After a moment, she gathered the presence of mind to close it, hoping somehow he hadn't been able to see how caught off guard she was in the darkness.

"Luke," she repeated. She wasn't sure if she had ever heard his first name before, and when she said it aloud, she was surprised by how quiet her voice sounded.

Through the darkness, her eyes met his, which picked up the glint of moonlight just like the crests of the waves in the ocean. She reminded herself that it was *forbidden* for WAVES to fraternize with the Navy men—and everyone knew what they meant by that. It wasn't friendly conversations the Navy was trying to discourage. It was this . . . whatever *this* was.

Then her mind began to race, wondering what she should do next. Part of her told her to run back the way she'd come as fast as she could. The other part . . . well, she didn't like what the other part wanted.

Before she could decide, Luke grinned. "What's your first name, Palmer?" he asked.

"L-Lottie," Lottie stammered. "Charlotte," she added, as if that might build back some of the formality that they had just cast to the wind—and give her some more dignity in his eyes.

"Lottie," Luke repeated. Then he looked back out at the water. "You found one of the best beaches on the island," he said. "I've always loved this beach."

"It's beautiful," Lottie said.

"It hasn't always looked this way," Luke replied.

"What do you mean?" Lottie asked.

Luke didn't answer, staring out at the dark water.

Lottie glanced back at where he had been sitting, still curious about what in the world he had been doing on the beach.

Her eyes had adjusted to the darkness of the cove by now to the point where she could make out where Luke had been sitting.

To her surprise, it didn't have the natural shape of a rock. Instead, it had the straight lines of something man-made, even though it had the bulk of one of the big rocks scattered around it.

She took a few steps up the beach, drawn by curiosity. And as she did, the shape Luke had been sitting on suddenly came into focus.

It was the wing of a plane. Luke must have

been sitting on it when she first jogged into the cove.

"It's a plane!" Lottie exclaimed.

When she looked back at Luke, he didn't even glance at her, as if he hadn't heard her say anything at all.

Lottie felt a lurch in her stomach. She'd known of the carnage that must have happened here, in the attack on Pearl Harbor. But to see it firsthand . . . it was a chilling reminder of what might still happen, all over the world, if they didn't find a way to win this war.

She padded back down the beach to Luke's side.

When she got there, he turned to her and locked eyes with her again.

Lottie braced herself to hear the awful story that must have lain behind that plane, whose fuselage had been blown apart, and whatever had happened to the pilot.

"What is this?" she asked.

Luke shrugged. "We grounded this old plane a few years ago," he said. "Just didn't have anywhere to stash it on the base. So it wound up here."

Lottie bit her lip, thinking that the plane wasn't the only thing that had ended up on this beach.

Luke took a deep breath. "I guess that's how we all end up one day," he said. "No matter how fast we fly."

Lottie could hear the weariness in his voice, but

for some reason her chin came up at the sound of it. He had every reason in the world to be weary. But that didn't mean he knew everything about the world.

"Well, if this is how we end up," she said, "it's better to fly than stay on the ground."

Luke looked at her, surprised. For a long moment, he seemed to be seeking something in her eyes. Then he smiled. "Maybe so, Lottie," he said. "Maybe so."

Then he looked up at the galaxies spread before them, over the ocean. "Aren't the stars beautiful?" he asked. "You never see them the way you can over the ocean. There's too much light on land."

Startled, Lottie nodded uncertainly.

"Sometimes," Luke said, "I think, maybe if I just souped up a powerful enough engine, I could build a plane that would take me up there." Lottie looked at Luke while he gazed at the night sky. He looked peaceful. "Out among the stars. Beyond all of this. Just leave it all behind."

Lottie looked up at the stars as well.

Then Luke turned to her.

"Do you ever think anything like that?" he asked.

He scanned her face now the same way he had been scanning the stars, as if he were looking for something incredibly important. And as if he were a little lost himself.

For a moment, she was caught by his dream, imagining a freedom that would catapult them up beyond this world, into something else, hopefully something better.

But she fought the feeling back. It was strictly forbidden, she reminded herself, then repeated the word, as if she might forget it: *forbidden*.

Instead, she stepped away. "I think I better be getting home," she said. "I don't want to miss curfew."

"Oh," Luke said, surprised. "Sure."

Lottie tried to give him something approaching a smile, then started off jogging back down the beach, the way she had come.

With every step, she could feel something pulling her back, toward Luke.

But she kept on, determined not to give in to her thoughts, until her feet hit the macadam of the parking lot again, and she put her shoes back on for the drive home.

Eighteen

Lottie breathed in a sigh of relief as she walked into the hangar.

Early morning light poured through the windows, but the big bay doors hadn't been opened yet, which was exactly how she wanted it.

She'd had strange dreams all last night: That she was in the thick of a battle and dodging falling pieces of metal between deafening explosions. That she was hiding in the crevice of a cove, waiting for a chance to rescue someone stranded on the beach, but the fire never let up enough for her to rush out and help them. That she was working in the shop as a battle raged around them, but no matter how hard she worked, they could never provide as many planes as the Navy needed.

And other dreams that were in some ways even more disturbing. Dreams where she and Captain Woodward—Luke—were walking and talking, dressed in civilian clothes, as if they were old friends. He listened as she told him the story of her life, and she listened as he told her his. And at some point, he even held her hand.

She tried to tell herself it was just a dream, but mixed with the strange memories of the evening, it was hard to tell the difference. And she didn't want to be confused in her feelings for her commanding officer.

The best remedy, she'd decided, was to get to work as soon as she woke up and give herself a good strong dose of the Captain Woodward she knew best: the one who spent most of his time ignoring her or telling her what she'd done wrong. She knew how she felt about that version of Captain Woodward.

And it would be good, she thought, as she stepped into the deserted hangar, to have a minute or two to herself, just working with an engine, which had problems she understood and could fix, before he got there.

She headed over to the shelves where she stowed her toolbox every day, collected it, and headed over to the plane she'd been working on the day before, a Hellcat fighter with one gun out. She hadn't worked with guns before. The men hadn't liked the idea of having her work with it, because they didn't think girls mixed with guns.

She was eager to get a good look at it and educate herself without their interference.

But as she crossed the hangar, heading toward the Hellcat, she had the eerie sense that she wasn't alone. It was so strong that she stopped in her tracks and did a full 360-degree turn, scanning the place for anyone else.

That's when she heard it: the murmur of another human voice.

She followed the sound of the voice cautiously to the back corner of the hangar. There, she found Luke, still fully dressed from the night before, asleep on a low cabinet that was almost wide and long enough to function as a cot.

Asleep, but not quietly.

He lay on his back, one arm thrown up over his eyes, as if trying to protect himself. Beneath it, Lottie could see his face contorted into a pained grimace. She looked closer and realized that it was wet. From sweat, perhaps, or tears. Maybe both. She shivered.

And he murmured a constant babble of sounds. None of them resolved into actual words, but it was clear how agitated he was. As Lottie approached, he began to cry out in his sleep, as if someone were hurting him.

"Captain," she said.

In response, he only cried out louder.

"Luke," she tried, raising her own voice and taking a step closer.

But Luke just thrashed where he lay, as if she hadn't said anything.

So Lottie walked right up to his makeshift bed, took his shoulder firmly in her hand, and began to shake him.

"Luke," she said. "You're dreaming. Wake up."

Even with Lottie's speaking at the top of her

voice, shaking him as hard as she could, it took him several seconds to wake up.

When his eyes finally did open, they were full of such horror that Lottie almost looked over her own shoulder to see if something awful was coming up behind her.

Instead, she locked eyes with him. "Luke," she said. "You were having a dream. You're okay."

"Lottie," Luke said.

It wasn't lost on Lottie that she'd only told him her name once, but he remembered, even waking up from a dream like that.

She shoved the thought from her mind.

Slowly, the horror faded from his expression. In its place was a sorrow so deep that Luke closed his eyes again and laid his hand over them. He fumbled for her hand on his shoulder, then closed around it, like a child hanging on to a favorite toy after a bad dream.

Lottie sat beside him awkwardly, wondering what in the world she should do now.

Then she heard footsteps behind her.

Instantly she scrambled to her feet, cursing her luck in her mind. It didn't matter which one of the men had surprised them. It would look bad to any of them.

When she turned around, she was only slightly relieved to see it was Cunningham. His wiry, gray eyebrows were only mildly raised, but she still didn't like the look of it.

"Palmer," Cunningham said.

Suddenly, Luke was on his feet behind her. When she glanced up at him, his face had transformed into the competent, commanding mask of Captain Woodward.

"Roger," Luke said to Cunningham. "Good morning. Palmer here decided to come in early and caught me napping."

"All right," Cunningham said in a tone that indicated he'd decide for himself later what he might think about that. "Well, we'll let you get to it."

Then he began to saunter off.

Lottie hurried off after him, too embarrassed to give Luke even a backward glance.

All through the day, she watched Cunningham. She knew he wasn't one of the gossips in the hangar, but she also knew he'd only need to tell one of the other men in order for the whole story to spread around the shop like wildfire, and with a lot of ugly embellishments that had no bearing on what had really happened.

From time to time, her face would flare up at the thought of the shame she'd feel if that happened. "Appearances matter," her mother used to tell her.

And below it all ran the same low hum inside her at any thought of Captain Woodward—Luke. She was suddenly aware of his presence in the shop. Even when he was clear on the other side of the hangar, it was as though she could feel a tether between them. And if she let herself think of the look he'd given her when they'd met on the beach, she forgot everything about the engine that was sitting right in front of her.

She told herself not to think about it. The best cure was to ignore these gnawing feelings. But, she discovered as the thought intruded on her mind all through the morning and into the afternoon, that was easier said than done.

She knew Cunningham had a habit of staying late. He was a lifer at Pearl Harbor. He liked to remind them that he'd been there since the place opened, if he felt they weren't working as hard as they could or giving him the respect he deserved. He ran the shop as if he owned it himself and not the Navy. And no matter how conscientious a mechanic was, Cunningham could still find a reason to snoop around their station and discover something that needed straightening up after they were done.

For Luke's part, he had spent the entire day acting not just as if he'd never met Lottie before, but as if she didn't even exist. That was perfect, in Lottie's estimation. She didn't need him doing anything that would add to any speculation from Cunningham, or any of the other men.

But by the end of the day, she knew she was going to have to talk to Cunningham about what had happened.

As her father had always said, the best way to deal with a problem was head-on, man-to-man.

Or woman-to-man.

So Lottie, who had been there before all the other men arrived, waited until all the other men, except Cunningham, had left.

By this time, the sun was sinking in a gorgeous haze of pink and orange, filling the entire hangar with warm light.

After the last mechanic slipped out the door, heading for the mess hall, Lottie went over to Cunningham, who peered with disapproval at the patch job some of the men had left half-finished on the belly of a wounded bomber.

"Chief Cunningham," Lottie said.

Cunningham didn't even look away from his inspection of the patch. He answered her with a noncommittal grunt.

"I just want to make sure you understand," Lottie said. "There was nothing untoward happening between me and Captain Woodward. I just came in early, and he was—" She paused, not wanting to give away Luke's secrets. But not telling this one, she reasoned, could hurt both of them.

"He was having bad dreams," she said. "Yelling. I was just trying to get him to wake up."

The statement hung in the air, making Lottie shift uncomfortably.

But to her surprise, Cunningham nodded. Then

he turned to her and met her eyes. His were no longer suspicious but kindly.

"Captain Woodward was here during the attack," he said quietly.

"Pearl Harbor?" Lottie said in shock. Then she realized that, to someone who had actually been here, those words didn't conjure up just the surprise attack, but so much more: friends, places, and work they'd devoted their lives to and loved.

From the way Cunningham nodded, she could see at once that he had been here on that terrible day, as well.

"This wasn't our shop, then," Cunningham said. "That shop is gone."

Lottie shivered. Instantly, she understood what that meant, what Cunningham was trying to tell her.

Luke had survived a direct hit of the bombing.

"Real good friend of Captain Woodward's died that day," Cunningham said. "Wesley Pine. Got caught under a bird he was working on when the bomb dropped. Luke managed to get him out, but he was too busted to move any more. Died in his arms before they got there with their stretchers."

Lottie's heart turned over at the thought.

Cunningham shook his head. "Course, there were others. Still, I think Pine's death hit him the hardest. He hasn't been the same since," he said. "For a long time, he had a lot of trouble with sounds, surprises. Any kind of surprise. That's why they sent him back to the mainland, for rest."

Lottie nodded.

"Maybe we should have let him get some more rest," Cunningham said, looking out at the fading colors of the sunset. "Maybe we should have let him sit the whole rest of this thing out. If I had a thousand men just like him, that's what I'd do."

Lottie stared at the crags of Cunningham's kindly old face, as everything she'd ever thought about Captain Woodward came apart and began to rearrange itself in her mind, around these new pieces of his story.

Cunningham sighed. "But I don't," he said. "This war's too hot now. And it's only going to get worse. We need all the men we can get. I had to have him back here.

"Because," he added, "there's no one like Woodward."

He clapped Lottie on the arm.

"I'm glad you cut one of those nightmares short," he said. "And I'm glad it wasn't one of the other men who saw it."

His face crinkled into a grin that let her know what had happened that morning in the hangar would stay between them. Then he looked at his watch.

"Get out of here," he said. "You can just make dinner if you run."

Nineteen

Lottie squinted as she stood on the deck of the carrier. The strong Hawaiian sun had come out in full force that day. The wind was whipping the tendrils of her hair that had escaped from the bandana and tight knot she always pulled it back in when she was working, as she stared up into the propeller of the busted bomber.

Over the past few weeks, the deck had steadily filled as their shop put bird after bird into fighting shape, replacing bad gears and calibrating electronics. Now there were only a few slots left on the carrier deck. The shop had been working almost around the clock to get all the planes possible onto the ship before it went out, along with dozens of others scheduled to head for the brewing conflict in the Pacific.

But they hadn't been working so fast to get just the birds on the ship. After the carrier moved out, there wouldn't be much of a shop. The demand for manpower was so high in the Pacific that most of the men Lottie had been working with had been assigned to deploy—they'd be shipping out along with the planes they'd fixed.

That only made sense. There was no reason to keep a whole mechanic's shop working hundreds or thousands of miles from the real conflict.

Putting them on the carrier itself was the best way to keep the pilots safe and get the planes back in the air as quickly as possible, even if a battle was raging around them.

Of course, Lottie hadn't been assigned to deploy with them. The Navy might have tolerated women in their secretarial pool, or even in the mechanic's shop, if they fought hard enough. But there was no place for one on a carrier—or in battle.

So when everyone else shipped out, she'd be one of the few who stayed on. It gave her a lonely feeling, thinking of rattling around in that big hangar with just a skeleton crew. But their reduced number also raised a fighting spirit she didn't tell anyone about, especially the other women at the barracks.

While the other women seemed content to share news and speculation about the coming conflicts, most of them hated the idea of battle. A lot of them were nervous to be as close to the fighting as they were.

But a part of Lottie was itching to fight. Maybe it was because, more than the other women, she'd worked side by side with men in the shop. She hated the idea of their going off without her, taking risks without her—putting their lives in danger without her. If someone had been willing to put a wrench, or a weapon, in her hands, she'd have been just as ready to take it as any of the men.

She'd heard how men in service grew deeply loyal to their units, wanting nothing more than to stick with them, whether they were under terrible fire or not. She felt that way about her unit—the men in the shop—leaving without her. About Luke's leaving without her. Deep in her heart, she felt a strong desire to protect her country, and her freedom, just like them.

In the meantime, they still had to finish the last planes that could fit on the carrier. Every one counted. And every one had to be perfect.

That was why Lottie was there now. Pilots had started to fly short flights from the base runway to the carriers, delivering finished planes. Sometimes Chief Cunningham made the runs himself.

Cunningham hadn't flown a plane for the Navy in a long time. But for the short hops to the carrier—basically a takeoff, lazy circle around the bay, and landing—he often volunteered without complaint.

Today, Luke had sent Lottie along with him. It was a welcome relief to have a break from trying to do her work without thinking of him. Now, though, with the fresh, salty breeze, she couldn't help but wish it'd been Luke, and not Cunningham, sitting next to her in the cockpit. Her stomach lurched at the thought.

The maintenance department on the ship had sent a message over saying the propeller on one of their TBM Avenger reconnaissance planes had been catching when it started up. They'd given it a crack on board, but it was such a serious problem they wanted some expert eyes on it.

"You look it over," Luke told her. "I think we can get it back, no problem. But I can't leave the shop while we're working around the clock. I want you to be my eyes. You can do that?"

It wasn't really so much a question as a statement.

And without hesitation, Lottie had nodded.

Then she'd jumped into the next plane Cunningham was flying down to deliver to the carrier, so she could get on board and get a look at the Avenger herself.

Maybe she should have been worried about the fact that it was her job to decide whether the Avenger was safe to fly back in, not for some faceless pilot, but for both her and Cunningham.

But what had really worried her, on the flight over, was the fact that she'd never set foot on the carrier before. The men on land at the base had had time to get used to seeing some female faces around. But the carrier was still a man's world, through and through.

And now it was her assignment to convince all the mechanics on board that she knew how to do something not one of them had been able to do themselves.

Lottie had seen this kind of problem before.

If she was right, it was simple, but deep in the propeller, so that most of the obvious fixes, even by a seasoned mechanic, wouldn't work. In any other circumstances, she'd have been sure. But in this case, she had to get into the plane and fly in it back to base.

So she climbed up the ladder to the propeller and removed the variable-pitch hub case, exposing the gears. There it was: a dislodged gear.

"What's she doing?" one of the carrier's mechanics asked Cunningham, who was standing at the foot of the ladder. "Gonna wind it by hand?"

Cunningham didn't say anything, but she could imagine his smug expression: a cross between annoyance and anticipation of what this guy's reaction would be if she could get it working.

Lottie fastened the stray gear back into place, at least enough so that they could get it to the shop, where they could tear the whole thing apart.

Then she climbed down the ladder.

"You might want to get out of the way," she told the mechanic beside Cunningham, who was already following her out of harm's way.

"You sure about that, honey?" the mechanic said with a leering grin.

Ignoring him, Lottie gave the thumbs-up to the tech in the pilot's seat, who had been waiting for her signal to fire the engine to test the prop.

Instantly, the engine roared to life—with the propeller spinning.

The mechanic on the ground scrambled out of the way. "You got her fixed!" he yelped.

"Not quite," Lottie said. "Just a patch-up. Once she's loaded off the boat, we'll need to get her back to the shop and tear it apart to make sure it's fixed once and for all."

When they got back to the shop, Lottie strode in with an air of satisfaction. But she'd hardly had a moment to savor it when she saw Luke coming toward her.

"Palmer," Luke said. "Glad you're back. Come here."

Dutifully, Lottie went over to where he was standing, close to the lip of the repair bay, where the shadows of the hangar gave way to the bright Hawaii sunshine, and tried to pay attention to anything else in the world but how close Luke was.

To her surprise, he immediately climbed up on a nearby stool and began to whistle and clap to get the hangar's attention. The dozens of men in the shop began to gather 'round. As they did, Lottie's own heart started to slow down.

"As you know," Luke said when they were all assembled, "the carrier is shipping out tomorrow. You men have all done tough work here. We'll have twenty more planes on board than the commander ordered, because of your work in the past weeks. And I don't have to tell you, those twenty planes could be the difference between victory and defeat."

A low cheer rose up among the crowd.

"As you also know," Luke said, "most of us will be shipping out with them, on the carrier or support ships. Including me."

Another cheer rose up.

Lottie scanned Luke's face, looking for any trace of the vulnerable man she knew lay buried beneath the surface.

Is he really ready to go to battle? she wondered. A nagging voice inside her knew that he wasn't. And her heart twisted at the thought of what might happen to him if he was sent back into the fight while he was still struggling with the nightmares she'd seen in his eyes. But war raged on, whether the men were ready or not.

"We'll be leaving a skeleton crew in the shop," Luke went on. "If you haven't got orders to ship out, you know who you are."

A few of the men looked at each other. Lottie glanced at them as they did, hoping to get a sense of who she'd be working with.

"Cunningham will be running the shop while I'm gone," Luke said. "And Palmer will be his second-in-command."

The room suddenly fell silent.

Lottie's head spun.

"I'll expect nothing but the absolute best standard you're all used to providing in my absence," Luke added. "Because believe me, I'll be back to check up on everything you've done."

He grinned, then clapped his hands. "All right," he said. "Get back to work."

As the men shuffled away, Lottie looked up at Luke, in shock.

"What's the matter, Palmer?" he asked. "Don't tell me you don't think you can do it without me."

For some reason, this challenge focused Lottie's mind. She lifted her chin. "I can," she said. And at the same time, she started to feel a bit of indignation. Where did he get off, putting her in charge without ever even talking to her about it? Maybe he thought it was some kind of compliment and she should be grateful for whatever she could get from him. But she deserved more respect than that.

Luke raised his eyebrows. "So why are you still standing here? You out of work to do before the carrier goes out?"

"No," Lottie said.

"I didn't think so," Luke said, and grinned.

As Lottie headed back to the plane she'd been working on, she heard a voice she didn't recognize. "Hey, Palmer," he said.

When she turned, she found herself face-to-face with a mechanic she'd never talked to before, whose name tag read *Redmond*.

"Guess you're the captain's favorite," he said. "Wonder how you managed that?"

By the lift of his eyebrows, he made it very

clear how he thought she'd managed to become Luke's favorite. Her cheeks flared with heat.

"Redmond," Lottie said with as much authority in her voice as she could muster.

Redmond looked at her in shock, as if she were some kind of savant for knowing his name. Apparently he'd forgotten it was prominently displayed on the chest of his overalls.

"You staying here once the carrier goes out?" she asked.

Almost reluctantly, Redmond nodded.

"You think you'd make a good boss?" Lottie continued.

Redmond wasn't sure of the answer to this one. He just looked at her, calculating.

"You see that Avenger out there?" Lottie said, nodding at the plane she and Cunningham had just brought in from the carrier. "I'll tell you what. You get that thing up and running, I'll make you the boss. Deal?"

Redmond couldn't bring himself to say no, but he wasn't about to try his hand at the Avenger on his own, either.

Lottie just stood there for a long moment, making sure that he, and all the men around him, had the time to take the situation in.

"I didn't think so," she finally said, then turned on her heel and smiled as she walked away.

Twenty

"You know," Maggie said with a twinkle in her eye, "when all these men ship out, we're going to finally have the run of the place."

She was scanning a civilian club that was currently bursting at the seams with women and Navy men. One of the big carriers was shipping out tomorrow, and the men were doing everything they could think of to celebrate what for many would be their last day on land for God knew how long.

"Can you imagine it?" Maggie asked, turning back to Lottie where the two of them were ensconced, at one corner of the long tiki bar, and raising her eyebrow.

Lottie took her own look around the room, which was filled with tiki decorations: carved wooden faces, flickering flames hidden behind gold lampshades, and local girls dressed in short skirts and leis.

"Probably a lot less of this tiki motif," Lottie guessed. "And we might let these waitresses work in tuxedos, like a respectable maître d'."

"Or make the maître d's wear leis," Maggie said with a grin. Then her face turned serious as she looked around the place.

She didn't need to tell Lottie what she was

thinking. Despite the joking, the dancing, and even the singing that broke out from time to time in the raucous club, nobody could really forget that the war never stopped.

And that many of them would be on their way to the heart of it, tomorrow.

There was nothing any of them could do about it now. Except for enjoy themselves tonight, as much as they could, because they didn't know when they'd have the chance again. But still, shadows passed across many faces in unguarded moments. When it happened, everyone else quickly glanced away, because they all understood themselves.

Lottie remembered one of her last engagement parties, the one where she'd run into Robert heading off to war. No one had had a care in the world, except for Robert. All the needs of those in her social circle back then had been taken care of. There were so many diversions and frivolities. She'd never wanted for anything.

The mood at this party was very different. But for some reason, Lottie felt more at home here, despite the danger everyone faced. Or maybe she felt at home *because* they were all facing danger together, not despite it.

"Anyway," Maggie said, "I think we might miss them after all."

Then her face crinkled into a mischievous grin. She gestured to the surrounding crowd, as if she were a maître d' herself, introducing guests to a large and tempting smorgasbord. "What do you think?" she asked, looking over at the faces of the many young men gathered there, in all shapes and sizes, from all backgrounds. "Any in particular that you're going to miss?"

The face that rose up in Lottie's mind, instantly, was Luke's. As soon as it did, she felt uneasy, foolish, and strange.

She didn't like the feeling that her mind, or maybe her heart, was mixing up business and pleasure without her permission. She hadn't been lying awake at night like some silly schoolgirl, nurturing hopes of a romance with her commanding officer. In fact, she'd done just the opposite, doing her best to avoid him and stay out of his way.

Lottie had never been the kind of girl to go chasing after a man. And she certainly hadn't joined the Navy to find one. Her heart squeezed at the sudden thought of Eugene back home, a wave of guilt resurfacing. There was some small part of her that felt she owed it to *him* not to entangle herself in a complicated new romance.

She hadn't ever told Maggie, or any of the other women, about her feelings for Luke, or the private moments she'd shared with him. She and Maggie had become such good friends that it felt strange not to share with her about something that important. And the other girls in the barracks were in the habit of swapping stories about their own little crushes and flirtations, some of which Lottie suspected might end in full-blown marriages, if this war ever ended.

But her story with Luke wasn't like any of theirs. What could she tell the girls about him, even if she wanted to? That he was harder on her work than any of the other trainees'? That he spent entire days pretending that she didn't exist? That he only gave her compliments about her skills as a mechanic?

And the deeper things between them—the strange way he'd looked at her on the beach, as if he were hoping something he saw in her face might actually save him, and the frightened, wounded noises he'd made when she caught him sleeping in the repair hangar—those felt far too personal, too serious and deep, to be swapped in exchange for their tales of seamen who brought them little presents at their desks or complimented them on the cut of their uniforms.

Maggie shifted in her seat and suddenly looked away. Lottie realized that the same sorrowful shadow must have fallen on her face. Maggie searched the crowd, and Lottie guessed she was checking to see if there was some specific person who had caught Lottie's eye.

But as she looked back and forth, from Lottie to the crowd, it became clear to Maggie that the answer didn't lie out there. Maggie slapped the counter.

"All right, Palmer," she said. "Why the sad face? Did one of these clowns break your heart? Do I need to do some reconnaissance of my own, before all these jokers move out?"

Lottie shook her head and smiled.

As she did, a tall, handsome soldier with blue eyes and black hair almost stopped in his tracks, caught by her expression.

But Lottie simply didn't have the wherewithal to think of what to say to him tonight.

"All right," Maggie said, waving him by. "Move along. Move along."

Behind him, his buddy gave the tall soldier a shove, and the tall soldier disappeared into the crowd, looking for a more welcoming greeting from someone else.

"Although," Maggie said, "I have to say, I might have talked to that one myself."

As Maggie gazed after the departed young man, Lottie felt a tap on her shoulder.

When she turned, Luke was standing there, his expression serious.

He looked so different in his street clothes, a light blue shirt and a pair of blue jeans, that it threw her off balance. Her heart suddenly started beating harder, her breaths short.

"Palmer," he said. "I've been looking all over for you."

Lottie glanced at Maggie.

"Palmer," Maggie repeated in a voice full of

amusement. "Just when I thought you were out of surprises."

"Maggie," Lottie said. "This is Luke—I mean, Captain Woodward. Captain Woodward, this is my friend Maggie.

"We work together," Lottie said, by way of explanation, turning back to Maggie.

By now, Maggie was staring at her with an amused expression.

"Mm-hmm," Maggie said, nodding. "I'm sure you do. You know what? I think I saw someone over there I need to go talk with."

"Well, no," Lottie began to protest, but there was no stopping Maggie, who swanned off into the crowd, perhaps in the direction of the tall seaman who had just grinned at them.

Lottie half-hoped that when she looked back, Luke would have disappeared, too. Then Lottie wouldn't have to figure out what to say next. And she'd have some time to deal with the rush of emotions that had welled up in her at the sight of him.

But there he was, as solid as ever.

"It's kind of noisy in here," he said. "You want to see if it's any better outside?"

"Sure," Lottie said. Out of habit, she tried to stuff her hands in the pockets of her overalls, a tic she'd developed in the shop whenever she tried to ward off her uncomfortable feelings. But there were no pockets in the dress she was wearing.

And she suddenly realized that she was wearing pearls and not her usual jumpsuit.

The end of the bar was near a side door. When Lottie agreed, Luke nodded at it, and an instant later, the two of them were standing outside, under the bright light of the Hawaiian moon, which broke and sparkled on the ocean beyond the beach where the club was perched. Lottie wasn't sure if it was the view that took her breath away or something else.

"Look familiar?" Luke asked.

For a long moment, nothing looked familiar to Lottie. Apparently standing outside in the dark made the whole world seem new and strange.

But then she realized what he was talking about.

The club was set on the far edge of the beach that the officers loved to frequent. The one where she'd run into Luke that night, just a few weeks before.

"Care for a walk on the beach?" Luke asked.

When Lottie hesitated, he grinned. "I'll be there, in case you run into any strange men."

"Are you trying to say you're not strange?" Lottie managed to shoot back.

Luke's blue eyes crinkled as he smiled. "Nope," he said.

The two of them had crossed onto the sand, which slid through Lottie's pumps as they padded down the beach. She pulled them off and let her toes sink into the sand.

"I didn't get the chance to talk with you," Luke said. "Before I made you head of the shop."

"I noticed that," Lottie said, frustration stirring in her heart. Was this all just about work, after all? A flood of embarrassment coursed through her.

"You think you can handle it?" Luke asked.

"My commanding officer does," Lottie said, keeping her eyes fixed ahead. "Or he wouldn't have made me second-in-command."

Luke tilted his head as the waves crashed beside them. It hadn't taken them long to reach the cove where she'd found Luke that other evening.

"You mind getting your feet wet?" Luke asked.

In answer, Lottie darted ahead of him, across the wet sand at the foot of the rock outcropping that hid the cove from the rest of the beach.

"Hey," Luke said when he'd followed her into the curve of the cove. "I've got something for you."

Lottie turned, curious.

In his hand, he held a thick metal ring.

"It's the O-ring," he told her. "From that first engine you worked on. I want you to have it, for luck."

Lottie held her hand out, palm up. The gesture felt vulnerable, almost childlike. She couldn't believe that he'd kept it all this time.

Luke placed the O-ring in her hand. She had expected it to be cool, like the metal in the shop. But it was warm from the heat of his hand.

Surprised, she looked up at him.

He was staring at her again with that same searching look he'd given her when they'd met at the cove before by accident, scanning her face, but in a way that made it seem like he was looking for something deeper, something hidden far within.

But this time, he began to lean toward her, his eyes still locked with hers, his face moving closer and closer to her lips.

Lottie stood there transfixed, her own heart racing. She wanted so desperately to lean toward him, to feel his arms wrap around her in an embrace.

But just before he reached her, Lottie stepped away.

"It's against policy," she said softly, looking down. She hadn't realized until this moment just how much she wanted this. How much she wanted him. A floodgate gave way to her pent-up emotions, and they tried to carry her with them. It took everything inside her to keep the distance between them.

"When this is all over," she said, looking back up with a small smile, "you come back and collect that kiss."

She could see from the way Luke held himself that something was drawing him to her just as powerfully as she felt drawn to him. But just like her, he didn't allow himself to close the distance. She could see from his face that he knew she was right. "Lottie," he said, in a way that took her breath away. "It's my last night."

"No, it isn't," Lottie said firmly.

The way Luke looked at her then almost tore her heart in two. He looked so pained, so fragile, that she hardly recognized him. "You haven't seen what I've seen."

Lottie's hands had wanted to reach out for Luke, and her lips had wanted to kiss him. Now her heart tugged toward him, like an anchor to a moving ship. This was the closest he'd ever gotten to talking with her—really talking with her—about the things she knew he still wrestled with in his dreams.

"Maybe I haven't," she said. "But I don't believe the things you've seen are the only things you'll ever see."

He sighed and turned to walk closer to the water. As he passed, his arm grazed hers and an electric jolt shot through her.

"You're going to be a great leader," he said, looking out into the black abyss.

Suddenly, the faces of the men back in the shop flashed in her mind and a wave of mortification coursed through her.

"Is this why you promoted me?" she asked, almost in a whisper. She still felt unsteady on her feet from the power of feeling him so close to her. But the thoughts and questions that had begun to crowd her mind made it easier for her to resist him. "Because you have feelings for me?"

But when he turned around, his expression was insulted, almost pained. In an instant, her words had broken whatever spell he had seemed to be under.

"Palmer," he said, suddenly in the familiar tone she knew as "Captain Woodward." "What kind of CO do you think I am?"

"I guess I don't know," Lottie said, her voice rising.

"Then what kind of a *man* do you think I am?" Luke asked. "You really think I'd play with our pilots' lives by promoting someone who wasn't ready?"

Lottie looked deep into his eyes, searching for answers. But the longer she looked, the more she realized there was a lot she didn't know about Luke. And, she was finding out tonight, there was a lot she'd thought she'd known that wasn't right.

"It's just—" Lottie said, her voice softer. "I never thought you . . ."

Luke squinted. "Well, Palmer," he said. "There was a reason for that. I guess you thought I was pretty hard on you. Right?"

Lottie nodded, a bit of fire flashing in her eyes at the memory of all the times he'd corrected or dogged or outright ignored her.

"Well," Luke said, "first off, I wasn't about to let my best new recruit get lazy or overconfident.

Or let her get away without learning anything she might need to know. You can't tell me you haven't learned anything while you've been working with me."

Lottie nodded. It was true. She'd learned more in her months working with Luke than she had perhaps ever in her life.

"But there was something else," Luke said.

"What?" Lottie asked.

"I didn't want to cause any trouble for you. If the men got any hint I thought you were anything but a new recruit, it would have been over for you."

Lottie thought back to the comments she'd heard the men making about her promotion. Luke was right. They'd jumped to those conclusions even when neither of them had given them any reason to.

"Well, then, let's not give them a reason," she said. The words came slowly as she worked this through in her mind. Nothing, no one, was more important to her than this mission. If Luke truly thought she was qualified, then she was going to do this the right way. Without a moment to lose her nerve, Lottie straightened and cleared the lump forming in her throat.

"Godspeed, Captain," she said quickly as she turned and briskly walked back up the beach so he wouldn't see the tears streaming down her face.

Twenty-One

The aircraft carrier had been anchored in the harbor for so long, and was so incredibly large, that it had become a piece of the landscape in Lottie's mind. As long as she had been there in Hawaii, the big ship had been a feature of the bay. And when it began to move at last, it felt to her, standing on shore among so many of the other WAVES and sailors who had come out to see them off, like a piece of the island or an outcropping in the bay had just broken loose and begun to float out to sea, against all the laws of time and space and physics.

Part of her felt pride in the moment. Almost half the birds on board had passed through their shop. And even from this distance, she could see that they were spaced a little tighter than on some of the other carrier decks she'd seen—a testament to the fact that their shop had managed to churn out those twenty extra planes.

But the pride took a distant second to the deep ache that had taken over her heart when the carrier first began to move.

"It's like watching a mountain head out to sea," Maggie said beside her.

Lottie nodded silently. She hadn't expected to be able to tell which man was which when the carrier moved out. She'd seen it from shore a million times, and she knew that the deck was so far away that in general the forms of the sailors who milled around on it were as indistinguishable as ants.

But in the crush of women who had come to watch the carrier ship out, she and Maggie had wound up next to someone who had an old, Navy-issue captain's lookout glass, a short brass telescope that looked like it had been kicking around since several wars before this one.

"They put us girls in charge of all the ancient stuff in the storage warehouse," the woman told anyone who would listen. "So when I saw this, I thought, *I know where I can use that!*"

Lottie wasn't one of the women who was constantly jockeying to take a look through the glass, but it eventually got handed to her.

When she looked through it, the figures on the deck of the ship suddenly sprang toward her. Instantly, she could make out the makes of the planes on deck, and see the individual uniforms of the men and what they were doing: testing that the planes were safely fastened to the deck; leaning over the railing to get a last look at shore; running down the bridge, probably with an order from the admiral who was standing high above, his white uniform blazing in the early morning Hawaii sun.

"See anything, princess?" Maggie asked.

And then, clear as day, there was Luke. He was already hard at work, with the side of one of the birds open to expose the engine within. And of course, a machinist's mate whom he'd already corralled into service, running here and there on his orders.

As she watched, the carrier's horn blasted a friendly toot, in farewell to the harbor that had been its home for these last few weeks.

Luke looked up and back at shore. And through the glass, Lottie had the unmistakable sense that, even over all that distance, their eyes had met.

"Hey," Maggie said, watching her expression closely. "You all right?"

Shaken, Lottie nodded, then handed the glass back to the woman who had given it to her, wishing that she'd just passed it on rather than taking the turn to look through it herself. It did no good to dwell on things she couldn't change.

But Lottie still couldn't erase the image from her mind.

The men on the deck, which was receding instant by instant as the carrier moved out of the bay, had shrunk to specks because of their true distance from shore.

But however Lottie tried, she couldn't forget which one specific speck he was. And as it grew smaller and smaller, as the carrier crossed out of the bay and headed out to sea, her heart constricted so tightly that she didn't know what to do.

Everything in her told her that she should do anything in her power to stop what was happening.

But at the same time, she felt paralyzed by the absolute knowledge that there was nothing she, or anyone else, could do to stop the carrier from moving out—and the war itself from churning on.

When the carrier began to look like a child's toy, dwarfed by the sheer size of the ocean and the endlessly distant horizon beyond, Lottie turned away from the view of the water. She felt like something that had been holding her up had just fallen away.

Maggie, who was still at her side, looked at her closely. "All right, princess," she said. "Back to work."

At this, a thought that had been wiped from Lottie's mind by the spectacle and excitement of the departing carrier suddenly straightened her back.

She didn't have the luxury of crawling into a hole to rest this ache away, no matter how much she might have felt like it.

The shop would be open this morning, just like always. And she was the one who had to take charge of it.

"See you," Lottie said.

"See you," Maggie said, her gaze still questioning.

Squaring her shoulders, Lottie started off toward the repair bay without another backward glance at the sea.

When she arrived, Cunningham was the only man in the hangar.

"You didn't go down to the harbor?" Lottie asked.

Cunningham shook his head. "I've seen it before," he said in a tone that let Lottie know that he was worn down by the harsh rhythms of war. Lottie suspected he'd seen a fair number of men leave on those ships and never return. "Why don't you give out the assignments today, Palmer?"

"Aye aye, sir," she replied.

Lottie took in a deep breath and walked over to the station where Luke used to stand, ready to command the men. It felt strange to take his place. And even stranger that he wasn't there to see her do it. The ache she felt at missing him in this space, where he was always nearby, was almost overwhelming.

She steadied herself by looking down at the muster list.

Lottie hadn't exactly made friends with any of the men in the shop.

But over time, she felt she had fallen into a steady pattern of respectful partnership with some of the men she'd worked with. Men whom she could trust to have her back, or at least take her orders, now that she was in charge of the shop.

Not one of those men was on the list.

But there, near the bottom, was Pickman's name, the last one she would have chosen for herself if she'd had any choice in the matter at all.

She looked around the hangar. Even though they'd just sent the whole ship out, loaded with planes, there was already more work to do. Two planes had come in overnight.

And on the other list Luke had shown her, of planes slated for repair but still in transit to the base, she could see almost a dozen more, beside the list of ten men they still had on staff.

It might not have been a heavy load if the shop were full of mechanics. But with the skeleton crew she had to work with now, they'd have to continue working at a good clip to get these planes back into shape and back into action.

The war didn't stop, it seemed, for anyone.

She looked up at the sound of footsteps. Several of the mechanics had wandered in at the same time: Jameson, whom she knew to be quiet and responsible; Harris, who was a loudmouth but was their resident welding wizard; Johnson, whom she'd never worked with before. And Pickman.

They looked around the hangar much like she had, with a mixture of wistfulness and surprise.

All of them had probably just come down from the bay. They seemed to feel the same way she had: listless and a bit restless.

Then they looked at her.

Lottie had felt the weight of responsibility as she got up that morning and as she walked down alone to the hangar.

But until all those eyes turned to her, she hadn't realized how important this moment was. If she didn't take command now, and quickly, she might never be able to earn the men's respect again.

The thought of failure was sickening. Her biggest fear was having to come into the shop, day after day, with a group of mechanics whom she couldn't command. But the idea of Luke's coming back to his shop and finding it in disarray was worst of all.

And there was only one solution to that. She needed to make it clear that she deserved her position of authority. And she needed to do it now.

As she glanced over the faces of the men, her gaze slid more quickly past Pickman. She didn't like the fact that he was there, she realized, so she was trying to pretend he wasn't.

But when she realized that, she looked back and locked eyes with him.

"Pickman," she said.

"Yeah?" Pickman replied.

Lottie considered demanding he come back

with a more respectful reply, but all she could think of at the moment was what Luke might have said: *"That's 'aye aye, sir' to you, recruit."* And she didn't want to give the men a chance to laugh if she demanded they call her sir—or ma'am.

Instead, she narrowed her eyes, lifted her chin, and pointed at the first busted plane that had come into the shop the afternoon before, a seaplane with the name *Mary Alice* emblazoned on the side.

"The *Mary Alice*," she said. "Report says it's not drawing fuel, but it was sluggish in flight before that. I want a full workup of the basic systems to see if it's something more than just the fuel line. By lunch."

This was a big ask. It would take some doing. It showed she knew what needed to be done and that she expected things to keep happening in the shop as fast as they always had.

But Pickman was a complainer. And he could change the tenor of the whole morning by pushing back.

She and Pickman watched each other.

Then Pickman shrugged.

"You got it," he said, and headed for the seaplane.

Jameson raised his hand for permission to talk.

"Jameson," Lottie said, hiding a smile.

"I got experience with those seaplanes,"

Jameson said. "Captain Woodward had me rebuild two of them, when I first got here."

Lottie gave a curt nod, and he trailed after Pickman.

Then Lottie looked back down at her list, a feeling of relief washing over her as she decided how to allocate the remaining men for the day.

Maybe, she thought, this would work out after all.

Twenty-Two

Lottie sighed as she pushed through the crowd that was milling about outside the mess hall in the Hawaii twilight.

She was exhausted after her first day in the shop, and all she wanted to do was go back to the barracks and drift off into a deep, dreamless sleep.

But the base was crawling with newcomers. Since they'd deployed so many troops, the Navy had sent in replenishments, getting ready to ship out themselves on later carriers.

A big group had arrived today, Lottie had heard, from training bases all over the continental United States. And it seemed like every single one of them was now standing between her and her bed.

As she wove through the crowd, she let her mind wander to her bed back at home: covered with down pillows and duvets, all wrapped in cotton so fine it might as well have been silk. The flowers on her bedside table, always fresh no matter the season. And the ever-shifting moods of the tree beyond her window. What she wouldn't have given for just an hour of sleep in that bed. Or just one more glimpse out that window.

In her shapeless jumpsuit and bandana, Lottie felt pleasantly invisible.

She would have never been able to slip through a crowd like this unnoticed before the war, she thought wryly. People were always saying it was amazing what the war could do to change you. And in this little way, at least, it was true for her.

"Lottie!" she heard a voice calling. "Lottie!"

The sound gave her a strange feeling.

She had just managed to pull free from the knot of men and had taken a few steps down the dim path toward the women's barracks.

But somehow the sound of her own name, said that way, made her feel as if she were suddenly back in Michigan, feeling the evening settle in around her on the shores of a lake, instead of on the cusp of one of the world's great oceans.

And it made her feel as if she were a different, younger woman.

For an instant, it froze her in place.

Then, before she had a chance to even see who had spoken, she was enveloped in a bear hug.

As soon as the arms closed around her, she knew whose they were.

Eugene had picked her up off her feet and was laughing joyfully.

When he put her back down, she looked at him, dazed.

"Oh, I can't believe it. Your mother said you were stationed at Pearl Harbor," he said, his breath short. "But when I checked into it, I heard the place was huge. I'm only here for a few hours before they ship us out. I never dreamed I'd actually get to see you."

Lottie was overwhelmed by a rush of warmth at seeing the man she'd cared about for so long.

Here, in uniform, he suddenly looked different. She realized how tall he was compared to the men around him, and how handsome, with his dark hair and dark eyes. And there was something new about him, too. Although she couldn't put her finger on exactly what it was, he reminded her of Robert, who had come to their engagement party in uniform so long ago. There was some new intention in the way Eugene carried himself. Some seriousness now, where before there had only been joking. She took a step forward, drawn to him.

And then she remembered.

The last time she'd seen him had been the night before their wedding. The wedding she'd run away from, without ever telling him goodbye to his face. And the Eugene standing before her was not the one she had always known. She'd made him a stranger, by leaving him.

Who was he now? she wondered with alarm. Was he angry at her? Still hurting from what she'd done? Was there any chance at all that he might be as happy to see her as she was to see him?

As all of these thoughts collided in her mind, Eugene pulled her away from the crowd, over to a low stone wall, about the right size to sit on, overlooking the water of the bay.

"You'll have to tell me everything," he said. Then, as he looked over her greasy dungarees, his brow knit in confusion. "What have they done to you?" he asked.

"They made me a mechanic," Lottie said.

Eugene threw back his head and laughed heartily. Then he spread his hands in surrender. "I guess you were right all along. Who am I to argue with the US government?"

"I'm second-in-command of my shop," Lottie said. "Since the captain shipped out."

"Of course you are," Eugene said. "I wouldn't expect anything less."

He stared at her fondly.

"Eugene," Lottie began. "I'm sorry. I—"

Eugene gave his head a firm shake. "You don't have anything to be sorry for," he said. "You were right. I did some long, hard thinking after you left. My calendar had been cleared for a few weeks, for some reason," he added with a grin. "So I had a lot of time to think.

"And what you did inspired me to join up," he went on. "I realized that I didn't want to sit this war out, either. Part of me knew I was hiding behind Dad. I never asked him to get an exemption for me. But I never told him no, either.

And I never felt quite right about that. I think some part of me always wanted to do something more, but I'd ignored it. Until you made that impossible."

He reached for her hand and squeezed it.

It felt so familiar, so warm and tender, that tears sprang to Lottie's eyes.

"Hey," Eugene said. "This is good news. It's not *supposed* to make you cry."

Lottie took a deep breath.

"I'm just so glad to see you," Lottie said.

"Me too," Eugene told her. He glanced at the sky. "Maybe someone arranged it for us, better than we could have ourselves."

"Maybe," Lottie said with a smile.

"I wanted to tell you what it had all meant to me, before we shipped out," Eugene said. "What you mean to me. No matter what happens, you helped me see what I really wanted in life."

Lottie didn't know what to say. But before she needed to say anything, Eugene drew her into another hug. For the first time since she'd joined the Navy, Lottie felt as if she were back home, safe and known.

But as they drew apart, someone shouted his name. "Grantham," a voice bellowed in the darkness. "Where'd you go?"

"Duty calls," Eugene said.

Lottie gave him one last squeeze. "You be careful," she said.

Eugene grinned at her. "Always," he told her, and jogged up into the darkness to meet the men he'd trained with.

Lottie sat on the stone wall, reeling.

It had been a wonderful surprise to see Eugene. A weight she hadn't even known she was carrying, of sorrow and guilt over their wedding, seemed to have slipped from her shoulders.

But in its place was a new, nagging anxiety. It was one thing to risk her own life. It was another thing to know that Eugene—someone who had always been so precious to her—was now also at risk in the war.

As she stood to walk back, finally, to her own barracks, she felt as if the ground had shifted in some permanent way beneath her feet.

The words he'd used to thank her—*you helped me see what I really wanted in life*—also echoed in her mind.

And as they did, they raised questions as well.

That was why she had left their wedding behind. To look for something more than the life she'd known. And she'd definitely found something different.

But was it what she wanted? she wondered, looking down at her grease-stained dungarees and thinking ahead to the next day, when she'd have to put on a brave front to the men in her own shop again.

She felt a profound sense of purpose. She was

doing her duty to her country. She was doing what was right. But what was waiting for her after the war—if this war ever ended? Lottie suddenly realized that she'd never thought about what came after.

What, she wondered, walking down the dark trail, did she really want in life?

Twenty-Three

"Look at that!" one of the men said, stabbing a grubby finger at the crumpled map that someone had spread out among the tools on a worktable in the hangar.

The spot he was pointing at was Iwo Jima, a volcanic island surrounded by the sea of blue off Japan.

Luke, Eugene, and thousands of other men on the base had already been gone for well over a week, headed toward the battle that was brewing there.

Luke's ship had steamed out of Pearl Harbor heading for Operation Detachment, a plan to capture the volcanic island and use it as a staging ground to invade Japan's main islands. It would be a bit of payback for the damage the Japanese inflicted on Pearl Harbor.

And according to the chatter that Lottie heard echoing through the women's barracks, from the women who were privy to the communications channels, the US military was hoping a conquest in Japan would turn the tide of the war.

In the shop, the men worked harder than Lottie had ever seen them work before, as if they were fighting some kind of battle themselves. Because they didn't have the kind of volume they'd been working under in the days leading up to the deployment, they'd put the entire shop into spic-and-span shape—although Lottie dared anyone in the shop to make a joke about how cleaning up was women's work.

But they weren't just putting things in order. They were getting things done. In a single day, earlier that week, they'd put three planes into fighting shape.

"I think you broke a record today," Cunningham had told her as the men filed out of the hangar that night.

"No," Lottie had said instantly, "we sent out seven in one day when Captain Woodward was here."

"When Captain Woodward was here," Cunningham had said, raising an eyebrow, "we had five times as many men."

"The Japanese ain't gonna give that up without a fight," one of the other men said now, looking grimly down at the map.

"You think any of those little islands are gonna take a crack at a dozen Allied battleships?" someone asked.

"You never know," Pickman said. "The Japanese are tough."

On any other American base, he might have been called unpatriotic. But this was Pearl Harbor. The statement brought a moment of sober silence.

But the news of the morning was so exciting

that nobody could stay quiet for long. According to the radio report, the Pacific fleet had finally launched their campaign. And they'd already swept onto Iwo Jima, where they were sealing their victory on land, as the men at Pearl Harbor spoke, a thousand miles away.

"But look at this," Hanson said, pointing his finger at another spot on the map.

The eyes of all the men in the shop followed his grease-stained finger as it landed on the Japanese mainland. It was across an expanse of water. But not an uncrossable expanse.

"How far does that put us from Japan?" someone asked.

"Close enough," Hanson answered.

Around the circle, smiles broke out and heads began to shake.

"We can do that," someone said. "Easy."

Hanson grinned. "I think you and the big brass been doing some of the same math," he said.

"And it'll be planes we put in shape," Lottie said, "that make those runs."

A round of cheering broke out among the men. Several of them actually clapped Lottie on the back with so much enthusiasm that she had to steady herself against the impact.

Except for Cunningham.

He stood to the side, watching the excitement with a mild smile. But he made no move to celebrate himself.

"You know something we don't?" Lottie asked him.

Cunningham gave his head a decisive shake no. "I just know war," he said.

"All right," Lottie called. "Back to work. Back to work."

"What are you talking about?" Hanson said. "They won't even have any firepower to throw at us. There won't be any more planes to fix."

"Well," Lottie said, "we've got planes now. And until we hear otherwise, we're gonna fix them."

Hanson headed off to his station with a nod and a grin.

The mood stayed buoyant all day in the shop, and even Lottie's thoughts began to wander toward what had seemed unthinkable even a few days before—the idea that the war might be over one day soon.

What would it mean to return to real life, after all this was over?

What would her real life look like, without this war?

What would Luke be like when he returned? Would he have shed some of the weight he always seemed to carry on his shoulders? Or would it be even heavier, with everything else he'd seen?

Would the changes she saw in Eugene last—or would it be nothing more than jokes and games with him again?

And what about her? This life she'd carved out for herself, bossing around a group of male mechanics on an island on the edge of the world—was it really anything more than a passing dream?

Was there anywhere for her to go, after this great crisis of the war was over, other than back to exactly where she'd come from? She'd never fit there in the first place, trying to make small talk at garden parties and care about the pattern of the most recent dress. And with everything she'd seen and done now, it would be even more impossible.

But what other kind of life could she build for herself?

She walked back to the women's barracks, lost in thought, wondering what Maggie's take on today's victory would be.

But when she slipped in the door and began to make her way through the rows of bunks to her own, she realized quickly that the mood among the WAVES was surprisingly somber.

All over the place, girls were standing around whispering in hushed voices. Lottie saw one who was actually crying, tears streaming down her cheeks, and not making any effort to wipe them away or dry them.

She went right past her own bunk, heading for Maggie's, a sick knot forming in her gut. Maggie's work in the offices meant that she often knew more about what was going on in the rest of the world than most. She wasn't in the habit of shooting off her mouth about any sensitive secrets. But it sure looked to Lottie like whatever was going on now wasn't much of a secret anymore.

She found Maggie sitting on her own bunk, hands on her knees, staring off into space. Maggie's eyes were suspiciously bright—and she didn't immediately greet Lottie with one of her trademark jokes. Something was wrong.

Lottie sank down on the bed across from Maggie.

"Maggie," she said. "What's going on?"

"It looked good," Maggie said, staring at something beyond Lottie, over her shoulder. "This morning. It looked like we won."

"Did we *lose* the battle?" Lottie asked.

As Maggie processed the question, her face contorted as if she couldn't get the answer to add up, no matter how hard she tried.

Then she gave a smile that was so strange it was by far the most disturbing thing Lottie had seen all day, on any of the distressed faces of all the women she had passed on her way to Maggie.

"We can't lose now," Maggie said. "We sank three of their battleships. Hundreds of planes. We landed more than seventy thousand men on that old rock."

"So it's over," Lottie said, breathing a sigh of relief.

Maggie shook her head. "The Japanese don't think so," she said. "They're falling back to caves from the volcano. It could take us weeks to clear them."

"But we can do it," Lottie said.

Maggie raised her hand and let it fall, as if that were the last thing in the world that mattered to her right now.

Even though all the news she'd heard so far only seemed to be good, Lottie's heart felt even more dread than it had when she first walked in.

"Maggie," she said, and reached for her friend's hand.

At the human touch, Maggie's eyes finally met Lottie's. When they did, tears began to slide down both of Maggie's cheeks.

"Maggie," Lottie said, her voice low. "What did we lose?"

"The men," Maggie said, her voice dissolving into tears. "Our men."

Twenty-Four

"Nurse," the man said again. "Nurse."

He'd called it out the last time Lottie walked past, carrying a wad of bandages down to the other end of the overflowing hospital ward. And now that she was returning, coming back down the seemingly endless rows of wounded men, in bed after bed, he called it again—even though she wasn't a nurse. But she, like many of the women on the island, was spending all her spare time trying to ease the burden of caring for the huge number of wounded who continued to pour into the base.

Lottie had thought that there wasn't much that could tug at her heart anymore these days. Not because she didn't care, but because her heart was so tired. She'd seen men crying out in pain and men missing limbs, men with their eyes bandaged who might never see again, men crying out for their mothers or wives or girlfriends, men who just sat and stared, men who cried in silence, over wounds that were all too obvious, or perhaps others that not even a doctor would be able to see.

Lottie, like most of the women on the base, had been there for all of it—after working all day in the repair shop, which was overflowing now with planes that had been battered to bits in the fighting.

Putting the planes back in action took up her days. But for all the other waking hours she still had between eating and sleeping, she volunteered what time she had in the wards with the wounded, just like many of the other WAVES. Hawaii was the closest US holding to the fighting in Japan, so a great portion of the wounded had been landed there.

And the number of wounded was huge.

The Allies had won the battle of Iwo Jima. But the Japanese, as Pickman had observed, were tough fighters. It had taken the Allies several weeks to declare victory. And in the meantime, the losses had been terrible.

Over seventy thousand men had landed. Almost seven thousand of them had been killed in fighting. Over twenty-five thousand more were wounded.

And to Lottie, it sometimes felt like every single one of them had landed here, back in Pearl Harbor.

It was hard to feel anything, when there was so much suffering.

But what struck her about this man was that he didn't seem to really expect that anyone would answer him. He kept saying "Nurse," again and again. But his eyes didn't fix on anything as they roved the ward. And he didn't say it as a command, or even a plea. It was almost a childlike tone, as if he were a boy who had just learned the word and was repeating it to himself, half wondering what it meant.

Over the past few days, the women working in the wards had realized that if they stopped to talk to everyone, they'd never be able to help the ones in the most distress. And this man didn't look to be in any kind of immediate danger. So under normal circumstances, Lottie would probably have walked on herself.

But something in his tone made her stop. Maybe because the exhaustion and the loss of hope she could hear in his voice reminded her of something in herself.

"Yes," she said, going over to his bed.

She hadn't looked closely at the man before she stopped. You couldn't afford to, not if you wanted to get anything done. And so much of what you saw when you looked closely, either at the men's wounds or at their faces, was unbearable. So she'd gotten in the habit of keeping her eyes forward, on where she was going, not all the suffering around her.

But now that she looked at the man, she could see that he wasn't much more than a boy. Maybe not even as old as she was, with freckles on his pale face and a mop of straight brown hair over brown eyes.

It took him a moment to realize that someone had stopped for him, finally.

"Nurse," he said.

Lottie took his hand, scanning the man for his wound. She didn't immediately see one, which wasn't a good sign. If his arms and legs were still whole, that meant he was suffering from some kind of internal wound. The doctors might have patched him up, but that didn't mean they'd really been able to patch up whatever the bullets or shrapnel had torn up inside him.

When she took his hand, he met her eyes. Suddenly, his face lit up in a beatific smile. It had been so long since she'd seen a smile like that that Lottie felt her knees begin to buckle. Quickly, she sank down on the bed beside him.

"Nurse," the young man breathed, as if it were the name of an angel.

"I'm Lottie," Lottie said matter-of-factly. "What's your name?"

"Ben," the young man said. "I'm from Detroit. Where are you from?"

At this simple question, tears sprang into Lottie's eyes. Embarrassed, she blinked them back. What was she doing, letting herself cry, when this man was in so much more pain than she was?

"Detroit!" she said, trying to make her voice sound as cheerful as it would have if she'd just met him at a party. "That's impossible! I'm from Detroit."

She wouldn't have thought Ben's smile could get any bigger, but somehow it did. "I think there's room for both of us in Detroit," he said. His eyes wandered a bit, and Lottie wondered if he'd just had a flash of pain. But then they connected with hers again.

"Only thing I can't understand," he said, "is how I never met you before."

"What do you do in Detroit, Ben?" Lottie asked.

"I'm gonna work at Palmer Stamping," Ben said, pride flaring in his eyes. "That's where my dad works. He says when I get back, he can get me a job, for sure."

Lottie's heart turned over at the name of her father's company. If Ben's dad had any trouble finding him a spot, she resolved then and there, she'd find him one herself.

"It sounds like you've got a lot to look forward to," she said, taking his hand and squeezing it. "You've just got to concentrate on getting better for now."

Ben gave a wry smile. "If you tell me how to concentrate on growing myself a new stomach, I'll do my best," he said.

Lottie had a sinking feeling. He had internal wounds. And to a vital organ.

"You rest," Lottie said.

"And pray," Ben said.

"That's a good idea, too," Lottie told him with a smile.

Lottie managed to make it down to the end of

the aisle before another man called her name. This time, the voice was coming from the next aisle over, just a few beds from the end.

Lottie gave her head a little shake. She couldn't get in the habit of stopping for every man who tried to get her attention. Nothing would ever get done around here if all the women did that. The best thing was just to get back to what she'd been doing before, toss a little smile and nod that direction, and keep moving on, unless it became clear something was really wrong.

And if she did that, she thought to herself, maybe she'd be able to shake the aching sensation of loss, even as she walked away from the bedside of one of her hometown boys.

But then she realized: Whoever it was wasn't calling for a nurse, like the boy from Detroit had been. He was calling her name.

The instant Lottie turned her head, her eyes locked on the only face in the whole place that she recognized.

Eugene lay on a cot several rows over.

And he was smiling.

The sensation of seeing his familiar face, safe and sound, in this ward full of hardship and suffering and hard work, was overwhelming.

She completely forgot any semblance of professional demeanor and rushed over to his side just like she might have when the two of them were kids.

A moment later, she was kneeling beside his bed to give him an awkward embrace, the two of them laughing and talking at the same time.

"How did you—?" she began.

"I'm so glad—" he started.

They both stopped, looked at each other, started again, stopped again.

"You first," Eugene finally said, his eyes crinkling around the edges as they always did when he smiled.

"What are you doing here?" Lottie asked.

It was a familiar question, one she'd asked him a thousand times. But as she asked it this time, a feeling of dread washed over her.

There was only one reason that Eugene would be here: he was wounded.

And the fact that as she drew back from his arms and looked at him, he looked just as solid as he ever had wasn't necessarily a good sign. Was he suffering from internal wounds, just like Ben?

Lottie turned her head, looking for the answer to her own question.

And found it, with a sickening lurch that seemed to knock the whole world off its axis.

"Eugene," she said, reaching blindly back for his hand.

"It's all right, Lots," Eugene said as she took in the sight of him and everything it meant. "I'll be okay."

But Lottie was already shaking her head. How could he be okay? What could he possibly mean?

Because under the fresh sheet, where Eugene's left leg should have been, was nothing but empty space.

Twenty-Five

"Next thing I know," the young soldier told Lottie, "you'll be telling me that if I just eat enough of this Navy-issue Spam, I'll be able to grow wings."

Lottie pursed her lips to hide her own smile. "I didn't say any such thing," she told him. "I told you to drink up that pineapple juice, because the vitamins will help you heal."

Ben, the boy from Detroit, shook his head.

"I'd drink it, Lottie," he said. "I love the taste of that juice. And even if I didn't, I'd drink it for you. But . . ."

Lottie set the glass down on the table beside him again.

"But what?" she asked.

"It hurts," Ben said, and turned his face away on the pillow.

"Well," Lottie said, trying not to entertain the memories of all the other boys she'd cared for with internal wounds over the last week, and all the ones who were no longer in their beds, because they hadn't survived. "It hurts when we heal, too."

Ben tilted his head, considering this. "Maybe," he said. Then he nodded over her shoulder, in the direction of Eugene's bed. "Now get out of here," he said. "Have you visited your old friend yet?"

"I'm about to," Lottie said. But first, she bent down and gave Ben a little kiss on the cheek.

This had become her habit, ever since Eugene had arrived back on the base: she worked all day in the shop, then came to the wards full of wounded, where she worked as long as she could, just as she had before he arrived. But then she sat with Eugene for a while before she went back to her own barracks, long after midnight, to try to sleep.

Eugene, when she reached him, somehow managed to seem just as polished and debonair in his Navy-issue patient's robe as he ever had in the most expensive drinking jacket she'd ever seen him in.

Every time she saw him, she wondered how he managed to pull it off. He could comb his own hair and shave his own face, but why did his bed always look neater than the other men's, and his clothes so much less rumpled?

As she came up, she saw him lay aside a letter.

"News from home?" she asked with a smile.

Eugene nodded as she sank down beside him.

"Everyone still doing well?" she asked, trying to keep her voice cheerful, as she always did when she came to see him.

Eugene had always had a good poker face. But she still noticed a slight jump in his eyebrows and widening of his eyes. And when he nodded, he nodded just a fraction too slowly.

"What?" Lottie said. "Is something wrong?"

"Have you heard from your mother?" Eugene asked.

"I got a letter from her a few days ago," Lottie said. Throughout her time in the WAVES, her mother had kept up a steady stream of messages from home, full of the same cheerful news and mild gossip. And Lottie tried to answer her when she could—which was less and less often these days. The pressure of leading the shop wore on her even in her dreams, and it took up so much mental space that she could barely think of anything else. And even then, she was constantly worried that there were things, important things, that she had forgotten—details that might affect the lives of countless men. "She sounded fine."

Another raise of Eugene's eyebrows.

"What?" Lottie demanded. "Is she sick? Is Daddy all right?"

Eugene nodded and patted her hand. "They're fine," he said in a completely unconvincing tone. "They're both healthy."

"They're not fine," Lottie said, reading his expression.

Eugene took a deep breath and squeezed her hand. He looked at her with sympathy. "This . . ." he said, obviously choosing his words carefully. "This war hasn't been easy for them."

Instantly, Lottie understood what he wasn't saying. It was her. She was what wasn't fine in her parents' world. And from Eugene's expression, she could see that she wasn't the only one paying the price of her choice to join the WAVES. For Eugene's expression to be so somber, her parents must have been under considerable strain.

"Are they . . . ?" she began, but couldn't bring herself to finish the sentence.

Eugene just gazed back at her. "You can imagine what it's like for them," he said. "Your father never talks about it. Your mother doesn't talk about anything else."

He didn't need to say anything more. She'd been trying to avoid the knowledge for months, but suddenly, she knew exactly what it must have been like for them: how helpless they must have felt, and how frightened.

"I haven't had much time to think," she said, a pang running through her heart at the thought of her parents.

And even in the stolen moments when she did have a second to think, she realized, some of her thoughts never seemed to settle.

Like her thoughts about Eugene, which just whirled and whirled in the back of her mind, never seeming to find a place to land.

Having him on the base felt like a member of her family had just arrived—and was in trouble. The men around him assumed that she must be his girlfriend. In Eugene's current state, she had no intention of disabusing them of that notion.

But things were unclear, even in her own mind. She'd been Eugene's girl for years, and his friend for as long as she could even remember. And even the fact that she'd left town on the day of their wedding, bringing all their plans crashing down, didn't seem to change the easy way they got along and how well they knew each other.

It seemed so natural to be with him. As the world fell into chaos around her, full of twisted metal and broken men, he was the one spot that still seemed familiar—and good.

Had she made some kind of terrible mistake, all those months ago?

Was this God's way of bringing them back together, giving her a second chance at happiness, after all she'd gotten wrong?

She didn't know.

But like clockwork, every day, she came to tell him good night, as she did now, and talk for a while.

Eugene looked up and smiled when she settled down on his bed, but she could see the pain in his face. So much about Eugene was just the same as it always had been, but the pain was new, a constant strain that he never complained about but that Lottie couldn't ever stop seeing, even when he smiled.

"Hey there, Lots," Eugene said as she sank down beside him. "How was your day in the trenches?"

Her day had been tough. They'd had more planes to work on than men, and for some reason any part anyone had asked her for all day seemed to have gone missing or not have come in yet. But that was par for the course.

The real problem was the strain—not just of being in charge, but of Luke's absence. Not just of Eugene's wound, but of the whole war. And not even the war, but her own days and nights turned upside down and blending together after days and days with little to no sleep. She'd taken the job Luke entrusted to her confident that she could do it. But she felt more and more uncertain. And the longer Luke was gone, the more dread built up in her heart.

And the more tired she got. She thought she'd worked hard before Luke left the shop to her and Cunningham, but she hadn't had any idea what hard work meant before then. The labor itself was so demanding that she worked just as hard as the men. The hours were longer.

And there was never time to sleep when work was done—not with the flood of wounded men, and Eugene waiting for her every evening. She was so worn out that she could feel parts of her mind shutting down; she barely had the energy or imagination to think. And she was sometimes surprised to find her hands still sure and steady when she worked on an engine.

But none of this compared to Eugene's missing leg and the physical pain she frequently saw reflected in his face.

He didn't like to talk about it. But he said it helped when she told him stories. So every day, she armed herself with a new batch of tales, regaling him with everything that had happened since the two of them had been separated. It distracted him from the pain, and it also built a bridge between them, over the only significant time they'd ever spent apart in their lives, so far.

And the men around him had gotten used to listening to her spin her yarns, almost as if she were a favorite nighttime radio show, there in the flesh.

And since her day had been uneventful, Lottie had decided to tell the tale of an unlucky recruit whom Luke had decided one day wasn't taking his job seriously enough. The young man wasn't filing the rivets on a wing thoroughly and didn't seem to believe Luke when he told him that could have a big effect on the plane's drag, and even the way it flew.

So Luke had assigned him to buff the rivets of every plane in the place, which had taken the kid the better part of a week.

"Captain Woodward" was a favorite character

of Lottie's audience, growing to something like Paul Bunyan proportions as she told story after story about his unusual methods. And it was a comfort to remember the days when Luke had been firmly in charge of the shop. No matter how much she might have rankled under his leadership at moments, she had never realized how much he was carrying—until she tried to carry the same weight herself.

But tonight, as Eugene's eyes crinkled at the story, his pain momentarily forgotten, and the other men around her broke out in guffaws, she heard a voice she didn't recognize.

"Did you say Woodward?" it asked. "Captain Woodward?"

Lottie felt her stomach lurch as the hair on her arms rose in a combination of expectation and fear.

Her eyes darted to the man who had spoken. A few beds down, there was a new man, a little more battered than the soldiers who had been recovering for longer. He had a bandage around his whole head and a bright red cut across his cheek.

"That's right," Lottie said, reaching for Eugene's hand, which closed around hers comfortingly.

"I'm real sorry about that," the man said.

"Sorry about what?" Lottie asked, surprised by the high sound of her own voice.

"I went into action with Captain Woodward at Iwo Jima," the man said. "We lost him."

"Lost?" Lottie repeated.

She glanced at Eugene, who met her eyes, a different kind of pain in them than in his.

The man nodded. "I'm real sorry to tell you," the man said again. "He was riding as engineer in a bomber that went down."

He shook his head as Lottie's fingers closed ever tighter on Eugene's hand.

The man looked her square in the eyes. "He never made it back."

Twenty-Six

"Nothing?" Lottie asked. "You didn't find anything?"

Maggie, who was carrying an empty basin full of fresh bandages, shook her head. She had just arrived in the ward, after a full day in the office. And as soon as Lottie saw her, she'd taken a detour over to meet her.

"I'm sorry," Maggie said. "I checked every list we've got. Twice."

Lottie took a deep breath. A week ago, when she'd first heard the news that Luke's plane had gone down, she'd gone to Maggie, who had access to classified reports and manifests in her office. Maybe the man in the bed near Eugene's had gotten it wrong. He'd known another Luke, or another Woodward. Or maybe he'd even known her Captain Woodward, but he'd made a mistake about what had happened. That would have been easy to do, she told herself, in the midst of the chaos of war, when the man was wounded himself. Maybe his injury had even done something to his memories.

In her mind, she continued to grasp at straw after straw, until Maggie came back with the word: Luke was, in fact, on the list of men missing in action in Iwo Jima. Last contact, in a downed bomber. Just like the man had said.

"Missing," Lottie had said. "So they still might find him."

She could see from Maggie's face that this was only a faint hope. But Maggie didn't know Luke. Not the way Lottie did.

Lottie hadn't liked watching the other men in her shop go off to battle without her. And she knew the men who had stayed with her didn't like being left behind, either.

Now, at the thought that Luke was missing—perhaps gone forever, or perhaps just stranded on some harsh rock half a world away from everything he called home—the desire to be there, wherever *there* was, became unbearable. Lottie would have done anything to get to where he was.

The only problem was that nobody knew where that might be. Except for Luke himself, if he was even still living. Against all odds, Lottie believed that.

So she began to pray. It seemed unfair to ask God to watch out for just one when all of the men who were wounded or missing from that battle had people who cared about them, at least as much as she cared about Luke. But she couldn't help the way her thoughts turned to him, again and again. And when they did, she sent up tiny prayers that, wherever he might be, God would take care of him and watch over him.

It was so much easier than coming to terms with the fact that he was really gone.

But over the course of the week, the pain of not knowing, and the pang became more and more unbearabl this morning, Lottie had caught Maggie ... barracks as the women were milling around, all getting ready to go to work.

"Can you check for me again?" Lottie had asked. "Just one more time?"

"Check what?" Maggie had asked.

The question of where Luke was, and how he was, had been so central in Lottie's mind all this time that she could hardly believe it wasn't the first thing everyone else was thinking of too. Or that Maggie, at least, could have had any question about what she was talking about.

"Luke," Lottie had said. "Can you find out where he is?"

"Luke," Maggie had repeated.

"Captain Woodward," Lottie had said.

Maggie's eyes had suddenly widened in understanding—then softened with a pity that Lottie didn't like.

"Sure," Maggie had said gently, buttoning up her jacket. "I'll check again."

But she hadn't found anything.

Lottie glanced around the ward, as if the answers she was looking for might be somewhere nearby. Everything looked just the same as it always had. And yet, everything felt different.

"Well," Lottie said, "we can check again.

ᴊe by next week they'll know something ᴊre. Maybe—"

"Lottie," Maggie said. She kept her voice low, but by the tone, Lottie could tell she had something serious to say. She met her friend's eyes. And when she did, something Lottie saw in them made Maggie glance away.

"I'm sorry," Maggie said. "I'll check again if you want me to. I'll check as much as you want. But I have to tell you, I look at these lists all day long. And on the casualty lists from Iwo Jima, missing doesn't mean missing. I haven't seen a single missing man recovered alive. If their status ever changes, it only ever changes to deceased." She reached for Lottie's hand and squeezed it. "I don't want to be the one to tell you this, honey," she said. "But I don't want to be the one who doesn't tell you. If he's listed missing . . ." She took a deep breath. "He's gone."

Lottie had tried to tell herself, over and over again, that she had to face up to the fact that Luke might never come back. But telling herself that in her own mind was different from listening to someone else say it aloud. Somehow, that made it real—not just a thought that she could change or chase away, like any other thought.

And she was stunned by the wave of emotion that washed over her at the fact that Luke was really gone. All the small, familiar ways that her heart had been opening to Eugene during his convalescence were suddenly swept away by the power of her feelings for Luke.

Luke, whom she had never even kissed. Luke, who believed in her more than anyone she'd ever known. And whom she would never see again.

She thought back to their last conversation.

It's my last night . . .

She would take back so many of the things she said that night. And she would say so many things she hadn't.

Tears sprang into her eyes. Maggie drew her into an awkward hug, the basin with the bandages caught between their bellies.

But as the two of them drew back, Lottie heard her name. One of the other WAVES, a woman she didn't know, was striding down the row of beds. "Palmer," she called urgently. "Lottie Palmer."

Lottie's first thought was that something must have happened to Eugene as well. Her heart lurched as if the ground under her feet had just given way.

"I'm here," she said. "That's me. What's happened?"

"He's taken a turn for the worse," the woman said. "He's asking for you."

Panic rose inside her. She couldn't handle another loss today. Maggie squeezed Lottie's hand as Lottie turned to follow the woman through the ward, toward Eugene's bed.

But just before they got there, the woman turned down a nearby aisle.

It wasn't until she was standing at the foot of his bed, and Ben smiled up at her, that Lottie realized who the woman had been leading her to.

"Ben," she said, sinking down at his bedside.

The soldier from Detroit gave her the same beatific smile he'd given her the first day they met.

"I been waiting for you," Ben said.

"Oh yeah?" Lottie said, smiling. "Are you going to take me out for a walk?"

Ben smiled again. "Maybe later," he said. His eyes drifted across her face, then focused on something behind her, something she knew wasn't actually there. "Maybe you can meet me there."

The woman who had brought Lottie to Ben's bedside leaned over to whisper in her ear. "The doctor said he doesn't have long," she said.

At this, something stubborn rose in Lottie. She couldn't do anything about losing Luke, or about Eugene's leg. But Ben was right here, in front of her. Close enough that she could hold his hand in hers. And she didn't plan to let him slip away, too. Not today.

As the woman had been speaking to her, Ben's eyes had closed.

"Don't you dare leave, Ben," Lottie said. "I just got here. I'm not going anywhere."

"That's nice," Ben murmured with a smile. "I'm glad you're here."

But as he finished speaking, something started to feel strange about his expression. It was the kind of smile that could easily appear on a face and disappear just as quickly. But on Ben's face, it just stayed.

It only took her a moment to realize he was no longer breathing.

"Ben!" Lottie cried.

The men on either side of her glanced over from their own beds.

Behind her, the nurse who had brought Lottie over put her hand on Lottie's shoulder.

Lottie broke into tears.

The nurse knelt beside her and gently pulled Lottie's hands from Ben's. "Not here," she said, her voice low. "Not here. The other men."

At a tug from the other woman, Lottie rose in a fog, obediently following her until they reached the door of the ward.

The other woman pushed it open, letting a gust of hibiscus-scented sea air sweep over them.

"Take a walk," she said. "Come back when you're ready."

Blindly, Lottie stepped outside and began to walk. She crossed the entire base, to the perimeter gate, but she didn't stop there. Nodding at the guard, she walked out into the darkness, hugging the coastline, gazing out over the dark water that churned in the choppy ocean beyond, and thinking about all the things that lay under and beyond it.

For a long time, it was as if she were walking through a world she'd never seen before. Nothing looked familiar to her, not even the coast. She felt as if she might have even landed on some other planet, one she'd never seen before.

Then, suddenly, she knew exactly where she was.

The curve of the land against the sea felt like home.

But why did it suddenly seem so familiar?

Looking around, Lottie saw the little club at the edge of the cove where the WAVES and seamen had spent so many raucous nights. And the curve of the beach below, where she and Luke had run into each other.

Without hesitating, she made her way down the beach and along the damp shore to the cove.

It was foolish, but she couldn't help looking up to the twisted hunk of metal she'd first found Luke sitting on and down to the shore, in case he'd beaten her there again, as he had before.

But there was no sign of him.

Lottie took a deep breath and walked up to the spot where she'd found him before, in the shadow of the busted wreck from the attack on the island.

She knelt in the sand and pulled something out of her pocket: the O-ring he had given her from that engine in San Diego, which she had carried with her ever since.

It wasn't much, but it was the only thing she had of his.

This war had already taken so much from her. She couldn't let it take her spirit as well.

God, she prayed. *I don't know how to let him go. Please help me find the strength. Please help us all.*

Kneeling beside a large rock, almost the shape of a gravestone, she dug up a few handfuls of sand, until she reached more sand that was damp and hard-packed. She dropped the O-ring in.

It was something real she could do, here and now, to mark the pain that twisted in her chest, something that wouldn't slip through her hands the way Ben's spirit had even though she was sitting right beside him. The way Luke had always seemed to slip away from her whenever they got close.

She suddenly understood why she'd been pushing her emotions away for so long. The longing for Luke was so strong she thought it might split her in two. And when it receded for a moment, everything else rushed in—the exhaustion and worry about the shop, and a deep fear that she wouldn't be able to hold it together there, not even for a minute longer. Missing her mother and father, and the twist of guilt and sorrow at the thought that she'd caused them so much pain, after all they'd done for her. And an ache over Eugene and the things that could never be restored—his leg, and the innocent love they'd shared from their childhood, which seemed so far away now.

For a long time, she knelt there over the O-ring, her tears dropping into the sand. Then finally the shaking in her shoulders subsided.

She lifted her chin, spread sand over the gift Luke had given her, and stood.

Looking out at the dark water, she said another wordless prayer—for Luke, for Ben, for herself, and for everything they'd all lost.

Twenty-Seven

Eugene looked up when she came down the aisle the next morning and grinned.

But there was a clear question in his eyes, mingled with concern for her.

"Good morning, Lots," he said.

"Hey," she said, setting down the pieces of toast she'd brought him from the mess hall. The men in the wards were fed reasonably well, but she always liked to bring him anything extra she could. He'd even started to joke that it wasn't fair for her to bring him extra food, because he couldn't get around to work it all off—a joke that always made her heart twist with pain, while she tried to smile.

"I think that strawberries finally went out of season on the mainland," Lottie said, unfolding the napkin she'd brought the toast in. "We're back to pineapple marmalade."

Eugene's brow furrowed. "If they'd served me pineapple marmalade at the Ritz last year, I'd have been tickled pink. But I don't think I'll ever need another bite of it, after all this."

Still, he crunched into the toast with a grateful smile.

"How are you doing?" Lottie asked, as she did every morning.

Eugene nodded and took another bite, just as if they were an old couple, seated at opposite ends of a long table, with nothing much else that needed to be said between them, after so many years together.

But then he gave her a searching glance. "What about you, Lots?" he asked.

Lottie understood the question—and why he didn't ask it more directly. He couldn't have helped but notice that she hadn't come to visit him last night, as she always had every night since he'd arrived here again. But how could he ask why she hadn't come? He was in such a vulnerable position, totally dependent on her kindness and friendship. He wouldn't want to seem like he was complaining that she hadn't come to visit him. He wouldn't want to do anything that might drive her farther away.

"I'm just tired," she said, trying to give him a smile. "Do you remember the boy I was talking to? The one from Detroit?"

Eugene nodded. "He wanted to go to work in one of your dad's factories."

"He died last night," she said, her head bowing as she said it. "We've just lost so many people."

"And your friend, too," Eugene said gently.

Lottie looked up, confused. Did Eugene know something about Maggie? Had something happened to her, as well?

But when she met Eugene's eyes, he clarified: "Captain Woodward."

Until she heard his name said aloud, Lottie had almost convinced herself that she had been able to bury her feelings for Luke with the O-ring, in the sand on the beach.

But the wave that crashed over her when Eugene spoke his name was so overwhelming that she actually reeled a bit, even though she was already seated on the side of Eugene's bed. And it wasn't just that the wave of sorrow and loss knocked the wind out of her. When the pain finally receded, it left her feeling like it had knocked everything out of her. Her whole heart and even her whole mind felt hollowed out, with nothing left other than a dull ache that she slowly realized pulsed every time her heart did.

Lottie took his hand and kissed it.

Eugene's eyes widened in surprise.

"Lots," he said, his voice questioning and soft.

"I'm coming home with you," Lottie told him. "I decided last night. As soon as you're well again, we'll go together."

Eugene squeezed her hand gently. As she looked into his eyes, tears sprang into her own. "I want us to be together," she said. "And we don't have to have a big wedding, like we'd planned. We'll go to the justice of the peace on the way home and tell them when we get there."

Lottie looked into Eugene's eyes, realizing that

she'd been so overwhelmed with the demands of the war and the shop that she hadn't really seen anything clearly for—she didn't know how long.

And she could see from Eugene's expression that he hadn't missed that, the way he never missed anything.

"Lots," he said quietly. "I've dreamed of hearing you say that. That you wanted to come back."

Gratefully, Lottie squeezed his hand. "I'm ready," she said. She bowed her head. "Maybe I never should have left," she added.

Eugene collected both her hands in his own. For a long moment, the two of them just sat like that, together, the way they had a million times before, before their broken engagement, before Eugene's injury, before anyone had ever even dreamed of this war.

Then Eugene spoke again. "But I've known you all my life, Lottie Palmer," he said.

Something in the way he said it made Lottie look up in surprise.

When she met Eugene's eyes, they crinkled into his familiar smile. But now that smile was tinged with a pain she hadn't seen even in all the days that he'd been struggling to recover from losing his leg.

"What do you mean?" she asked.

"The life I thought we were going to live," Eugene said. "The life I wanted to give you:

parties, and jet-setting. A house on the lake and a house in Florida, and one in Maine. Chauffeurs, and cars we don't fix ourselves." Still smiling, he shook his head. "You aren't cut out for it. You never were."

Lottie opened her mouth to protest, but Eugene raised his eyebrows with a faint smile, and she fell silent.

"Sometimes I used to think I knew you better than you knew yourself," Eugene said. "Looking back, I realized maybe I should have seen what happened coming."

"But we don't have to have that kind of life," Lottie said. "We could do anything we want."

"Maybe," Eugene said. "My life's certainly going to be different than I'd planned now."

Lottie looked down at the place where his missing leg should have been with a pang.

"But that's not what I'm worried about," Eugene said.

Lottie's brows drew together. "Then what?" she asked.

"Lottie," Eugene said. His tone was so serious that for a moment Lottie thought he might propose to her again. Instead, he said, "Do you love me?"

"Of course I do!" Lottie exclaimed.

But then she paused. In that moment, she suddenly knew exactly what Eugene was asking her. And she knew that, in her pause, she had answered the question, without even wanting to. But she still pressed on. "We've been through so much together," she said. "We know each other so well. There's no one I care about more than you."

Eugene didn't say anything for a moment. He just watched her, letting what she knew and he knew sink in, for both of them.

Then he gave her another faint smile. "That's not enough," he said. "For me, or for you."

"But—" Lottie began.

"All this, the war," Eugene said, looking around, "it wasn't just a whim for you. It was just the beginning. If it hadn't been the war, it would have been something else. You were built for more than any of us ever knew. More than you do, maybe. And your adventures are just beginning. I don't want to stand in the way. And I can't wait to see what you'll do next. You'll just have to promise to come back and tell me about them now and then, the way you're always reporting on how you're whipping those guys into shape down in the repair bay."

By now, tears were rolling down Lottie's cheeks. "I got you into this," she said. "If it weren't for me, you might not even be wounded. It's only right that I take care of you."

Eugene raised his eyebrows and shook his head. It was strange, but a look of amusement had come into his eyes. "Lots, I've got a lot more to go back to than most guys in this place," he said. "This isn't the end for me, either."

Lottie wiped at her eyes.

"And you know something else?" Eugene said.

Lottie shook her head.

"I don't regret a thing," Eugene told her. "It's my country. It's my duty, too. And I'm not sorry I came to fight for it. No matter what happened. And no matter what happens next. All right?"

Lottie nodded. But in her heart, she felt nothing but a deep, throbbing ache.

Eugene looked up at the clock high on the ward's wall.

"You better get out of here," he said. "It won't do if the boss is late."

Twenty-Eight

It wasn't until Lottie was standing at the edge of the water that she realized she hadn't gone to the repair hangar after she left Eugene, but walked in a fog of confusion and hurt and guilt through the maze of runways and base buildings to the water. There wasn't a beach to speak of at Pearl Harbor, but she'd managed to find a quiet spot of shore, anyway, a little strip where the water of the bay sloshed quietly against the concrete footings of the building behind her.

But with the harbor in front of her, the nondescript buildings behind her quickly faded from her mind, replaced by her own thoughts and memories.

They were overwhelming.

Eugene hadn't said a word to her in reproach, but she had plenty of that for herself. It had all seemed like such an interesting game to her, hadn't it, playing at being at war? And for a while, she'd been able to pretend she wasn't just a selfish princess. Because what kind of princess would ever get her hands dirty fixing greasy, busted engines?

But that hadn't been war, Lottie realized now. War wasn't being the only woman in a workshop full of men. It was the absence of all those men who had once crowded her shop. It was not knowing when many of them would ever come back, and knowing some of them never would. It was Eugene, trying to smile through the pain of a wound that would never heal, no matter how long he waited.

And Luke. What if she'd made it harder for him to do his job, instead of easier? What if she'd been a distraction, instead of a help? The sickening question of which plane he'd been in when it went down came to her. Had it been one she worked on? Was she sure her work had been good? What if she was part of the reason he was gone? What if she had cost the lives of any other men, men whose names she didn't even know?

She looked out at the sparkling water, wishing she could cry, but although her heart twisted in her chest and she found it hard to take a full breath, her eyes were bone dry.

Something in her tugged her back to Eugene: the part that always wanted to return to the familiarity of their long friendship. But even though her thoughts were raw and fractured, she knew that wasn't the answer. He'd be kind to her, and he'd talk with her as long as she wanted. But in the end, nothing he'd said would change. She knew him well enough to know that. She even knew that he was right. She couldn't give him her heart, because she didn't even know it herself.

What she wanted to go back to, she realized,

was something that was gone forever now—the life she had left behind when she walked out her door on the morning before their wedding. She wanted to go back to a world where he still had both of his legs. She wanted to go back to a world where he was the best and safest person she had ever known.

Even more than that, she wanted to go back to a world where she hadn't lost or hurt them—not Luke, not Eugene, not anyone else.

She couldn't turn time back and take back everything she'd said and done, she thought. But she could at least quit now, before she hurt anyone else.

And all the dreams she'd had, all that fire in her belly about wanting to change the world or be part of something—it all sounded just like nonsense to her now, a child's wish that didn't mean anything in the cold light of day, against the harsh backdrop of war.

Her mind flashed back on the time that Luke had tried to tell her about the realities of war and the ways it might change her. She'd thought she was helping him remember the good in life, helping him somehow by reminding him they couldn't give up the fight. But now she realized she was the one who should have been listening to him all along. Nobody could change any of this. And anyone who tried would just end up like her—worn down and lost.

God, she prayed as the waves danced toward the horizon and splashed against the concrete she stood on. *Please forgive me for everything. Please forgive me for my arrogance, my vanity. There's so much I thought I knew about the world, but I'm learning that there's so much I don't understand. Please keep me from doing any more harm. Please help me.*

Tears began to run down her face. Gratefully, she wiped them away, feeling some of the tightness in her shoulders and pressure in her chest leak out of her along with them.

And when they were gone, her decision became clear.

I'm going home.

She started back toward the women's barracks. As she passed the turnoff to the repair hangar, her thoughts flitted briefly to the men, who should all already have been there.

They might wonder where she was for a few minutes. But that wouldn't stop them from diving into the work. Who was she to have believed anyone needed her?

When she got back to the women's barracks, it was deserted. Everyone else was already out, at their posts.

Lottie pulled her bag out from under her bed and began to pack. It didn't take long; most of her personal effects were already stored neatly in her Navy-issue satchel.

When she was finished, she slung the bag over her shoulder and looked around at the rows of empty beds.

Maybe the Navy would come after her if she went AWOL. Or maybe no one would even notice.

She only knew one thing: she had to get out of here before she did any more harm—to herself or anyone else.

But as she walked down the aisle, to the exit door, someone threw it open. The bright Hawaii morning light that poured inside was so strong that Lottie actually threw up her arm to shield her eyes.

Then the door thudded shut, and Lottie lifted her chin again, planning to give whoever it was a quick nod before she passed her by and made her escape.

"Where are you going?" Maggie demanded.

As the sting of the sun left Lottie's eyes, they focused enough to recognize that Maggie's eyes were full of tears.

With all they'd been through together, even the tough days at basic training, she'd almost never seen Maggie shed a tear. In fact, Maggie had been the one who told Lottie not to let her own tears show.

Lottie's heart grew even heavier at the sight. Had she already hurt another one of the people she cared about, before she even managed to get herself off the base?

A host of explanations and excuses leapt into her head, a jumble of words to make Maggie understand that it wasn't her fault and that Lottie had to do what she was doing, even if it would be hard to go and be separated from her.

But before she could say any of them, Maggie broke out in a sob and wrapped Lottie in a hug.

Startled, Lottie leaned in and returned the hug.

"I can't do it," Maggie said as she shuddered with tears. "I can't do it anymore. It's too much. I just can't."

Slowly, it dawned on Lottie that Maggie didn't know anything about what Lottie was about to do. Something had happened to Maggie. Something that, judging from Maggie's reaction, sounded awful.

"Maggie," Lottie said. "What happened?"

Maggie pulled away from Lottie, but she didn't do anything to stop the tears rolling down her face, and her voice was still high and tight with emotion.

"Those men," she said.

Lottie felt a burst of protective ire rise up in her. If someone had been bothering Maggie so badly they'd reduced her to this point, they were going to hear about it from Lottie.

But as Maggie went on, it became clear that she was worried about the men she was talking about, whoever they were—not angry at them.

"It's too awful," Maggie said. "Everything

about this war has been awful, but this is too awful. Those poor men. They did so much—and—"

She dissolved into tears again as Lottie led her to a nearby bed, where the two of them sat down, with Lottie's arm around Maggie.

"I don't understand," Lottie said gently.

Maggie took a deep breath.

"There are men from the battle at Iwo Jima lost at sea," she said. "I just got the word of it in the comms office. We've been getting updates ever since I went in this morning. And they're awful."

"What happened?" Lottie asked, steeling herself for the worst.

"They were captured in the fighting, but they managed to escape," Maggie said. "I think they must have been shot down, but when they got free, they found a Japanese boat that had been damaged in the fight and took it over. They managed to get back into US waters, living on the rations on board. But now the engine's died, and they've been drifting for days. All the food's gone, and they're almost out of water. But the radio's still working. They've been signaling ever since they took the boat last week, and they just finally caught an Allied pilot on a flyover."

"But that's good," Lottie said. "They survived."

Maggie shook her head, tears filling her eyes again. "But they won't," she said. "They've drifted too far. They're too far from our ships.

It'll be days before anyone can reach them by sea. And we can't do a rescue by air that far out to sea.

"The pilot kept circling so he could stay in touch with them," she said, her face crumpling. "But he couldn't land. And they're so far out that eventually he had to head back to base, so he didn't run out of fuel himself."

Lottie took a deep breath as the horror of the situation sank in for her: Men who had survived so much and fought so hard to do it. The joy of finally raising a friendly voice on the radio. And then the bitter disappointment that, for some of them, help still couldn't come in time.

"Some of them are wounded," Maggie said. "Bad. Without food, without water—who knows if they'll even be alive tonight?"

She squeezed Lottie's hand.

"They came so far," she said before dissolving into tears. Lottie gently put her hand on Maggie's back and rubbed it comfortingly.

Then Maggie looked up, and a thought that hadn't yet crossed her mind finally surfaced.

"Lottie," she said. "What are you doing here?"

But Lottie shook her head.

Because all of a sudden, she wasn't leaving anymore.

Maggie couldn't see any way to save those stranded men.

But Lottie did.

Twenty-Nine

"What do you think?" Lottie asked.

Cunningham squinted up at the wings of the plane they were both standing under.

They weren't in the shop. They weren't even in one of the standard hangars, where planes that were already in good shape waited to be deployed.

The two of them were standing out behind the repair hangar, amid the piles of twisted metal and parts that the men sometimes came out to during the course of the day, either to find a piece of metal big enough to hammer or solder into some shape they needed, or to drop off some part that was too busted to work on whatever bird they were currently repairing.

The plane they were looking up at was the only whole one out there, a PBY Catalina flying boat. Legend had it that it had been pulled out of Pearl Harbor near the mouth of the freshwater Aiea Stream after the attack. Lottie had always figured that was a tall tale they told her since she was the new girl, hoping she'd be dumb enough to repeat it to someone else as truth.

But now that she looked at it more closely, she started to wonder. She'd seen the paint on planes damaged by a lot of things—bullets, impact, heat, and actual fire. But she'd never seen a finish that looked quite like this—still smooth, but with all the sheen gone, almost as if it were a piece of beach glass. And were those barnacles on the tips of the wings?

None of that mattered, though, as much as the base of the Catalina. Under the hold, the belly of the plane was curved: the aquatic landing apparatus of the flying boat.

"We got her so she fired up once," Cunningham said. "But we never put her back in working order. There weren't much call for her. Too small to do much good."

"How many men do you think she'll hold?" Lottie asked.

Cunningham squinted. "Plenty," he said.

"Do you think it could take ten?"

Now Cunningham squinted at her.

"What are you up to, Palmer?" he said.

Quickly, Palmer brought him up to speed.

Cunningham's stoic face didn't flicker, but she could see his eyes narrow in concentration. He peered up at the plane, then gave a quick nod. "She can fit ten, eleven," he said. "If that's what it takes."

"Well," Lottie said, glancing up at the cockpit, "what are you waiting for?"

"You think it'll start?" Cunningham asked.

"Only one way to find out," Lottie said, nodding up at the plane.

Cunningham took that as an order. He swung up

into the cockpit and a minute later was flicking at the controls.

Lottie took a deep breath, waiting for any sign of life to cough out of the engine.

But before she even really had a chance to hold it in, the engine didn't just cough—it roared.

She could hear Cunningham's yelp of laughter even over the growl of the engine. "Hot damn!" he called. "She's alive!"

Ten minutes later, they'd wheeled the water bird around the back of the hangar and in through the main bay.

As the men around the shop looked up, Lottie hopped on a stool and waved them all over. Quickly, she explained the story Maggie had told her less than an hour ago. As she did, the faces of the men grew serious but determined.

"She runs," Lottie said, slapping the side of the plane. "So that's something. But I'm not going to put a pilot up in this thing without a full inspection. And she's only got a range of a thousand miles as built. So we're gonna want to find a solution for the fuel."

"I thought you said the men were only eight hundred miles out from Hawaii," Pickman said.

"That's right," Lottie told him. "But there's not going to be a fuel depot in the middle of the Pacific for the pilot to refuel before he brings those men back."

She slapped the side of the plane again, then

gave orders for each man to take responsibility for doing a full check of the various systems: structural integrity, fuel, engine, controls.

"Every minute counts," she said as they scrambled to get their tools.

Then she turned to Cunningham. "Now we just need a pilot," she said.

For a long moment, the two of them looked at each other. Lottie knew what he was thinking, because she was thinking it herself. She'd proved herself to the men in this shop. But if she went to command asking for a pilot, especially for a scheme like this, there was a good chance she'd get laughed out of the place before she even began.

A man might get laughed at, too. But he wouldn't face the same trouble Lottie would. Nobody there would think he shouldn't even be in the room. And with lives on the line, it was no time to gamble.

"It's a crazy idea," Cunningham said carefully. "But I could talk to someone."

"Go," Lottie said. "Get me a pilot. I'll have a plane by the time you have one."

The months-long saltwater bath the plane had taken might not have had the magic rejuvenating properties advertised by some of the more ambitious local Hawaii hotels, but it didn't seem to have done nearly as much damage as Lottie would have thought, either.

"It's not the water that does the damage," Pickman told her. "It's the air."

Whatever the case, with all the men crawling over the Catalina, working as fast as they could, they made short work of her. To give the plane more range, they patched together a daisy chain of fuel tanks. A choke in the engine, which Lottie initially thought might mean a busted gear—or one that had rusted into oblivion—turned out to be fixed by nothing more than a bit of oil and the removal of a large clump of seaweed from the engine block. Pistons were greased, filters were changed, a bit of damage on the wingtip was soldered back into place.

By the time Cunningham returned, about an hour later, the engine of the old seaplane was humming, and one of the guys was climbing around on the roof, trying to clean off the thick film of dirt that had accumulated on the windshield after months of disuse.

Lottie was glad to see Cunningham had actually gotten someone from command to come to the hangar. He could have easily returned by himself, and told her their plan was turned down, sight unseen.

But that was about all Lottie liked about the look of the guy who walked in with Cunningham.

He was a big, bluff officer, a good ten years older than Lottie, in full Navy blues, and he didn't even take off his sunglasses when he stepped deep into the shadows of the hangar.

At the sight of him, the men from the shop

scrambled into place and offered a series of clumsy salutes, the pride in the incredible work they'd just done clear on their faces.

But the officer, whose name tag read *Hoyt,* barely glanced at the plane.

Instead he gave Lottie a full once-over, looking her up and down as if she were the main attraction at some seedy dance hall.

Then he looked up at the plane, his lip curled.

"Cunningham here insisted I come down and get a look at this," Hoyt said. He shook his head. "You really got her running?"

Lottie nodded at one of the nearby mechanics, who jumped into the cockpit. A moment later, the engine purred to life.

At the trace of a smile that passed over Hoyt's lips, Lottie's heart leapt. But then he looked back at Cunningham.

"I'm sorry, Cunningham," he said. "We appreciate the effort, but I can't send a pilot up in this bird. There's no way she's ready for flight."

"She's ready, sir," Lottie broke in.

Hoyt raised his eyebrows, obviously annoyed by her interruption. Then he turned to her with all the condescension of a superior officer putting a lackey who'd stepped out of line back in place.

"I think Cunningham and I can handle this, miss," he said, not even meeting her eyes.

"Palmer is second-in-command here," Cunningham said quietly. "Sir."

It wasn't clear if Hoyt didn't hear him or just chose to ignore him. But in any case, Hoyt didn't look at anyone in particular when he made his next announcement.

"I've been on Navy boats for over a decade," Hoyt said. "And I've never even let a rowboat set sail with so little time for inspection."

"With respect, sir," Lottie said, "boats and planes are different. And I stand behind this inspection. I'd go up in her myself."

Hoyt's lip curled, as if he were briefly relishing the thought of dispensing with Lottie by sending her up in a faulty plane.

But then he shook his head. "This is a matter of life or death," he said. "We just can't risk it."

"It is a matter of life or death," Lottie broke in. "For those men out there. And there are at least ten of them. Isn't it worth risking one life if we could save all of them?"

Hoyt's eyes narrowed. "None of my pilots are at risk now," he said. "And those men out there on the water—" For the first time since he'd walked into the hangar, Lottie thought she saw a flicker of humanity in his gaze. "We don't know any of them are still alive. Or that they still will be when they get there, even if they are now. I can't risk my men's life on the chance."

"But—" Lottie protested.

Hoyt held up his hand. "These are the realities of war, miss," he said, with an emphasis on the *miss.* "I don't expect you to understand. But this plane won't be flying today. You can continue with whatever work this unit was supposed to be doing, before someone came up with this crackpot plan."

"Sir—" Cunningham tried, but Hoyt was already striding out of the hangar.

Lottie felt hot tears come to her eyes, but at the same time, the eyes of every man in the place now turned to her. She couldn't even blink them back without their seeing how upset she was. So instead, she raised her chin and took a deep breath.

Then Cunningham cleared his throat.

"You know," he said. "I flew in the last war."

Lottie turned to him, openmouthed. "You did?" she asked.

Cunningham nodded. "They say I'm too old for active duty now," he said. "But that don't mean I forgot how to fly a plane."

Pickman whooped. "Johnson," he called. "Fuel her up!"

"You think you can get your friend to give you the coordinates of those men out there?" Cunningham asked.

Lottie nodded and picked up the hangar phone.

"I'm gonna go find us a pair of jumpsuits," Cunningham said.

"Wait," Lottie said. "What do you mean 'us'?"

Cunningham grinned. "You think I'm going to make a flight like that without the best engineer in this shop?" he asked.

Thirty

Lottie held her breath as the plane nosed out of the repair hangar.

She'd been in dozens of planes before, both commercial and private, because her father and his friends were all fascinated with flight, to the point where Lottie used to tease her father that next he should order his engineers to design a flying car.

But she'd never been in the cockpit in a plane this big. And she'd never before tried to take off against the express wishes of the US Navy—which meant that if they got into any trouble, they'd also be operating without backup.

But she didn't feel afraid. She didn't even feel thrilled. She just felt the all-consuming calm of total concentration.

In the cockpit, she and Cunningham were as high as the second story of the buildings that surrounded them, so she could see the half-deserted runways and lanes of the base well enough to get a bird's-eye view—and to passionately wish they were completely deserted.

"Never done this without flight control before," Cunningham called over the noise of the engines. He looked up at the empty blue sky. "But I don't think we'll have much competition."

Until they got to the runway itself, nobody paid them much mind.

A few of the passing seamen took a second squint at the bird, simply because the deeply rounded belly of the flying boat was such a different profile from the standard planes they were used to seeing.

But nobody took one look at them and went running off to make a report, as Lottie half-feared someone might.

The other half of her feared that no one would stop them. And that in a few minutes she'd be flying in the air in a bird that hadn't been flown for years, heading for a rescue mission she had no idea how to accomplish. In some ways, it'd be easier if they did get caught, so that she wouldn't have to figure out everything that came next if they actually did manage to take off.

It wasn't until they nosed onto the actual runway that heads began to turn. Men who had been lazily fueling up planes, or standing around waiting for orders, were suddenly at true attention, not just the military version of it, when an unfamiliar plane entered the runway unannounced.

A few of them stood in shock. Some began to wave and yell. But an instant later, Cunningham gunned the engine. He and Lottie hurtled forward, toward the blue of the bay. And just before they sank into it, the lift of the wings kicked in, and the plane began to rise.

Cunningham and Lottie looked at each other, grinning.

"You think they'll come after us?" Lottie shouted over the roar of the engine.

Cunningham shrugged. "They ain't gonna shoot us down," he said. "So they'd have to come with us. Which means more help for the rescue."

The twinkle in his eye said he'd take those odds.

But as the plane leveled out over the wide sea, the two of them fell silent, both focused on the distant horizon and the men they were trying to reach, far beyond what they could even see now.

The broad expanse of blue sky and blue sea that stretched before them was vast. It took Lottie's breath away.

Somehow, the sea and sky proved just as varied as any land, with just as many colors and changes. And Lottie was glad for them. As she let them fill her senses, everything else fell away. For the first time she could remember, all her problems seemed to get smaller, as she realized how minuscule she was in the face of the ocean. It was a fact that could have scared her and made her feel insignificant. But somehow it came as a comfort, that this sea was still rolling on, despite all the troubles of everyone back on land.

But still, the thought of the men they were headed for, stranded in their tiny boat, even tinier themselves, and at the mercy of such a vast ocean, was a continual pinprick in her heart.

The only conversation she had with Cunningham was his reports on their progress—three hours out, two hours, one. And the closer they got, the more impatient Lottie became. Every second counted now. Couldn't the plane go any faster?

Anticipation grew in her heart as they flew through the final hour, all trace of land now left far behind them.

But as the quad engines purred through what should have been the last half hour, on the horizon, they could see a storm, a dark, angry patch in the otherwise clear line of sea and sky, which the sun was now beginning to sink down.

Lottie watched it, trying to judge the path Cunningham was on. The storm was so small and the horizon so long. It seemed impossible that they'd have to go through that spot, of all the spots they could see.

"We going to miss that?" she shouted over the roar of the engine.

Grimly, Cunningham shook his head.

And then, faster than she would have ever imagined, they were in it.

The sun was still up. But inside the storm, it was as if night had just set in.

Lottie squinted and tried to scan the ocean below. With this little light, and this much rain and wind, Lottie began to worry they wouldn't be able to see the boat, even if they made it to the exact coordinates. And she worried even more about what this kind of a storm had done to the boat's position. In clear weather, they should have been able to see for miles, which meant they'd have had a good chance of finding the little ship, even if it had been blown quite a bit off course. But in this kind of a blow, Lottie didn't know.

Cunningham just narrowed his eyes, heading steadily for the setting that Maggie had given them.

And then Lottie saw it.

It wasn't easy to pick out through the steel-colored waves and the sheets of rain that poured down around the plane, sometimes flying in at an angle from the wind, directly into the glass shield of the cockpit.

But it was a ship, as plain as day. A small one, more the size of an independent fishing rig than what Lottie would have thought of as a military vessel.

It spun lazily in the water, like a child's toy left in the tub after a bath. It flickered in and out of view, depending on the ferocity of the wind and the waves. But it was a ship. It fit the description. And it was just where it should have been.

"It's there!" Lottie called, pointing out her window. "I see it."

For the first time since he'd taken the controls, Lottie saw a look of relief pass over Cunningham's face. But just as quickly, he steeled himself for the task still at hand.

"I can't land anywhere near them," he shouted over the noise of the engine and the storm. "With waves this big, we might swamp the boat with our wake."

Lottie nodded.

Cunningham was already descending in the direction of the ship. He jutted his chin out, toward a patch of water just beyond it. It didn't look too far now, just a scrap of space from this distance, but by the time they landed, it would be hundreds of yards. "I'm going to try to get just past it," he said.

Lottie braced herself as the plane bounced and groaned, losing altitude through the worst of the storm.

But the landing was different than any she'd ever experienced. Even in the heart of the storm, the ship staggered from the sudden resistance of the water, and the sound increased from the slap of waves on the hull.

She and Cunningham had worked the plan out in advance: she'd be the one to climb down into the hold, open the hatch, and take a launch out to get the men. But when they'd made the plan, neither of them had imagined that she'd be doing it in the midst of a storm.

"You all right, Palmer?" Cunningham shouted.

She gulped at the thrashing sea around them. But she nodded.

"It don't look good out there," Cunningham said. "Maybe I should go."

Lottie rose from her seat, shaking her head.

"No way!" she said.

"You're a fast learner," Cunningham said with a smile.

"Not that fast," Lottie said, pushing past him, heading for the belly of the plane. "If we lose me, some men might still make it here and get home. If we lose you, we're all done for."

"Palmer!" Cunningham called as she was about to disappear into the plane's cargo area.

She stopped and looked back.

"Go get 'em," Cunningham said, and grinned.

Thirty-One

When Lottie first managed to push the large hatch in the belly of the Catalina open, she could clearly see the outline of the stranded ship, a solid chunk through the sheets of rain, even over the choppy surface of the waves.

The boat she planned to take to the other ship was a light inflatable. It didn't have much bulk to keep it from being tossed around once it got into open water, but it was light enough for her to drag over to the hatch herself.

Lottie dropped it into the water without much problem because the lip of the hatch was so close to the waterline itself. She looked back toward Cunningham in the cockpit and sent up a prayer for his safety. If the weather shifted even slightly while she made her foray over to the wrecked ship, the plane itself could swamp. She and the men would be stranded in this vast stretch of ocean where no one else would ever find them again.

But she had come so far that there was no way she was giving up now. Once the boat hit the water, she didn't even take a second to consider or hesitate. She just jumped straight down into it herself, then turned back to swat at the door to the hatch, closing it as much as she could against the sheets of rain that were still pouring down.

It was when she felt herself bobbing on the angry sea that the vertigo hit her.

Reeling, she sank down into the inflatable raft and began to paddle. To her relief, despite the choppy water, the little boat jumped forward, away from the shelter of the plane, into the rain.

But when she looked up to get a sighting of the stranded boat she was heading for, it had vanished.

Nothing was in front of her but stony-gray waves, mist, and rain. Panic swelling in her chest, she looked back—just in time to see the plane behind her disappear in the mist.

God, she prayed, plunging forward into the unknown, not sure if she was about to hit the wreck in the blinding spray or rush past it completely, into open water she'd never find her way back from. *Help.*

A wave slammed into the inflatable raft, knocking it off the wobbly course she had set based on her last sighting of the ship, and knocking Lottie off the seat she had been crouched on. The force of it didn't just make her lose her grip on the paddle she was holding. It threw her body half out of the boat. For a sickening instant, Lottie had a glimpse of what it would be like to be lost in these waves. Then she mustered everything she had and pulled herself back up onto the raft.

Kneeling in the water that was already sloshing

in the floor of the raft, Lottie bit her lip and blinked back tears. Then she scrambled back to her seat.

When she did, the ship was dead ahead, so close she had to swerve to avoid banging into it.

"Hey!" she started yelling. "Ahoy! Hello!"

She had no idea what a real sailor would say in this situation. She was just trying to make as much noise as she could.

The hull of this ship was low to the water, too. It was a little cutter whose deck was only about six feet off the surface, probably designed to do exactly what Lottie was doing now—transport men from one big boat to the next—but for a much larger ship.

But in the noise of the rain, those six feet made all the difference.

Lottie could feel her own words blown back at her by the wind, even as she continued to shout. Was anything she was saying even making it up to the deck, let alone inside, where the weakened men were probably taking whatever shelter they could get from this terrible weather?

Beside her was a toolbox, fastened into the side of the raft. Looking for something that might help her make noise, she flipped it open and found a small air horn resting on top. She pulled it out and pressed the button, creating a blaring, bleating sound that she thought might have traveled all the way back to Cunningham in the flying boat.

Up on the silent ship, though, nothing happened.

Lottie blasted the horn again.

This time, a face appeared on the lip of the ship, pale, with a mop of dark hair.

Lottie waved. "We're here to take you back!" she yelled, gesturing to the boat. "Come down! Get in!"

By now her little launch had bumped up so close to the ship that she could see the consternation on the man's face. Instead of looking glad to be rescued, he looked as if he'd seen a ghost.

A moment later, another face appeared beside him. This one was just as pale, but dotted with freckles.

"Harry," the dark-haired guy said to the freckled one. "You see this? Am I seeing things?"

"Is it a mermaid?" Harry said in a tone of wonder.

Lottie stomped her foot on the floor of the boat impatiently. "I'm a Navy WAVE," she yelled. "There's a seaplane waiting for you a few hundred yards out. But we have to go now!"

For a moment, the men stared at her in shock, rain running down their faces. Then they both disappeared.

But an instant later, they were back, surrounded by a dozen other faces. A rope ladder dropped over the side of the ship, and men began to scramble down it, some of them working their way steadily, others missing a step and collapsing onto the men who had already made the raft. A few of them whooped with laughter at their good fortune. But most of them seemed to be using everything they had just to stay awake and upright.

There were still faces peering over the edge of the boat, waiting for help, when the raft began to swamp.

"It's too many!" one of the men on board yelled. "Come back for us."

On the raft, two of his buddies had already begun to bail.

"Get in!" Lottie called back. "We can't make this trip twice!"

The last remaining passenger couldn't even make the ladder himself. Instead, two of his buddies lowered him down the side of the boat, wrapped in a hooded raincoat and attached to a plank, and the other men in Lottie's launch reached for him and drew him in. He lay so still that Lottie was afraid he was dead, and she could see fresh blood spreading over the belly of his uniform when the raincoat fell open, bleeding like ink onto paper in the rain.

Then his two buddies dropped into the boat behind him.

"That's everyone," Harry shouted to Lottie. "We're all here."

"Where are we going?" someone else called

from the rear of the raft, which was riding even lower in the water with the full load. That meant it wasn't getting tossed as much by the waves. But it also meant that even a small swell put them in danger of getting swamped.

Lottie was grateful to see, though, that now all the healthy men had joined the bailing, throwing water out of the bottom of the boat with anything they could find, including their own hats.

In answer to the man's question, Lottie gestured to what she hoped was the Catalina, now lost in the mist again.

Then the men pulled the oars free from their locks and began to paddle, guiding the little launch in a large, lazy circle away from the side of the ship where they had spent so many hopeless days. As they pulled away, the ship seemed to nose after them, almost as if it wanted to come along, too.

Lottie's heart rose in her chest as they plunged toward the unknown, into the mist. But just as they reached the top of the circle their path was describing on the waves, she caught sight of the Catalina again, up and off to the left.

This time, when they set a course for it, it never disappeared from sight again. But when they reached the hatch in the belly of the Catalina, the water wasn't as cooperative. The waves were so rough that the men in the fore of the raft had to jump and scramble just to get a grip on it. And even once they had purchase on the hatch, two of them together couldn't pry it open until a third joined. The force of all three finally got the hatch to swing wide, although it knocked one of them off their feet. Then two of them scrambled up into the belly of the plane and reached out to pull the wounded man aboard.

Harry, who seemed to be one of the ones in the best shape, held out his hand to help Lottie out last.

"I'm not sure you need a hand," he said, "after what you just did." But he extended his anyway.

"I'll take all the help I can get," Lottie said.

When she set foot back in the belly of the flying boat, everything she'd just been through finally hit her. She swayed and might have fallen if two of the men hadn't put their hands out to steady her, while another pulled her launch in and fastened the hatch against the rain and the wind.

"You okay, princess?" one of them said.

Lottie barely had enough energy to stay on her feet. But a fire rose inside her. And she shot back, "I'm nobody's princess."

Even more than their helping hands, the looks on the men's faces steadied her. They were gaunt and hungry, clearly in more need than she was, whatever she'd just been through.

"We've got crackers," she said. "And water. It's not much, but—"

"It's more than we've had," one of the men

said as Lottie hurried over to the box of supplies they'd thrown into the plane before they left, hoping as she did that the provisions wouldn't be completely soaked. "Thank you."

"Not too much at once," one of the men called.

"Ah, doc," another said, waving the advice away.

"That's right," the first man said. "I am. And you don't want to eat too much when you've been starving. It's a good way to get sicker than you even are."

As the other men fell on the crackers and canteens of water, Lottie's glance landed on the wounded man, who hadn't stirred. She grabbed a canteen and knelt beside him in the water that now sloshed in the belly of the plane, and gently brushed aside the hooded raincoat hiding his face.

His features were gaunt and ghostly white. His lips were cracked and had turned a purplish hue. But still there was something so familiar about him. She hadn't realized until this instant that some part of her, some crazy, hidden part, had been hoping she might find Luke among these shipwrecked men. It was such a silly dream that she hadn't even let it break the surface of her mind. But now the twist in her heart told her she had been holding that hope somewhere, in some secret chamber. She held the canteen up to his lips and let the smallest amount drip in.

"Wake up," she whispered, almost as a prayer. Then the man's eyes opened.

"Lottie," he said.

Suddenly, her breath was knocked out of her.

Lottie stared back into Luke's eyes, not sure if she was dreaming or awake. She felt flooded with heat and frozen at the same time. Blindly, her fingers found his and closed around them. His grip was so weak that tears sprang to her eyes.

"Doctor!" she said, looking up for help.

One of the men detached himself from the rest as another looked after him. "It's Woodward!" someone cried. "He's awake!"

"He hasn't been awake for a day and a night," the doctor said, coming over.

As he knelt beside Luke, Lottie heard a voice calling from above. "Palmer!"

It was Cunningham. And she knew what he wanted. As the plane rocked under them and the rain pelted down on the hull, there was no time to waste. They needed to get these men home.

It took everything she had to let go of Luke's hand. If his eyes had still been open, she might not have been able to do it. But they had closed again, as he'd slipped back into oblivion.

Taking a deep breath, feeling as if her limbs weren't really her own, she climbed back up into the cockpit.

"Am I glad to see you," Cunningham said with a toothy grin.

Lottie's mind flashed to what he must have been through in the past few minutes. That drop that she had felt when she left him behind and struck out on the open waves, that sense that she might soon be the only living person for miles— she could imagine he had lived through his own version of that, himself.

She knew better than to think he'd ever put it into words, if he had. But his big smile said it all.

"They ready to go?" Cunningham asked. "I think we can outfly this storm if we take off now."

Lottie thought about telling him that Luke was down there, with the other men, but she could barely bring herself to speak the words out loud, in case she might break the spell that had somehow brought them together by putting it into words.

Instead, she nodded, then ducked back down into the hold. "Hold tight," she yelled. "We're taking off!"

Some of the men were already seated with their backs against the wall, exhausted by the trip. Some of them kept right on eating. The doctor crouched over Luke. Lottie went over to the hatch, made sure it was fast, and then headed back up to the cockpit.

"All clear," she said.

"Then get up here," Cunningham said. "We need to get out of here."

Suddenly, Lottie was exhausted. The last few steps to her seat beside Cunningham seemed like an uncrossable distance.

But these were the last steps, she told herself, on her way home. Once she took that seat, the next steps she'd take would be on solid ground.

With a sigh, she somehow found the strength to reach her station.

As she was about to drop into her seat beside Cunningham, something banged into the side of the plane, knocking her sideways on her knees. As she fell, her head struck the control panel.

"Palmer!" Cunningham said. "You all right?"

Then he let out an oath.

Lottie sat up, holding her head. From the alarm in Cunningham's voice, she was afraid that she'd split her forehead open. But she didn't see any blood on her hand. It just stung and ached where the blow had struck.

She settled weakly down into her seat, but when she looked at Cunningham to reassure him, she realized she was the last thing on his mind.

His eyes were fixed on something beyond the windshield of the plane. Something outside.

Thirty-Two

With a feeling of dread, Lottie turned to follow his gaze.

As she did, she heard a shriek of metal. It took her a minute to recognize the hulking form that now filled the entire windscreen of the plane.

It was the abandoned Japanese ship that she'd just rescued the men from. It had rammed straight into the hull of the flying boat. And as the abandoned ship bounced off, one of the propellers of the Catalina scraped all the way down its side.

"We can't take off," Cunningham said. "Not with that thing this close."

But almost as if he'd muttered a magic spell, the Japanese boat began to drift back into the mist, headed for God only knew where.

Cunningham took a deep breath and began to flip switches.

"Thank God," he said. "I'm getting us out of here before that thing comes back."

As he said it, the cockpit was filled with the comforting hum of a warming engine. But as the engine sound grew to the whine that could drive actual flight, it turned from the steady sound of a healthy bird to an eerie shriek.

"Shut it down," Lottie called. At the sound of

disaster, some part of her just wanted to rush to Luke. She wasn't sure if she wanted to go to him for comfort for herself or to comfort him. But in any case, she couldn't indulge it. She had to stay focused or none of them would ever make it home. "Shut it down."

Cunningham stopped the engines and looked at her. Then he said the dreaded words they both already knew: "Something's wrong."

Somehow, Lottie managed to lift herself out of the seat again.

But as she did, a surge of adrenaline rushed into her. She clambered back down to the hold, where she saw a single glimpse of Luke's face, which was still alarmingly thin and pale. But she didn't have time to think about that, rummaging through the boxes that lined the interior, looking for a kit of tools. She found a hammer and a wrench, stuffed them into the pockets of her overalls, then went over to the hatch.

When she opened it and looked up, she could see that the wing of the plane with the busted engines was close, maybe three or four feet beyond her reach. With water from the storm spraying in her eyes, she jumped as high as she could but didn't come close.

"Hey," Harry said behind her. "What's going on?"

"Help me," Lottie ordered. "Give me a leg up."

Harry looked up at the wing of the plane,

looked out into the storm, then obediently made a stair step for her with his hands. She planted her foot in it, but it still didn't give her enough height.

She slid back down into the hatch.

"I need to get up on that wing," she said. "Something's wrong with one of the engines."

Harry squinted up at the wing, then looked at her again. "Permission to pick you up?" he asked.

Lottie nodded.

Kneeling down, Harry caught her around the calves, then somehow managed to stand himself, giving her just enough height to clamber from the hatch up onto the wind-whipped surface of the wing.

At the first gust of wind, she flattened on her belly—the only way to keep from being knocked off. Then she crawled over to the closest propeller. Instantly, she could see what had gone wrong.

When the Japanese boat smashed into the Catalina, a spar had been driven into the propeller's engine. Jammed between the cylinders, it was cutting off power to the propeller.

Gripping the slick surface of the wing as well as she could, Lottie climbed down onto the busted engine.

The engine itself actually gave her more traction than the wing had, and for an instant, she clung to it gratefully as the water churned below, turning darker as night set in around them.

The metal spar had jammed deep into the works of the cylinder, and only God knew what kind of damage it had done along the way. In the shop, fixing the prop would have been a complicated operation, with testing, retesting, careful calibration.

But perched on the wing of a wounded seaplane in the middle of the churning Pacific, Lottie just began to yank. She pulled at the crooked spar with all the force she could manage, striking the wrench against it and leaning into it with all her strength, until it had begun to wobble loosely, and then pulled free, and dropped into the black waves below with a loud slap.

In a perfect world, she would have called to Cunningham for a test, scrambled down from the wing for safety, then gone back up to make adjustments based on whatever the test revealed.

But she knew Harry wouldn't be able to hear her over the roar of the storm, let alone Cunningham up in the cockpit.

So she just prayed that what she'd done would be enough.

Then she began to crawl back toward the hatch.

She made it all the way to the seam where the wing met the plane. Below her, she could see Harry's hands reaching out to draw her back in.

Gratefully, she judged the distance, exactly how she'd have to jump to make it back.

But as she did, a big roller washed up against the nose of the plane, knocking her off her perch.

She began to slide, and on the slick wing, there was nothing she could catch to stop herself. With a sickening drop, she fell past the hatch.

Angry water closed over her head.

The sudden silence underwater was a strange relief after the roar of the storm. But the water was so cold it almost knocked her unconscious. Her body alive with alarm, she struggled to the surface, but when she got there, all she could see was mist and more water.

In what seemed like the far distance, she heard men's voices shouting.

Then strong hands closed on the fabric of her uniform, and someone was dragging her back into the hold.

"You all right, missy?" someone asked.

"Is she all right?" someone else asked. "Is she alive?"

With a shock, Lottie realized that none of these men, whose lives she'd just saved, and who had just saved hers, even knew her name.

She sat up and gestured toward the hatch, struggling to get to her knees.

"Fasten it shut," she ordered. "We have to take off."

This time, she didn't even allow herself to glance at Luke as she clambered back up to the cockpit.

"Start her up," Lottie said.

With a nod, Cunningham fired the engine.

Lottie was too exhausted to feel the strain she might have felt otherwise, with the knowledge that whether the engine worked now or not could be a matter of life and a very unpleasant death, not just for her but for Cunningham and all those men in the belly of the plane.

She just leaned her head back on the seat behind her, listening.

A hum.

A whine.

And then—a slight wobble, but that was all. It might not have been perfect, but it would fly.

Cunningham grinned and pushed the bird forward, picking up speed.

Lottie took a deep breath and let her eyes fall closed.

Thirty-Three

"Your discharge will be immediate, Palmer," the officer behind the glossy desk said, looking across it unsmilingly at Lottie.

Beside her, Cunningham shifted in his seat, obviously about to burst.

Before he could, the officer raised his hand for silence. "But it will be honorable," he added.

"The Navy should be giving this young lady a medal," Cunningham growled.

But the officer's face remained impassive.

"You'll ship out tomorrow," he told Lottie, and stood, signaling that the meeting was over. "Thank you for your service."

Cunningham was on his feet instantly, and in a stance that showed he was ready to fight.

But Lottie rose slowly. It felt almost as if she were just in a dream, as if the officer and his giant, shiny desk weren't quite real.

They hadn't come for her while she was still recovering from the exhaustion and minor injuries of her rescue foray. But as soon as she'd been released from the sick bay, there had been an order waiting for her, to report on her activities.

As soon as she'd heard the tone the questions were asked in, she knew she wouldn't be part of the WAVES much longer. But she didn't plan to fight it. She'd already had her fight. She'd fought where it counted. And she'd left everything she had out there, on the field.

So now she simply nodded and turned to go.

She didn't even give a second glance to the secretary at her desk just outside the office. All Lottie wanted now was some peace and quiet, and as soon as she got outside, she promised herself, she could have it.

But when she came through the door, squinting slightly against the blazing Hawaii sun, she was greeted with a roar.

A small crowd was gathered outside, with a running jeep behind them. Lottie recognized the men from the boat, grinning and cheering.

"Recruit!" Maggie called, pushing through the crowd toward her. "I'm here to take you to your next assignment."

"Oh, really?" Lottie said. "And what's that?"

"You're ordered to report to a party at the club," Maggie said, stifling a smile. "We're all going. Double time."

Suddenly the men from the boat rushed her, lifting her up on their shoulders with a round of cheers—and not just them but the guys from the shop, including Pickman, who cheered the loudest.

When they put her down, Eugene was waiting in a wheelchair, a massive bouquet of flowers across his lap.

"The florist thought this must be for a bridal bouquet," Eugene said with a grin. "I told her it was something even better."

Gratefully, Lottie hugged him, the flowers smashing and giving out their lovely fragrance between them.

The club on the beach, as it always was, was packed to the gills when they arrived. But now that the tide of the war had shifted, with the Allies racing across Europe and the balance of power in the Pacific Theater changed, the mood was different than it ever had been before. The faces were older, and maybe wiser. They bore traces of suffering and sorrow, but they no longer carried the shadows of worry and death. They were still alive, still young—and they'd been given the gift of knowing how lucky they were just to be those two things.

Lottie danced and laughed with the rest of them as people pressed around her with congratulations, eager to hear her tell the story one more time.

But after they'd all been there for hours, she caught sight of someone on the other side of the club, and for an instant, everything stopped.

There, among the laughing crowd, was Luke. She glanced around, wondering if anyone else— Pickman or any of the others—had seen him as well.

But when her eyes fastened on the spot again,

it was only an ordinary seaman—and one who didn't look particularly like Luke to begin with.

Lottie shook her head. While she'd been waiting for the Navy to determine her case, she'd gone to visit Luke when he was recovering with the other wounded in the hospital. But unlike Eugene, he hadn't seemed thrilled to see her. At first she'd thought he was just too weak, but as he recovered, the distance in his eyes grew greater, until she finally got the message: he didn't want to see her. She didn't know the reason, even though she'd made a thousand guesses.

Maybe the things he'd said to her before he left weren't from the heart, but just the kinds of things men say to girls as they're going off to war. Maybe whatever he'd seen or been through in the last battle had been too much—and there wasn't room left for anything else.

So eventually, she'd stopped going. Still, in this moment, she couldn't help but think of him—and be grateful for everything he'd taught her. *Thank you,* she prayed silently, even as her friends laughed and celebrated around her. *Whatever happened, I'm glad I had the chance to know him.*

As the sun sank into the ocean, the celebration showed no sign of stopping, despite the official disapproval of the naval powers that be. But as the light drained from the sky, Lottie slipped out on her own, with something tugging her heart back to the cove.

She knew she wasn't the only one there who was missing someone. All of them knew what it was like to lose now. And in some ways, that made life more sweet.

But she needed a minute, now that she knew she'd soon be gone for good, to say goodbye once more.

It didn't take her long to reach the little cove, just down the beach and along the shore.

And when she got there, she stood in the wet sand, staring out at the ocean, until she heard a voice.

"Lottie."

Lottie's heart began beating in her chest, despite herself. She closed her eyes and willed it to stop. She could learn to be friends.

It was time to move on.

"Lottie," Luke said again.

She turned around and saw Luke standing before her, in civilian clothes, a white collared shirt with khaki pants rolled up to his knees, his right arm in a sling. He looked so thin, though some of his color had returned. And somehow wiser—but also, exactly the same.

Lottie blinked away the tears that rose in her eyes, shook her head, and looked back.

"I heard you were having a going-away party," Luke said with a small smile.

At the sight of it, Lottie's heart quickened. She hadn't seen a smile on his face in—she couldn't even remember. But she knew she hadn't seen one since she'd rescued him and the other men.

"Didn't think I'd let you leave without seeing you off, did ya?"

Lottie just stared at him, biting her tongue to keep from telling him that he was the reason they hadn't seen each other, despite what her heart truly wanted. But this was the first time he'd talked with her, really talked with her, in ages. And she didn't want to scare him off.

"I wanted to come in," Luke said. "But it was just so noisy." His face clouded. "I haven't been great with noises since . . ."

Lottie stepped closer. "What happened to you?" she asked. "Out there?"

"Our plane went down in enemy territory," Luke said. "It made such a big crash, there was no escaping them. So they captured us, but their camp was a mess, and it only took us a few days to escape. But we still couldn't get out of the battle zone, for weeks."

"Oh, Luke," Lottie said. "I'm so sorry."

"It was hell," Luke said matter-of-factly. "The fighting was going on all around us, but we had no comms, so we had no idea when it'd start and stop. Whose territory we were in. Who was shooting at us. We just knew they were always shooting. And if they weren't, there were always bombs dropping out of that clear blue sky. And so many dead, everywhere we went. But they weren't the worst part. The worst part was the wounded . . ." he said, his eyes taking on that distant look again.

Lottie blinked back her tears. She put a hand on his arm, then started to pull it away, not sure if she was overstepping. But before she could, his own hand closed over it, holding her hand there.

"There was only one thing that got me through," he said.

Lottie looked into his eyes, a question in her own.

"You," he said.

The wave of emotion that rolled over Lottie left her breathless. But as she swayed against Luke, he stepped away.

"When I saw you again, I just couldn't stop thinking about all the people I've loved in this world that I've lost. The idea of losing you—" His breath hitched, and he swallowed hard, clenching his jaw. Luke looked back at her with an intensity that made her heart pound. "There's nothing in this world that scares me more. I can't lose you, Lottie Palmer. I've got to take the risk. And I promise I'll walk through enemy lines a hundred more times to get back to you if that's what it takes."

It took her an instant to realize he was getting down on one knee.

"Lottie," he said. "Will you marry me? I have to ask now. I've never met a woman with spirit like yours. Or your stubborn, crazy hope. I tried to talk you out of it once, but I need it now."

Lottie just stared down at him, speechless.

Luke dropped his gaze. "I understand if you can't say yes," he said. "I wasn't much of a prize to begin with, I guess, and now . . ." He made a helpless gesture toward his wounded arm.

But now Lottie knelt in the sand beside him, wrapping him in her embrace. "Yes," she said through tears that now flowed freely. "Yes."

Then she kissed him. Suddenly, everything that had come before was erased—the war, his wounds and hers, all the time they'd spent apart, all the things she had learned and lost.

For perhaps the first time, Lottie knew she was exactly where she was supposed to be. And what life she was meant to live. Not the life that anyone else had planned for her, but the one she hadn't planned, and still couldn't—the one right in front of her. And the one they would figure out together.

When their lips finally parted, Luke gazed into her eyes.

"I'm afraid the Navy supply depot was clear out of engagement rings," he said, sheepish.

Lottie kissed him again. Then a thought sprang into her mind, and she scrambled to her feet.

Luke tried to hold her hand in protest. "No," he said. "Don't go."

But she grinned and pulled away, running up the beach.

When she came back, she was brushing the sand off the O-ring she had buried by the big rock there months before.

She pressed it into Luke's open hand.

"How's this?" she asked.

Luke kissed her cheek, and her other cheek. Then he slipped it on her ring finger and stared into her eyes.

"I'll get you a better one someday," he said. "I promise."

Lottie grinned and wrapped her arms around him, with no intention of ever letting go again.

"This one's perfect," she said.

Acknowledgments

Many thanks to my wonderful team at Simon & Schuster: Beth Adams, Kaitlin Olson, Meriah Murphy, Isabel DaSilva, and Morgan Hart; and to the team at Alloy: Laura Barbiea, Sara Shandler, and Josh Bank, who all helped bring this book to life and make it beautiful.

About the Author

CANDACE WATERS lives and works in Brooklyn. Her great-aunt and great-uncle were survivors of the attack on Pearl Harbor.

Center Point Large Print
600 Brooks Road / PO Box 1
Thorndike, ME 04986-0001 USA

(207) 568-3717

US & Canada:
1 800 929-9108
www.centerpointlargeprint.com